ALL WAS FAIR IN H[...]

The ravishing, red-headed Lady Sharon Clevenger was the
first foe Gillian faced in her campaign to defeat the unworthy women who sought to snare the Marquis of Landover.
Lady Sharon was dispatched with the aid of an intoxicating
potion at the right time.

The next challange came in the fetching form of the flaxen-
haired Miss Clara Fitzwilliam. Miss Clara was sent spinning
with the aid of a gentleman's kiss at the wrong time.

But now the exquisitely beautiful Lady Henrietta Armitage
had entered Landover's life again to claim his heart once
more. And this time Gillian knew that she had only her own
outragous daring to depend on to dislodge this woman who
was so clearly a perfect match for the Marquis—and seemed
so much more than a match for her. . . .

The
Indomitable
Miss Harris

Moose Jaw Book Exchange
and Prairie Leisure Emporium
117 High St. W.
MOOSE JAW SASK S6H 1H5
692-3674

SIGNET Regency Romances You'll Enjoy

(0451)

☐ **THE KIDNAPPED BRIDE by Amanda Scott.**
(122356—$2.25)*
☐ **THE DUKE'S WAGER by Edith Layton.** (120671—$2.25)*
☐ **A SUITABLE MATCH by Joy Freeman.**
(117735—$2.25)*
☐ **LORD GREYWELL'S DILEMMA by Laura Matthews.**
(123379—$2.25)*
☐ **A VERY PROPER WIDOW by Laura Matthews.**
(119193—$2.25)*
☐ **THE DUKE'S MESSENGER by Vanessa Gray.**
(118685—$2.25)*
☐ **THE RECKLESS ORPHAN by Vanessa Gray.**
(112083—$2.25)*
☐ **THE DUTIFUL DAUGHTER by Vanessa Gray.**
(090179—$1.75)*
☐ **THE WICKED GUARDIAN by Vanessa Gray.** (083903—$1.75)
☐ **BROKEN VOWS by Elizabeth Hewitt.** (115147—$2.25)*
☐ **LORD RIVINGTON'S LADY by Eileen Jackson.**
(094085—$1.75)*
☐ **BORROWED PLUMES by Roseleen Milne.** (098114—$1.75)†

*Prices slightly higher in Canada
†Not available in Canada

Buy them at your local bookstore or use this convenient coupon for ordering.

THE NEW AMERICAN LIBRARY, INC.,
P.O. Box 999, Bergenfield, New Jersey 07621

Please send me the books I have checked above. I am enclosing $_____
(please add $1.00 to this order to cover postage and handling). Send check
or money order—no cash or C.O.D.'s. Prices and numbers are subject to change
without notice.

Name_____

Address_____

City _____ State _____ Zip Code _____
Allow 4-6 weeks for delivery.
This offer is subject to withdrawal without notice.

The
Indomitable
Miss Harris

by
Amanda Scott

Ⓢ

A SIGNET BOOK

NEW AMERICAN LIBRARY

TIMES MIRROR

PUBLISHED BY
THE NEW AMERICAN LIBRARY
OF CANADA LIMITED

NAL BOOKS ARE AVAILABLE AT QUANTITY DISCOUNTS WHEN USED
TO PROMOTE PRODUCTS OR SERVICES. FOR INFORMATION PLEASE
WRITE TO PREMIUM MARKETING DIVISION, THE NEW AMERICAN
LIBRARY, INC., 1633 BROADWAY, NEW YORK, NEW YORK 10019.

Copyright © 1983 by K Lynne Scott-Drennan

All rights reserved

First Printing, November, 1983

    2   3   4   5   6   7   8   9

SIGNET TRADEMARK REG. U.S. PAT. OFF. AND FOREIGN COUNTRIES
REGISTERED TRADEMARK - MARCA REGISTRADA
HECHO EN WINNIPEG, CANADA

SIGNET, SIGNET CLASSIC, MENTOR, PLUME, MERIDIAN
and NAL BOOKS are published in Canada by The New American
Library of Canada, Limited, Scarborough, Ontario

PRINTED IN CANADA

COVER PRINTED IN U.S.A.

To Jim Richard Drennan
because he wants his name in a book

I

The front hall of the house in Berkeley Square was a spacious chamber with a minimum of furniture, boasting only an occasional table or two; a carved and gilt side table with scrolls, swags, and a grotesque mask, surmounted by a huge mahogany-framed mirror; and several small carved wooden single chairs. The focal point of the hall was a grand winged staircase that swept back from the center of the highly polished floor to a point halfway to the lofty painted ceiling before branching into a graceful, circular railed gallery.

Sunlight filtered into the hall through a magnificent Venetian stained-glass window located above the front door and depicting a classical welcome to Spring in shades of green and gold. Filling nearly the entire upper half of the front wall, the window arched regally as it approached the domed ceiling.

Seated upon the only other piece of furniture, a high-backed settle near the front door and opposite the imposing side table, were two young females. The first, sitting bolt upright with hands folded primly in her lap, was outfitted in a drab cloak over a gray uniform dress, her brown curls tucked neatly under a mobcap, and was obviously of the serving class.

The other young lady, presenting at least an outward appearance of poise and composure as she steadily regarded the grotesque mask on the table before her, was dressed according to the height of fashion in a bright green walking dress and tan kid half boots. A chip hat trimmed with daisies was tied firmly under her pointed chin with lemon ribands, and she wore gloves of a matching color. A fur-trimmed pelisse lay upon the settle beside her. She was Miss Gillian Harris, age nineteen,

7

and she had been sitting there cooling her heels for quite half an hour, having come in response to the curt summons that had accompanied her breakfast tray.

The author of the note, in firm black script, had ordered her to present herself in Berkeley Square without delay and had signed himself, briefly, though properly, "Landover." He was, in fact, Benjamin Charles Darracott, Marquis of Landover, a distant relation on her mother's side, and principal trustee for the Harris fortune. Gillian and her brother, Sir Avery Harris, nearly three years her senior, had met him on two previous occasions—the first a year before when he had paid a brief visit to arrange for the management of their Sussex estates after their parents' fatal accident, and the second but three weeks past, when he had greeted their arrival in London with the information that he had hired an elegant little house in Curzon Street where they would live with Amelia Periwinkle, the elderly widowed cousin who was Gillian's chaperone. In the ensuing time, Gillian herself had not so much as exchanged a word with Landover, though she had twice caught sight of his elegant figure at Almack's Assembly Rooms and several times riding or driving in Hyde Park.

If she wondered why, after such a summons, she was being left to vegetate in the hall, she was nonetheless not particularly anxious for the interview to begin, for she had an awkward feeling that she had made an error in judgment by convincing herself that, as a mere trustee, Landover would not interest himself in her activities. He had seemed so aloof that she had decided he would put no rub in her way while she suited her own wishes. Perhaps she had been a shade too gay, even daring. She rather feared he had heard of her latest escapade. She very much hoped he had not.

Gillian was not left many moments longer in doubt. The green baize door at the right under the staircase opened quietly, and a very properly attired butler emerged. He let the door swing to behind him and made his way with quiet dignity to the double doors by the side table. Pushing these open, he stepped aside to allow another man to emerge before entering the room beyond. The second gentleman, a good deal younger than the stately butler, cast a brief glance of appraisal at Gillian before passing on to another small door at the left of the staircase. The butler's words carried easily.

"You rang, my lord?"

A deep, mellow voice wafted its way to Gillian's ears from the interior. "Yes, MacElroy, you may show Miss Harris in now."

The butler turned and made a slight gesture to Gillian. Signaling her maid to remain where she was, she arose with careful poise, smoothed her skirts, and crossed the hall to the open doorway.

"Miss Harris, sir."

Looking up into the butler's gray eyes, Gillian thought she detected a spark of something like sympathy, which seemed to intensify when the deep voice spoke again. "Thank you, MacElroy. That will be all." Recalled to her senses, Gillian stepped over the threshold, thus allowing the butler to close the doors.

She found herself in a room smaller than she had expected and furnished with masculine taste. The wall to her right was filled with a long sash-door bookcase, while a hooded fireplace of dark walnut stood opposite her, its low fire crackling merrily. To her left, a set of triple casement windows flanked by maroon velvet curtains looped back with matching cords gave a view onto the misty square. In front of these windows, on a large Axminster carpet, sat the dominant article of furniture in the room, a tremendous pedestal desk of lustrous walnut with an inlaid top and ornately carved side pieces.

The tall, dark-haired gentleman who had risen from his chair behind this imposing piece now walked around to the front of it and indicated one of a pair of upholstered Kent chairs trimmed with brass-headed nails, which sat to either side of the fireplace. "Sit down, Miss Harris, and be so kind as to favor me with an explanation of the news with which I was regaled at my club last night, or rather," he amended, "early this morning."

Gillian stood where she was. Her face had been pale, but confusion now heightened her color. She had no idea which particular bit of news had reached his ears. In an attempt to cover her embarrassment, she straightened her shoulders, lifted that determined little chin an extra fraction of an inch, and in a nearly haughty tone, spoke the first words that came to mind. "My activities have not concerned you in the past, my lord."

"It must certainly appear that they did not," he replied grimly. "I realize without your telling me so that I have been remiss in my duties. But that is about to change. As you see, I *have* sent for you." He gestured toward the Kent chair once more. "Are you going to sit down?"

She shook her head. "No, thank you, sir. I prefer to stand." She could not sit down while he towered over her like the Grand Inquisitor, and it didn't occur to her that he might sit if she did.

"As you like." He leaned against the hood of the fireplace and folded his arms across his broad chest. At another time, she might have admired his well-cut coat of blue superfine, the tight-fitting cream-colored breeches, or the Hessian boots, polished to such a shine that she could see the reflection of the fire in them. At the moment, however, she did not notice such details. Nor did she contemplate what she had learned about him since her arrival in London from such undeniable authorities on the subject as his sister, Lady Harmoncourt, and her outspoken eldest daughter, Sybilla.

The Marquis of Landover was a gentleman who, according to these two well-informed ladies, knew himself to be one of the most eligible bachelors in London. His title and wealth were his two greatest assets, of course, but he was also handsome, polished, elegantly dressed, and generally easygoing. That he was also self-centered, often peremptory, always lazy, and interested primarily in his own comfort did not in the least disgust a single one of the horde of matchmaking mamas whose daughters were consistently urged to set their caps for him. He accepted such attention as his due and was not cynical, having realized long since that it was in the very nature of things for parents to desire to establish their daughters as creditably as possible. He had, after all, watched the procedure firsthand when his own parents had arranged Lady Abigail Darracott's marriage to Lord Harmoncourt, an earl in easy circumstances. Landover ignored the lures cast his own way for the simple reason that he considered himself, at thirty-two, to have several good years ahead of him before it became necessary to set up his nursery. When that time came, he expected merely to look about him for the most eligible damsel and to ask for her hand in marriage. That it might be denied was a possibility too absurd to be contemplated.

As head of his family, he had many responsibilities, but he employed a large and able staff for the purpose of sparing himself the necessity of dealing with any of them. Having accepted trusteeship of the Harris fortune only because he had been unable to avoid it, he had then visited the Sussex estates because he was required to sign various papers and because his sister bullied him into the trip, saying that while it would certainly be more convenient to authorize his man of business to act for him, it would be a gratuitous insult to the Harrises as well. The trip did not occupy him above three days, and as Sybilla had confided to Gillian, the feeling of having done a good deed made him feel quite pleased with himself.

His charges had not worried him at all while they spent their year of mourning in Sussex. However, just after the Emperor Napoleon was forced to abdicate and retire to his island exile, Sir Avery had written to say that he and Gillian wished to visit London. Lady Harmoncourt told them that Landover's first inclination had been to refuse funding, but her ladyship had informed him in no uncertain terms that it was time to present Gillian and that he had no right to deny them the pleasure of a London Season. Gillian, said her ladyship, had already been buried in the country for a dangerously long period of time and must, at the age of nearly twenty, be practically on the shelf. Under duress, Landover had finally agreed and ordered his secretary to arrange the details. He met with the young Harrises upon their arrival and, after introducing them to his sister, had seen them off to the handsomely appointed little house in Curzon Street, no doubt believing that nothing further would be required of him beyond an introduction or two for Sir Avery to such places as Jackson's Boxing Saloon and one or another of his clubs. He had clearly expected his sister to shoulder the burden of seeing to Gillian.

Unfortunately, Lady Harmoncourt, five years older than he, felt she had more than attended to her duty by bullying him into complying with Sir Avery's wishes. She had her promising first daughter to launch, with a second who would emerge from the schoolroom in time for next year's Season, and was not interested enough or generous enough to exert herself on behalf of a girl whose dusky tresses and rosy cheeks had a tendency to cast her own dear Sybilla's pale-blond beauty into the shade. Consequently, after bringing Gillian to the attention of her bosom bows Lady Jersey and the Countess de Lieven, thus assuring her vouchers to Almack's, she sponsored her upon the event of her presentation, then magnanimously escorted her to one assembly and two balls before leaving Gillian to her own devices. That these had been many and varied was no doubt the fact that had finally roused his lordship from his customary lethargy and the reason for the present confrontation. He crossed one shining Hessian over the other.

"Well, Miss Harris?"

Feeling her careful poise begin to slip away at his stern tone, Gillian raised her clear blue eyes to his. "I . . . I don't know precisely what you have been told, my lord."

He frowned. "What you mean to say, miss, is that you have been involved in so many escapades that you know not which of them is the reason for my summons this morning. Is *that* not so?" The ominous note in his voice caused a tremor somewhere in the neighborhood of her stomach. She nodded, feeling wretched and a bit frightened. He gave a sound very much like a growl as he straightened himself, hooked a thumb in his lapels, and took a step toward her. "I am speaking of your whereabouts last evening. Do you realize that if what I have heard about your activities is true, you may be denied further admission tickets to Almack's? The patronesses will not be pleased with that sort of conduct, you may be certain."

Gillian could not repress a slight gasp of dismay. To be barred from the assembly rooms at Almack's would cause her social ruin! Then, striving to regain her crumbling composure, she lifted her chin again. "You are perfectly right to be angry, my lord," she said. "I should not have gone to the masque. I see that now. But I thought it would be quite safe and that no one would recognize me, especially since I was not with Avery."

His hazel eyes hardened. "A matter that I shall presently discuss with your brother," he said dangerously. "You were recognized, Miss Harris, and in circumstances which do not enhance your credit. Lord Petersham recognized you and informed me of your presence at the gardens when we chanced to meet later at White's. He professed to have been greatly amused by your behavior, said he had observed you flirting outrageously with all manner of questionable persons and also mentioned that you were unattended by so much as an abigail, let alone a proper chaperone."

She dared to interrupt him, a note of near indignation tingeing her words. "I had an escort, sir."

"Ah yes. Petersham mentioned Lord Darrow." The touch of sarcasm in his tone brought flame to her cheeks. "According to Petersham, your so-called escort appeared only when one object of your flirtations allowed himself to be carried away by your charms. I collect that Lord Darrow interrupted his own dalliance long enough to draw the fellow's cork for him. For you to have been part of such a scene is beyond the line of what is pleasing, I assure you. Now," he finished sternly, "I should like an explanation, if you have one."

Gillian regarded him with innocent amazement. "But, sir, I have already agreed that I should not have gone to the masque, and in London no lady is ever required to explain or apologize for her behavior!"

"Who the devil told you that?" he demanded.

"Mr. Brummell, my lord."

It was Landover's turn to be amazed. "I beg your pardon?"

"Yes, sir," she replied staunchly. "He said a true lady of Quality should never have to apologize for her actions." She lowered her eyes to the floor in order to avoid meeting the wrathful expression she expected and thereby missed the glint of appreciation that crept into his eyes. Had she seen it, it would have surprised her, for no one had thought to mention that he might have a sense of humor.

His voice remained stern, however. "I doubt George meant you to take such a meaning from his words, Miss Harris. Whether he did or not, however, hardly signifies. He does not hold your purse strings. I do. And, by God, you shall favor me with an explanation of your conduct whenever I require one or suffer the consequences. Now, I should like to hear how you came to attend a public masque at Vauxhall Gardens as well as your own version of what transpired there." When Gillian eyed him speculatively, wondering how little she could tell him, he added firmly, "I want a round tale, if you please. It may help your memory to know that I have also sent for Lord Darrow."

Her mouth dropped open and her head snapped up. "You did not," she whispered, truly horrified.

"I did."

"Oh, my lord, I only wanted some adventure!" She clasped her hands together to keep them from clutching at each other as words suddenly began to tumble from her mouth. "I never thought to cause such a fuss. I have been used to a good deal of freedom in Sussex, even this past year, and the rules here seem absolutely cloisterish by comparison. Mrs. Periwinkle told me I was not to go to Vauxhall, and she can be so stuffy sometimes that I thought it must be an exciting place. I wanted to go so much, and the masque seemed the perfect opportunity, for I was certain I should not be recognized. Avery would not take me, so I teased Lord Darrow until he agreed to be my escort." A guilty frown fluttered across her brow, and she looked down at the floor again, muttering, "I told him you would not care what I did, that he needn't be afraid of you. He said I was absurd to think he feared you, but I think he had every intention of refusing my request before I said that. Anyway," she continued hastily, looking up at him again, "after we arrived, I began having such an exciting time that I didn't realize I had become separated from him until that odious man pulled off my mask and tried to kiss me." She blushed at the memory. "Lord Darrow came then and knocked him down. He took me home right after that . . . Lord Darrow, I mean." Her voice seemed to die away at the last words, and her throat felt uncomfortably tight.

"So that tale was true." He sighed, leaning back against the fireplace again and regarding her quizzically for some moments. "What about the so-called exploratory rambles I've heard you enjoy so much—without the company of either a footman or maid?"

That was easier. "Only until Avery said I truly must not," she answered. "I was used to taking long walks at home, and none of the servants here seems to enjoy the exercise. But I truly did stop when Avery said it was not the thing." She eyed him more hopefully.

"I see. So your brother does have his moments of sense. And

the episode at the Bedford House ball with young Feather-stonhaugh?"

She wrinkled her brow. "Do you mean when he kissed me?"

"Indeed. In a private room."

"Well, since it *was* in a private room, I do not know how it came to your attention, sir, but it was a small thing, believe me." She was feeling more sure of herself now. "He had obliged me by pinning up a torn flounce on my dress, so when he asked if he could have one kiss, I could see no reason not to oblige him in return. He is very nice."

Landover was unimpressed by her naiveté. "So nice, in fact, that he boasted later of his conquest to several of his friends." She regarded him in dismay, and he continued more gently, "Are you in the habit of bestowing kisses upon all the nice young men of your acquaintance?"

"Of course not!"

"You've no notion how that relieves my mind. But that brings us to the matter of your dress. I myself noted at Almack's that you had damped your petticoats."

"Why, 'tis the fashion to do so, my lord!"

"It is an unhealthy and indecent fashion that is thankfully on its way out, and I utterly forbid you to indulge in it further." He seemed to reflect for a moment.

"Is that all, my lord?"

Landover straightened himself again. "No, Miss Harris, that is not all, as you know very well, but it is certainly enough." He moved to the desk again. "Sit down." The tone was peremptory, and this time she obeyed him. He took the chair behind his desk and regarded her grimly. "I see now that I have been not only remiss in my duties but grossly negligent. It was clearly foolish of me to believe I could trust you and Sir Avery to conduct yourselves properly with only Amelia Periwin-kle to guide you. She is able to exert no authority over your brother, and I've come to believe that neither of them exerts much over you."

She leaned forward in her chair to protest. "Cousin Amelia has been very kind to us, sir. Avery and I hold her in the greatest affection."

"So great is your affection for her," he retorted, "that you deliberately disobeyed her, risking a social reputation that she has taken pains to help you achieve. Consider also the fact that you have chosen, on various occasions, to disport yourself with young men in a way that would put her to the blush at the very least, and that you have insisted upon following a fashion of which I'm sure she disapproves, and then dare to repeat that you hold any affection for her!"

Gulping down a sob, Gillian raised a gloved hand to her breast and twitched at her gold locket. "But we do care for her! We do! Please do not send her away!"

He grimaced. "I have no intention of sending her away. She is a woman of Quality. Her connections here are excellent, and she is a very proper person to act as your chaperone. However, it is evident to the dimmest intellect that she cannot control your behavior. Therefore, distasteful as it is to me, I must shoulder that responsibility myself." He breathed a long sigh and fiddled with a quill pen on the desk, watching her closely the while. She struggled to hide her resentment under a seemingly relaxed attitude, but his next words brought her upright with a wholly involuntary jerk. "My secretary has orders to see to the closing of your house. I have decided to remove you and your brother from Curzon Street at once and to install you here in Berkeley Square."

She gasped in disbelief. "Oh, no! You cannot be that cruel! I should be utterly humiliated, my lord, for people to think I cannot behave myself without you standing guard over me. And Avery is my guardian, not you," she added accusingly. "You cannot do this!"

"Sir Avery may certainly call your tune if he chooses to do so, Miss Harris, but I pay the piper for both of you. I most certainly can do this, and I might add that your brother's probable annoyance is a matter of the supremest indifference to me."

It was not a matter of indifference to Gillian. Much though she loved her brother, she had learned over the years to fear his infrequent rages. "He will be furious." She ended on a sob, as tears spilled down her face.

"It appears to me," Landover said gravely, "that you might have done better to think of that before you went to Vauxhall." She opened her mouth to protest further, but a gesture silenced her. "I have no intention of debating my decision with you,

Miss Harris. You have no choice but to obey me in this matter. Now, you have not come alone this morning, I trust."

Gillian shook her head silently. She was struggling to compose herself again.

"You left your maid in the hall?"

"Yes, sir." Her voice was very low.

"Good," he approved. "Then you shall send her to Curzon Street to deliver messages from me to Mrs. Periwinkle and Sir Avery. She can collect whatever you will need for the next few days as well. You shall remain here, for you are in no fit state to go anywhere at the moment."

And, indeed, she was not. The tears were still flowing despite her efforts to curtail them, but she made one last effort through barely stifled sobs. "Please, my lord, I will do as you wish—" She hiccoughed. "But could you not reconsider about Avery? Could you not allow him to remain in Curzon Street? None of this has been his fault!"

Extracting two sheets of his notepaper from a desk drawer, he answered harshly, "Compose yourself, if you please. I abhor being subjected to Drury Lane dramatics in my study. That house will be closed. I have already ordered my secretary to see to it at once. He will also arrange for the rest of your belongings to be transported here. As for your brother," he added in uncompromising accents, "he has been conducting himself little better than you have! I have good reason to believe he has contracted debts he will be unable to pay without diminishing his principal, and I know he associates with persons of questionable repute. It is high time both of you were brought to heel!" He watched to see if she would reply, but she had been shocked into silence. She had had no idea what her brother's activities included. She knew he hated "doing the fancy," as he called it, and preferred going about with his own friends to attending balls and such, but that was all she knew. Landover finished writing and sealed the two notes. Then he stood and pulled the bell. MacElroy reappeared with commendable promptitude, bestowing a speculative glance upon the unhappy girl before he spoke.

"M'lord?"

"MacElroy, take Miss Harris to her abigail. When she has delivered such instructions as she deems necessary, take her to

Mrs. Trueworthy, who will provide her with suitable quarters—the front blue bedchamber, I think. Miss Harris will be remaining with us for a time. Oh," he added as an afterthought, "you may also tell Mrs. Trueworthy that Miss Harris's brother, Sir Avery, and Mrs. Periwinkle will be joining us as well, later in the day."

"Very good, m'lord." MacElroy's face was properly blank as he ushered the now stiffly erect Gillian from the study. The abigail took one look at her mistress and jumped up from the settle, running to comfort her. The butler waited patiently while Gillian, firmly stifling her emotions and speaking with forced calm, gave young Ellen instructions regarding the notes, the clothes she would need, and apologies from herself to Mrs. Periwinkle and Sir Avery. Murmuring words of solace as well as a few choice epithets directed against those persons who decided without notice to take a domineering attitude toward poor lambs, Ellen fled to the carriage, and MacElroy was able to deliver his charge into the housekeeper's care.

That estimable dame, hearing that she was to show miss to a bedchamber, took one look at Gillian's tear-streaked countenance and raised an eyebrow toward the butler. Receiving some sort of answer to her unspoken question in the unbutlerlike shrug of his shoulders, she placed a plump arm around Gillian's waist.

"There, there, child. You come with me," she said soothingly, leading Gillian back into the hall and up the grand staircase to the gallery. Then, turning to her right, through a hallway leading to another stairway, and up this to the second floor, she opened a door onto a long carpeted corridor and continued to speak words of comfort until they had entered a charming bedchamber decorated in various shades of blue with flowered wallpaper and white hangings looped back around the spiral-posted bed. At any other time, Gillian would have been delighted. As it was, she took little notice of her surroundings.

II

Mrs. Trueworthy guided her to a blue silk-upholstered dressing chair and pushed her gently down. "Sit you here, miss. There's lavender water just yonder on the dressing table. I'll get it, and we'll bathe your forehead." Moving away, she added, "Mustn't let his lordship's tempers overset you. They are quick over, as you'll see. Now," she went on, liberally spilling lavender water onto her own large handkerchief, "just you blow your nose and compose yourself. He'll be expecting you down to a bit o' nuncheon, and though it's more than an hour off yet, still it wouldn't do to present yourself in this state, so you have a nice rest now. There's cold water in the jug on the nightstand and towels in the lower drawer of that chest. I'll send Bet—she's the chambermaid—in plenty of time." She paused briefly. "Will you be all right if I leave you now?"

Gillian had managed to regain control of her emotions by this time, so, removing her hat and gloves, she accepted the drenched handkerchief and assured the round, gray-haired woman that she would do nicely, thank you. Then, waiting only until Mrs. Trueworthy had closed the door behind her, she replaced the scent-laden handkerchief on the dressing table and moved to find a towel, determined to put herself properly to rights. After pouring water from the jug into the matching blue-flowered china basin, she soaked a corner of the towel and applied it to her face until she could feel the warmth in her cheeks abating. A bit more refreshed, she decided not to lie down, knowing that if she fell asleep, her eyes would be redder than ever when she awoke. Instead, she moved to the cushioned French seat in the window bay and settled herself, tucking her feet up and leaning back to gaze out on the activity in the street below.

There was very little of it. Only a few pedestrians were abroad. A fop with his spyglass ogled a girl of her own age walking with her abigail. Two elderly gentlemen strolled arm in arm through the small garden in the center of the square, and occasionally she would see a Corinthian or buck driving his high-perch phaeton or tilbury, or a heavy barouche would lumber past the house. But despite bright sunshine, the day seemed dreary, insipid; and boredom had begun to enfold her after fifteen minutes of this occupation when suddenly she recognized a familiar figure driving a spanking team toward Landover House. She watched with a twinge of conscience while Lord Darrow, looking precise to a pin in a dark blue jacket and cherry-striped waistcoat, with crisp blond curls neatly cropped and combed, pulled his team up at the front stoop. His tiger leaped to hold the leaders, whereupon his lordship jumped agilely to the flagway and, taking the steps two at a time, approached the front door.

Gillian waited impatiently, wondering what was taking place in the study between her escort of the previous evening and her temperamental trustee. She knew that Lord Darrow must have been as amazed as she had been to receive the summons from Landover, for she had been quite sincere when she had insisted that the marquis would not bother his head about anything she did. By dint of that insistence and the fact that she had teased him unmercifully, not to mention having ventured to doubt his courage, Gillian realized that she had practically forced his lordship to serve as her escort to Vauxhall Gardens. Reflection upon her experiences soon led her to the shame-ridden belief that her behavior had been prodigiously shocking, if not downright scandalous. She had flirted outrageously and had actually invited the attentions of the odious rogue whom Darrow had knocked so expeditiously to the floor. A fleeting vision of her parents brought tears to her eyes. They would have been disgusted by her conduct.

Hard upon that thought came another. Avery! What would he say to Landover's decree? That he would be furious with her was inevitable. He had refused to escort her to Vauxhall himself, partly because he preferred gaming to dancing, but also because he had disapproved of the idea, and she had purposely neglected to inform him when Darrow agreed to take her. Sir Avery had gone out early in the afternoon and did not even know she had made plans for the evening. Not that he had actually forbidden her to go, but she was certain he would not remember it that way, since he had no doubt assumed that by withholding his escort, he had effectively put a stop to it. Mrs. Periwinkle generally retired at an early hour on evenings when she and her charge were not engaged to attend some social function or other, and Gillian had not bothered to inform her that she did not intend to follow her example. A premonition entered her mind that someone might have something to say about that particular oversight before the affair was allowed to take its proper place in oblivion.

Lord Darrow emerged once more from the house. He looked shaken and spoke sharply to his tiger when he jumped into his phaeton. Gillian wondered again what Landover had said to him. But her thoughts were immediately turned in a new direction, for a second visitor hove into view from Charles Street. Clearly, her brother had received the marquis's message, and he looked as darkly fierce as a thundercloud storming toward the house.

Someone scratched on the door of her room, and at her command, a young housemaid entered, bobbing a curtsy. "If y' please, miss, I be Bet, and Mrs. Trueworthy said t' inform you a light nuncheon'll be served in ten minutes or so. Will you come now?"

Gillian's thoughts whirled. She had no wish to face her brother in his present mood, but she could see no way to avoid an encounter. Avery would simply come looking for her if she didn't go down. Mentally shaking herself, she forced a smile for the maid's benefit. "If you will provide me with a hairbrush, Bet, I shall be ready in a twinkling." The maid soon produced the required article, and Gillian forced her curls into order.

The small first-floor dining parlor to which Bet guided her was empty except for a footman who was laying a third place at the table. The maid seemed surprised. "Oh! I quite thought his lordship would be here, miss."

The footman answered her. "Mr. MacElroy says as how we're to hold service till the master rings."

"Perhaps you had rather wait in the green saloon, Miss Harris," suggested Bet.

"No, thank you," Gillian answered quietly. There was no point in delaying the meeting with her brother. "I'll wait here for the gentlemen." The maid bobbed again and slipped out of the room, followed by the footman. Gillian had not been left more than ten minutes with her own thoughts, however, before she heard masculine voices in the corridor. She was carefully examining some knickknacks on a wall-hung étagère when they entered. Avoiding her brother's eye, she swept the marquis a graceful, if silent, curtsy.

They sat down, but only Landover made any pretense of enjoying his meal. He made polite conversation in a lazy drawl and seemed amused rather than irritated by their lack of response. During a lull while the marquis requested a bowl of fresh fruit, Gillian glanced surreptitiously at Sir Avery, who was scowling at the half-empty plate in front of him. Despite the fierceness of that scowl, no one would deny that he was an extraordinarily handsome young man.

He had the same dark hair and blue eyes as his sister, but where her features were finely and delicately etched, his were sharp as though drawn with firm, bold strokes by a master hand. He was tall, broad-shouldered, and slim-hipped, and today he had dressed conservatively in buff pantaloons and a well-fitting chocolate coat. Even his neckcloth was neatly rather than extravagantly tied. Briefly, she wondered if he had affected the conservative look in hopes of mitigating Landover's displeasure, but the notion was quickly rejected. Avery was still experimenting. She had seen him in every outlandish fad that fashion permitted, but he had seemed lately to be favoring the mode and manners dictated by the famous Mr. Brummell. According to the Beau, whose word on the subject amounted to law, a gentleman was well dressed only when his clothes did not draw attention to themselves. Halfway through the last thought, Sir Avery glanced up, and Gillian suddenly found her gaze locked with his. There could be no doubt of his anger, and feeling guilty warmth flood her cheeks, she looked hastily down at her plate.

For the next few moments she concentrated upon pushing food around with her fork, making no attempt to attend to

Landover's remarks when he returned to polite conversation. Sir Avery replied in monosyllables, each one seeming to Gillian to underscore his displeasure with her. The strain was beginning to tell, and she was certain her nerves would be at screaming pitch in no time, but the moment she had dreaded came soon enough. When the footman began to pour a second glass of wine for the two gentlemen, her brother stopped him with a gesture and turned to Landover.

"May I be excused, sir? I should like to have a word in private with my sister." His voice was carefully controlled, but when Gillian glanced up at him, the hard glint of intent in his blue eyes caused her to pray fervently that Landover would deny his request.

"By all means, Sir Avery. Jeremy here," indicating the footman, "will show you to the green saloon, where you may be as private as you like." Gillian shot him a look of helpless accusation, to which he returned nothing more than a slight shrug.

"Thank you, my lord. Gillian, if you please?" Sir Avery waited impatiently while she took her time rising from her chair, then allowed her to precede him through the door. She hesitated on the gallery, waiting for Jeremy, who guided them to a front room several doors from the dining parlor. When the footman had pulled the doors to, she stood rigidly, her back to Sir Avery, waiting for the explosion. It was delayed only long enough for him to stride forward, grasp her by the shoulder, and whisk her around to face him. He gave her a rough shake. "How could you, Gillian!" he blazed, shaking her with increasing passion as he growled through his teeth, "Did I not warn you? Did I not say that Landover would not continue to turn a blind eye to your conduct? Did I not beg you to behave?" His voice rose considerably as he continued, "I should have taken a strap to you to force you to better conduct! By God, Gillian, you may take *that* and *that*, with my compliments, damn you!"

She reeled backward and fell in a heap against the settee behind her. Raising both hands to stinging cheeks and ringing ears, she burst into uncontrollable sobs.

"Gillian!" Sir Avery was on his knees beside her in a trice. "Gill, I'm sorry! Good God, did I hurt you so much as that? Let me see." He tried to pull her hands away from her face.

"Gillian! Let me see, I say!" He succeeded in bringing her hands away and scanned her face anxiously, but aside from heightened color and a red mark on either cheek, there was nothing to see that might warrant so much commotion. With narrowing eyes, he rocked back on his heels and said in a voice of chilling calm, "You are merely suffering from a fit of the vapors, Gillian, which can serve no useful purpose. If you do not cease that ridiculous noise immediately, I shall box your ears again."

Knowing from experience that he would not hesitate to make good the threat, she attempted to stifle her sobs and took a deep, steadying breath. It was no wonder her reaction had startled him. It had caught her by surprise, too. She did not generally lose control so completely when he raged at her. And it was not as though he had never boxed her ears before. He had done so since they were children. She looked up at him through tear-dampened lashes.

"I didn't mean to fall apart," she muttered gruffly. "I knew you would be angry, and I deserve that you should be, but I certainly never thought he would—"

"You just never thought at all," he interrupted sternly. "Landover is acquainted with the Regent, for pity's sake, not to mention he calls friends with Brummell, Devonshire, Brougham, the de Lievens, and anyone else of influence you might care to name. He may have a reputation for being lackadaisical, but they also say he's as shrewd as can hold together—he's rich as Croesus, after all—and he's known to have a solid streak of ruthlessness as well. He could scarcely continue to turn a deaf ear whilst you made yourself the talk of the *ton*. Here." He extended a hand and helped her to her feet, extracting a large linen handkerchief from his pocket and proceeding to mop her face with it while she stood meekly before him.

"I'm truly sorry, Avery," she said when he had finished. "What are we going to do?"

"Whatever he says we must do," was the unbending response. "I can tell you I don't relish the thought of another confrontation with him."

Gillian had forgotten for the moment that he, too, had had to face Landover's wrath. She blinked at him. "What did he say to you?"

He grimaced. "I'd as lief not go into the details, if you don't mind. Suffice it to say that he made himself quite clear. Either I retrench or I rusticate."

"Rusticate? You mean he would send you back to Sussex?"

"That's what he said."

"But he can't do that! He has no authority over you."

"Hasn't he?" There was a wealth of bitterness in the two words. "If our respected father had seen his way clear to leaving me my fortune without so dashed many strings attached to it, that might well be the case. But since Landover holds the purse until I turn twenty-five, he exercises a good deal of authority. I daresay I could defy him if he ordered me back to Sussex, but I'd find it deuced awkward to live in London with my allowance cut off."

"He couldn't do such a shabby thing! What would people think of him?"

"I doubt he cares a straw for that. Or for what they think of me, come to that. He has said I must sell my new curricle and pair and cancel any orders with my creditors that have not already been filled. And I am not to show my face at White's or any other gaming establishment until after quarter day, when he says I shall be able to afford such debts again." He allowed himself a wry smile. "When I dared to ask him how he expected me to pass the time until then, since I was not to be allowed to amuse myself, he said I should shoulder my responsibility as your guardian and strive to keep you out of mischief."

Gillian sighed. "I foresee that I shall be 'cabined, cribbed, and confined.' "

"*Macbeth*, act three," he chuckled, relaxing his stern air at last. "You begin to sound like Cousin Amelia and will be taken for a bluestocking if you aren't careful." He paused, then, taking her chin in his hand, tilted it up to gaze directly into her eyes. "I don't deny, puss, that I for one would just as soon lock you up, but I've a strong suspicion it won't be as easy as that. I shall be expected, instead, to dance attendance whilst you flit from ball to rout and back again. To think I swore that I would never set foot in Almack's. Knee breeches!"

She smiled ruefully at him. "You look very handsome in knee breeches. And Almack's is not so bad. The food is quite stale and unimaginative, of course, but the dancing is fun, and everyone who matters attends the assemblies. I wonder what Cousin Amelia will have to say to all this."

"She will smile and quote a line or two from the Bard, but I daresay she will not be much upset by the move," Avery replied wisely. "Her thoughts are centered much more firmly upon her social activities and obligations than upon her residence, so long as that residence is an appropriate one. Landover House will more than meet her requirements."

Sir Avery soon took himself off, wondering aloud how, since he had already promised to spend the afternoon and evening with some of his cronies, he could manage to do so without getting himself into trouble with Landover. He seemed pessimistic, but his prediction regarding Mrs. Amelia Periwinkle was soon confirmed by the arrival of that lady herself. Gillian had returned to her bedchamber, and when her chaperone arrived, Mrs. Trueworthy showed her straight up, then tactfully left them to their privacy. Mrs. Periwinkle, swishing orange crape and colorfully crowned with an improbable matching wig, fluttered into the room, her thin, shawl-draped arms outstretched toward Gillian, who came rapidly to her feet from the French seat.

"Naughty girl!" scolded the elderly lady in a twittering voice. "I cannot tell you how overset I'm become by your behavior. But every cloud engenders not a storm, you know, and a little fire is quickly trodden out. This house is utterly splendid and far better suited for our own entertaining than that tiny place in Curzon Street; therefore, we shall make the best of what the fates dispose."

Gillian clasped the veined outstretched hands and kissed the proffered well-powdered cheek. The sweet scent of orange blossoms enfolded her before she stepped away again with a tiny chuckle. " 'Tis not the fates, Cousin Amelia; 'tis Landover who disposes. But I apologize for cutting up your peace in such a way."

"Harp not upon that string, my dear. As the Bard of Avon so rightly said, 'headstrong liberty is lashed with woe,' but we'll not pluck that crow together now. Your Ellen is bringing the things you will need for tonight. You must cease to repine what cannot be changed, take yourself in hand, and look to the future."

"Tonight? Good gracious, cousin, I have forgotten. Who claims our company tonight?"

"Forgotten!" Mrs. Periwinkle wagged a reproving finger. "Then, remember thee, child. 'Tis the Countess de Lieven herself who expects us. A rout and a chance to meet her grace the Grand Duchess of Oldenburg. Poor Dasha says she is proving to be quite a problem, you know. A tiger's heart wrapped in a woman's hide."

"Cousin Amelia! The grand duchess is sister to the Tsar of Russia! What a thing to say!"

"Perhaps," agreed Mrs. Periwinkle, taking a seat and motioning Gillian back to hers, while adding dryly, "in this mealy-mouthed day and age. But true, nonetheless, as you will no doubt see before you are much older. She came here as soon as Bonaparte's defeat was certain to be effected, supposedly to await the Tsar's visit, but everyone thinks there was more to it than that."

"Like what?"

"Oh, the general opinion is that it was political, and the good Lord knows she's well enough suited to be involved in something of that nature, but I myself think it was nothing more than a desire to have a go at the Regent."

"Hasn't she got a husband?" Gillian asked. She had already heard a good deal about the grand duchess, but no one had mentioned a grand duke.

"Prince Oldenburg is dead," said Mrs. Periwinkle briefly. "His duchy was seized by that upstart Bonaparte when he annexed Holland in 1810. Which is why I think her grace is looking about for new blood. But Prinny thought her ugly, and she thought him ill-bred, and she has allowed her dislike of him to overrule whatever diplomatic considerations there might be, which, as you might realize, has made a good deal of trouble for the de Lievens."

Gillian could well imagine that it might. Count de Lieven was Russia's ambassador to England. It was his business to maintain good relations between the two countries, and it sounded much as though the grand duchess's behavior might undermine his best efforts. "But she cannot marry the Prince Regent, so what could she hope to gain from him?"

Mrs. Periwinkle shrugged narrow shoulders. "There has been

talk of a royal divorce, of course, but I think she meant only to impress him and, perhaps, hoped for his support in a liaison with one of his brothers. According to Dasha, the woman thinks herself irresistible. But she is very strong-minded and outspoken, just the sort of female Prinny dislikes most. Besides, once she saw that he could not admire her, she made a point of befriending Princess Charlotte and threatens time and time again to call upon the Princess of Wales."

"Oh dear," breathed Gillian, her eyes alight now with amusement. She was beginning to look forward to the evening ahead with a great deal more enthusiasm than she had hitherto felt. The enmity between the Prince and Princess of Wales was a matter upon which the whole country had taken sides, with nearly all the common folk and a large portion of the nobility favoring the Princess Caroline and condemning the Prince Regent for a lecherous, uncaring husband. And since he had announced his daughter's engagement to the Hereditary Prince of Orange, they had taken up Princess Charlotte's banner as well, thinking that now she would finally escape his tyranny. For the grand duchess to call upon Princess Caroline of Wales would be a calculated slap in the Regent's face.

"Just so," agreed Mrs. Periwinkle, who had been watching the various expressions flitting across her charge's face. "Somehow Dasha has managed to remain on good terms with Prinny as well as with the grand duchess, which says a good deal for her diplomatic skill, to my way of thinking."

And that was an understatement, thought Gillian, who had met the Countess de Lieven upon several occasions and liked her very much, despite having heard how haughty and cold she could be. She was definitely high in the instep, but her own relationship to the Russian royal family, as ward of the Empress, made others expect that sort of attitude from her. Gillian knew from firsthand experience, however, that she could also be charming and kind.

Ellen soon arrived with her clothes, and as she prepared for the evening ahead, she tried to imagine what the grand duchess would be like. For a brief time, however, it seemed that she would never know, for when she and Mrs. Periwinkle descended the grand winged staircase on their way to the waiting carriage, they were met in the lower hall by Landover, who was just coming in.

"Ah, Mrs. Periwinkle, I was hoping I might arrive before you had gone out. You look quite charming this evening," he added smoothly, casting an appreciative glance at them both. His gaze caused Gillian to feel more than usually self-conscious, and she was glad she had chosen to wear the deceptively simple white silk gown that showed off her soft complexion and glowing color to such advantage. That it also clung seductively to her tip-tilted breasts and curving hips was another of its assets, and one of which she suddenly felt blushingly aware, as Landover's gaze seemed to linger while his greeting was returned by both ladies.

"Did you wish to speak to us?" inquired Mrs. Periwinkle, recalling his attention as well as his gaze to her pink-satin-draped and turbaned self.

"Indeed," he answered briskly. "His highness has requested that I bring you to Carlton House later this evening. Therefore, I thought we would have our dinner together here before setting out."

"But we can't!" protested Gillian. Despite the thrill of an invitation to Carlton House, she was appalled by the prospect of Landover's escort, certain he would keep a sharp eye on her every movement to be sure she behaved herself. The very thought was simply mortifying. "We are promised to the Countess de Lieven," she added firmly when both of the others stared in disapproval of her tone.

Landover raised a questioning brow, and Mrs. Periwinkle responded to it apologetically. "I'm afraid that's true enough, my lord. Dasha has invited us both to meet the grand duchess. But it is only a rout, you know, and one need not remain above a half hour or so. I had thought to go on to the Bettencourt ball afterward, but there is no reason that we could not arrange to meet you at Carlton House instead, if that is what you desire."

He frowned heavily. "I cannot approve of Miss Harris's being seen in such company. It will do no good and might do much harm."

Gillian opened her mouth to protest again, but she was forestalled by Mrs. Periwinkle's gentle voice. "I collect that you refer to the grand duchess, my lord, but do you truly think it so dangerous? I myself had thought it would prove to be an excellent experience for her to meet someone of that sort in protective surroundings. For you must know that neither Dasha nor Monsieur de Lieven would allow the grand duchess to exert an adverse influence upon any of our young people.

"There is much in what you say, ma'am," agreed Landover, meeting Gillian's resentful glare with a measuring look of his own. "I still cannot approve of such an association for Miss Harris, but one would not wish to offend the de Lievens, of course, and since you have accepted the invitation, I suppose what must be, must be. I shall expect you, however, to keep a strict eye upon your charge. I would not wish that woman to stir coals with anyone so impressionable."

"Impressionable!" Gillian drew herself up indignantly.

Landover seemed about to respond when Mrs. Periwinkle chuckled. "How naughty of you, my lord, to bait poor Miss Harris so. Calm yourself, Gillian dear. His lordship was only funning. He knows, I'm sure, that you are to be trusted completely. Even if the grand duchess should allow herself to step beyond the line of what is pleasing, he and I know that you would never lower yourself to do likewise."

"Just so," agreed his lordship with an appreciative glint of amusement. "What will you do about dinner, ma'am?"

She laughed. "We shall endeavor to sustain ourselves upon lobster patties and croquettes, my lord. No one at Dasha's routs has any excuse to go hungry, I assure you. Now, how shall we manage to find you at Carlton House? I confess, 'tis an age since I set foot in the place."

"No need to worry, ma'am," he said firmly. "I shall collect you at the de Lievens' and carry you there myself. Shall we agree to meet at ten o'clock? I doubt that Prinny's own dinner will be concluded before then."

"In that case, sir, perhaps you had better fetch us at the Bettencourt ball. I had not meant to stay so long at the rout, and we did accept the other invitation as well."

He agreed, and Gillian was just expelling a breath of relief when he turned his attention to her again. "Where is your wrap, Miss Harris?"

"My wrap?"

"It is quite chilly out tonight. You surely don't intend to go all the way to Streatham Park in nothing more than that thin gown."

"Please don't be Gothic, Landover," she retorted crisply. "I never wear a wrap, and you are certainly too well versed on the subject of female fashions to expect me to wear a heavy pelisse. No one does that sort of thing. I should look like a milkmaid new-arrived from the country."

"Not a pelisse, but surely you have a suitable cloak," he responded in a reasonable tone. "It would be foolish to go any distance in such weather with nothing to protect you."

Once again, it was Mrs. Periwinkle who intervened. "Really, my dear, I told you myself that you ought to wear that lovely fur-lined silk cloak. It will be perfect with your gown, and it is quite stylish, I assure you."

"That settles it," Landover said sternly. "Will you fetch it yourself, or shall I send one of the footmen for it?"

Gillian's breast heaved with stifled fury at being so neatly outmaneuvered, but she saw immediately that it would do no good to argue the matter with him. There was truthfully nothing wrong with the silken cloak. It was merely that she preferred the freedom of being able to move from one entertainment to the next without having to go to the bother of fetching, then disposing of her wrap. By the time she had composed herself enough to inform him that she would get it herself, he had already sent the footman Jeremy to fetch it. Thus, the pale blue silk cloak was presented to him, and he draped it over her shoulders with an approving comment. So conscious was she of his touch, however, that Gillian scarcely heard what he said to her. Though it was the merest brush of his fingers against her shoulders, the contact was nearly electrifying. She dared not look at him, but hastily gathering the cloak about her slim figure, followed Mrs. Periwinkle and the footman out to the waiting carriage.

III

By the time the carriage had rolled across Westminster Bridge, Gillian was grateful for the protection of her cloak, though she would not have mentioned it for the world. Mrs. Periwinkle chattered idly about people she thought might be present, and Gillian answered when necessary, glad enough to let her chaperone bear the brunt of the conversation. Another four miles brought them to Streatham Park and the lovely, large white house standing in its own grounds that was the British residence of the Russian ambassador.

Linkboys scurried to and fro, directing the accumulating carriage traffic. It looked as though it would be a squeeze, Gillian thought, as she passed from linkboy to bowing, six-foot-tall footman. Monsieur de Lieven and his countess were standing at the foot of the stairs in the entry hall to receive their guests, and Gillian and Mrs. Periwinkle were greeted enthusiastically.

"Amelia! How delightful." Twenty-eight-year-old Dorothea de Lieven presented a cool, well-powdered cheek to her elderly friend and smiled at Gillian. Simply elegant, she was dressed in pale-apricot satin with a deep décolletage and tiny puffed sleeves that showed off her creamy skin to perfection. Her lovely chestnut curls were piled exquisitely atop her head, and her dark brown eyes sparkled. "How nice to see you again, Miss Harris."

Gillian responded properly, but Mrs. Periwinkle announced that they had come to see the grand duchess. "Like visiting a zoological exhibition at Astley's Amphitheater, Dasha. We've come to view the main attraction."

32

"Hush, Amelia," scolded Madame de Lieven in an undertone. "You must behave with exemplary propriety. 'Tis as much as my life is worth, I assure you. That woman causes nothing but trouble. But come, I shall introduce you to her myself." She leaned toward her husband. "You will do nicely without me for the moment, sir, but I shall not abandon you for long. I want to make Amelia and Miss Harris known to her highness."

Monsieur de Lieven smiled a bit stiffly at her but nodded before turning his attention to the next guest. Curiously, Gillian followed as the countess led them up the grand staircase. She wondered what Landover would have thought of Mrs. Periwinkle's remarks but dismissed the thought almost immediately. He, like everyone else, no doubt accepted her chaperone as an amusing but harmless eccentric. The countess moved into a small anteroom and paused.

"My dearest Amelia, you can have no notion," muttered Madame de Lieven in response to a remark from Mrs. Periwinkle. "She will not even speak to Bonsi." Realizing her comment had been overheard, she glanced ruefully at Gillian. "So I call my dear husband privately, Miss Harris, though to be sure, I should not do so publicly. You will forgive a momentary indescretion, however. We are all in such a taking." Gillian smiled. Relieved as she was that Madame de Lieven seemed to have heard nothing about her activities of the previous night, she would have forgiven her anything. But the countess barely acknowledged her smile before continuing, " 'Tis not enough that she should insult the Regent and drive us all to the brink of madness with her contemptuous tongue, but she has seen fit to bring the princess in her entourage tonight."

Mrs. Periwinkle's eyes lit with suppressed amusement. "I collect you mean Princess Charlotte and not the Princess of Wales."

The countess met her look directly. "How right you are to put the matter in such a light, dear Amelia." She let out a small sigh and seemed to draw her normal dignity closer about her, looking much more like the haughty young lady who was so familiar to London society. "I would do well to remember that things could be a deal worse. You know, of course, that she has threatened to *call* upon the Princess of Wales?"

Mrs. Periwinkle nodded. "And that Monsieur de Lieven said

he would resign his post if she did. It seems to have answered well enough."

"For the moment. But what am I thinking about? He will be wondering what has become of me, and here I stand like a stock." She ushered them quickly into a large and very crowded reception room, where the guests made way for them as they crossed to a group near the far wall. Gillian stared unabashedly at the two females who formed the focal point of that group.

The elder of the two was easily as tall as if not taller than the Countess de Lieven, and she was dressed in clothes that could only have come from Paris. Her light brown hair was coiffed in an intricate, rather fluffy style that was very becoming to her, and a fine pair of brown eyes glinted appraisingly as her gaze came to rest upon the approaching visitors. Catherine, Grand Duchess of Oldenburg and sister to the reigning Emperor of all the Russias, was younger than Gillian had expected her to be, and despite the Regent's opinion to the contrary, Gillian thought her to be a good-looking young woman. But then, she reminded herself, the Regent's taste ran to the likes of Lady Hertford and Maria Fitzherbert, both (in Gillian's opinion) quite old and rather shopworn.

The younger lady turned now to face them. Princess Charlotte, like her companion, was somewhat taller than most women, with a finely proportioned and well-developed figure, but Gillian's attention was immediately engaged by her winning smile and expressive blue eyes. Mrs. Periwinkle dropped a low curtsy, and Gillian hastily followed her example. The princess nodded graciously, then gestured rather impatiently with a slender hand for them to rise as the Countess de Lieven made the necessary introductions.

"Is this not a lovely party?" the princess asked Gillian, smoothing thick, soft, golden-brown hair back from her forehead.

"Indeed, madam. I have never been here before, and I am very glad I came."

"Well, Catherine says I do not go about enough," confessed the princess with a becoming hesitation in her words. "Of course, I am not properly out yet, since I have not been presented at court."

Gillian stared at her. Somehow it had not occurred to her that the crown princess would have to be presented like everyone else at the Queen's Drawing Room. "But why have you not been presented, if it is necessary?" she asked without thinking. "You are engaged to be married, after all. And you *are* seventeen!"

"Exactly what Catherine said," agreed the princess, casting an affectionate look at the grand duchess. "And my mother also, of course, though she has little to say to anything. I was to have been presented upon the occasion of my birthday, but when my father refused to allow Mama to attend with me, I refused to go. Now they say I am to be presented at the first Drawing Room in June. Though I do not know," she added with a small frown, "whether I shall still be betrothed at that time."

The grand duchess, overhearing her words, turned and laid a hand upon Charlotte's arm. "Everything will be as it should be, *chérie*. Your father is perhaps a trifle difficult at the moment, but so all girls your age would say, is it not so?" She smiled conspiratorially at Mrs. Periwinkle. "We with experience of such things, we know, do we not?" Mrs. Periwinkle said not a word, but the grand duchess went on as though she had agreed wholeheartedly, "Just so. I must tell you, my dears, that I have been disappointed in your Regent. Handsome as he is, he is also a man visibly used up by dissipation, and I am certain such must affect his temper in an untoward fashion. I find him rather disgusting," she added, much as though she were making a commonplace remark. Gillian felt her eyes widening, and she dared a glance at Mrs. Periwinkle to see what her reaction to such talk would be. That lady was regarding the grand duchess stiffly.

"Your opinion must always be an interesting one, madam, but this is scarcely—"

"Have I offended you, Mrs. Periwinkle? But how can that be? Is it not so that in your constitutional country one might speak as one pleases?"

"We have a strong belief in free speech, madam, however—"

"Then, I must tell you that I think your prince a vile libertine," the duchess pointed out, still in that casual, conversational tone. "His so-called affability is licentious, even obscene. I am, I assure you, far from being puritanical or prudish, but I vow to you that with him and his brothers, I not only often have to get stiffly on my stiffs, but I do not know what to do with my eyes and ears. A brazen way of looking where eyes should never go," she went on, shaking her head as she warmed to her subject in a way that struck dismay into Gillian's heart. "I do not know how the English must be made, that their women should stand such things. He becomes ecstatic over ribands, over diamonds, his fine plate, his good cook—like a child or an upstart."

"Please, madam," Mrs. Periwinkle began weakly, casting a worried glance first at her own charge and then at the princess, "would it not be better to—"

The grand duchess smiled sweetly. "Charlotte is well aware of my opinions, I assure you, and it won't hurt your Miss Harris to learn the ways of the world." She looked Gillian up and down appraisingly. "If she has met his highness, she knows I speak only the truth, and if she has not, it is just as well that she be forewarned. But perhaps you think we must not discuss such things at Madame de Lieven's so lovely rout." She shrugged expressively, then added with a smile, "Miss Harris, you must come to visit me at the Pulteney Hotel one morning. Her highness is often with me there, and she ought to cultivate friends of her own age. She is hemmed about by old women like myself."

Princess Charlotte laughed at such a reference, not seeming disturbed in the least by the grand duchess's candid assessment of her father's faults, but she augmented the invitation with one of her own. "We can be much more relaxed at Catherine's," she said. "But you must come to Warwick House, too. I shall send you a card." She smiled, and Gillian did not need the brisk nod from Mrs. Periwinkle to know that the interview was ended, and none too soon in that lady's opinion.

They turned and threaded their way through the crowd toward the buffet tables. "I thought the princess was very nice," Gillian said over her shoulder to Mrs. Periwinkle.

"Indeed," the lady agreed. "She is extraordinarily popular and has open, natural manners that can only command respect and affection. But that woman!" She paused, thinking. "Oddly enough, she seems to have put on her best effort for the princess. I wonder what she can be up to."

Gillian chuckled but broke it off as she came unexpectedly

up against another human body. "I beg pardon," she began, looking up, then blushing as she recognized the obstacle. "Lord Darrow! How . . . how nice to see you again," she ended lamely.

His lordship, nattily attired in a snug dark coat and an elegant salmon satin waistcoat, carried two glasses and had lifted them swiftly out of harm's way just before the collision. He lowered them now, giving Miss Harris a keen look through the long lashes shadowing his silver-gray eyes. "I saw you with her highness and the grand duchess and decided that after enduring such elevated company, you would require refreshment."

"Very thoughtful of you, my lord," commented Mrs. Periwinkle, accepting her glass with a careful look at both of them. "But I require sustenance, not mere refreshment. Will you accompany us to the buffet?"

"Gladly, ma'am." He stood aside politely to let her precede him, and as Gillian moved to follow, he bent toward her, speaking in a low tone for her ears only. "I should like a private word with you, Miss Harris."

Gillian glanced up at him, biting her lip. "I'm sure you would, sir. But this is hardly the place." He nodded toward Mrs. Periwinkle's disappearing form, and she followed hurriedly, conscious despite the noise around them of his footsteps just behind her. They rejoined Mrs. Periwinkle at the tables loaded with all manner of delicacies. She had certainly been right to prophesy that they could not go hungry. A footman appeared with a plate for Gillian, and she pointed out her choices to him, watching approvingly as he served her with hot broccoli salad, lobster patties, sliced pheasant, and nun's cakes. Then she followed as he led the way to an adjoining room where dining tables had been set up, grateful that she would not be expected to balance the loaded plate upon her knee while she ate.

Lord Darrow joined them, and although he refused a plate, he had accepted a mug of stout, which he now set down in front of him. Mrs. Periwinkle applied her attention to her food, and Gillian attempted to do likewise, but she was very conscious of Darrow's presence. "I did not expect to see you here tonight," she said finally.

He smiled. "It is not my normal sort of entertainment, to be sure, but my father was invited, and he insisted upon my company. It does not do to irritate the source of one's income."

The wry statement struck a little close to home, and Gillian could feel the warmth creeping into her cheeks again. She grimaced, self-consciously pushing lukewarm broccoli salad about with her fork. "I don't suppose you realize how apt those words are, my lord, but I feel that I must apologize to you for causing you to be subjected to such unpleasantness as you must have been as a result of my—" She broke off, bogged down in the stiff phrasing.

Darrow smiled again. "I've survived it, Miss Harris."

"But I know he must have been utterly horrid to you, and it was my fault entirely."

"Not entirely. I was angry, I'll admit, and it's as well I didn't encounter you upon my departure, but Landover was eminently fair. Said nothing I didn't deserve to hear. Never should have taken you to such a place and certainly shouldn't have left you to your own devices once I had."

"Such frankness becomes you, my lord," Mrs. Periwinkle said with a smile as she buttered a hot roll. "I am afraid that neither you nor Miss Harris behaved well in that particular instance. However, I trust such a thing will never again come to pass."

Darrow chuckled. "That I can safely promise you, ma'am. Landover has promised to break my head for me if I ever even contemplate leading Miss Harris into mischief again. And it's no idle threat. I've seen him at Jackson's. He spars with the old man himself, and he's got the most wicked right jab imaginable. Assure you!" He turned to Gillian again. "I'm sorry you had to leave your charming little house, but I don't suppose you will wish to discuss that." She shook her head, and he smiled. "Where is Sir Avery tonight?"

"He had an engagement for dinner with some friends. I think he will be home before we are, however." She didn't add that her guess was based upon the fact that the friends had originally planned to visit some gaming hell or other, a point her brother had mentioned rather bitterly just before his departure. "Why do you ask, sir?"

"Because I've no wish to meet him for a day or so," he said, laughing. "I've a strong notion he's as irritated over this business as Landover was, and I doubt he will restrain his feelings as admirably."

"But he does not spar with Jackson," she teased, "and you are of a size with him, my lord. I . . . I've seen your skill for myself. Surely you do not fear his temper."

" 'Tis true enough. He's the merest neophyte in the ring," he agreed. "Nothing but cross and jostle, yet it don't suit my dignity to engage in a brawl with a man who's got a right to be angry. Just as well to let him cool off a bit before we meet again."

"Plotting more masquerades, my children?" drawled a familiar voice behind Gillian. She stiffened involuntarily, and it was Mrs. Periwinkle who replied.

"Lord Darrow was kind enough to bear us company over our supper, Landover, and since it was at my invitation that he did so, I'll thank you not to scold. And if you were planning to attend this do, I wish you might have said so at the outset instead of planning assignations at Bettencourt Hall or Carlton House. 'Tis vastly confusing, my lord, and not like you in the slightest. How do you do, Mr. Brummell? And Lord Alvanley. How nice to see you again, sir. You both know my cousin, Miss Harris. And Lord Darrow, of course."

Greetings were exchanged, and Landover made his apologies, saying he hadn't realized until he met them at White's that Mr. Brummell and Lord Alvanley had accepted invitations to the rout. "George said he thought the change of air would do him good, so we all came in Alvanley's carriage," he added as the three newcomers pulled up chairs for themselves. "Have you met the grand duchess yet?"

"Indeed we have," said Mrs. Periwinkle, muttering under her breath, " 'Venom clamors!' "

The Beau's eyebrows flew up in mock dismay, and he exchanged a glance with Landover, who said smoothly, "You think the duchess a jealous woman?"

Gillian realized, not without a touch of admiration, that Landover had not only heard her companion's brief comment but recognized the source. So, apparently, did Brummell, for with a glint of mockery in his eye, he murmured dulcetly, " 'Poison more deadly than a mad dog's tooth.' " Mrs. Periwinkle shot him a look of approval.

"Just so. And I fear she aims her poison at the Princess Charlotte."

"Heard she was here," Alvanley put in mildly, taking a pinch of snuff from an exquisite enameled snuffbox. Though both Brummell and Landover were dressed conservatively in black pantaloons and jackets, crisp white shirts, neatly tied neckcloths, and a minimum of fobs and rings, Alvanley sported buff breeches, a chocolate coat, a brightly flowered waistcoat, and a Mathematical tie. His shirt points were so high that he could scarcely turn his head when Brummell commented that Prinny would not like to hear of his daughter's presence in the Oldenburg entourage.

"Then we must hope he does not hear of it tonight," Landover said. "What makes you think the grand duchess is spreading poison, Amelia?"

Mrs. Periwinkle glanced uncertainly at Gillian. Recognizing her predicament, Gillian spoke up quickly. "The duchess said a good many things that don't bear repeating, sir. I think Cousin Amelia merely thought she should not say such things in the princess's hearing."

Mrs. Periwinkle nodded gratefully, but Landover gazed at them both for a rather long moment before turning his attention to young Lord Darrow. "And what did you think of her, Darrow?"

"I have not been privileged with an introduction, sir. I know only what I hear."

"Can't know much to the good then," Alvanley declared. "Very pushing female by all accounts."

"Must have been spouting off about Prinny," observed the Beau with a nearly malicious glint in his eye. "Must say, she does make a shrewd assessment now and again."

"That will do, George," Landover said firmly. "We are all aware of your sentiments, but this matter could have serious ramifications. The princess is vulnerable."

Brummell shrugged eloquently. "She will survive, I imagine. Nice enough chit when all's said and done. Shame to give her over to that boorish fellow from Orange."

"She may not go," Gillian said without thinking.

"She will have no choice in the matter," Landover replied curtly, but his eyes narrowed, and he changed the subject.

Shortly afterward, they returned to the main reception room and circulated for a brief time. Then the Beau reappeared to inform Landover that he had spoken with three people, thus acquitting himself nicely for a rout, especially since one of them was a total stranger. "We can go now, my lords. Fifteen minutes longer, and we shall be bored to distraction."

Alvanley agreed, and Mrs. Periwinkle said that she and her charge must also be on their way as soon as they had made their adieux to the de Lievens. "Do you come with us, Landover?"

"I do. Alvanley and the Beau are promised at Clarence House, and if I go with them, I shall no doubt forget my duty, which is to see you both safely to Carlton House before the night is done. Shall we go?"

With the gentlemen taking the lead, it was but a matter of moments before the amenities had been seen to and the ladies were once more in their carriage. Landover seated himself opposite, his back to the horses, and they were off, the carriage lamps casting a dim glow over the three faces within.

Under cover of Mrs. Periwinkle's sprightly conversation, Gillian watched Landover. He seemed to be giving the elderly lady his undivided attention, so she felt perfectly safe in doing so. He looked precise to a pin and completely at his ease as he responded to a question regarding politics put to him by Mrs. Periwinkle. Within moments, their conversation had turned to the forthcoming visit of the Allied Sovereigns.

"What with Tsar Alexander and King Frederick William of Prussia coming to celebrate that dreadful Bonaparte's defeat, not to mention possible royal nuptials, this will truly be a Season to remember," Mrs. Periwinkle said cheerfully.

Gillian had little interest in the Tsar or the King of Prussia—though, to be sure, she was looking forward to catching a glimpse of these mighty personages—but she was rapidly developing a strong interest in the fate of the crown princess.

"I don't think we should count on a royal wedding," she said as a lull fell into the others' conversation.

"Would you care to explain that?"

Gillian scarcely realized she had spoken aloud, but she looked up at him now and answered directly. "The princess herself said so. I daresay she's having second thoughts about the Prince of Orange. I really know nothing more than that, but

I like her, and if she doesn't want to marry him, I don't think anyone should force her to do so."

"Your opinions must always be of interest to us, Miss Harris, though I would prefer that you not express them, as you did tonight, to such persons as Brummell or his ilk," Landover said, adding bluntly, "You are not to cultivate that acquaintance."

Gillian stared at him. "Mr. Brummell's?"

"Of course not," he growled. "Her highness's."

"Why not?"

"Because I say so. It can do you no good."

"My lord," she returned between gritted teeth, "you may control my purse strings, but I cannot allow you to choose my friends. The princess has very kindly said she will send me an invitation to visit her. I shall not refuse to go."

"Indeed, Landover, she cannot," put in Mrs. Periwinkle quickly. " 'Twould be to insult Princess Charlotte, and the only person who would approve such a thing is the Regent. Gillian has no reason to curry favor in that direction."

"No, certainly not," Landover agreed evenly. "I never meant either of you to attach such a meaning to my words. If the princess does indeed extend such an invitation, Miss Harris must accept. However," he added, speaking directly to Gillian, "you are to stay no longer than the requisite twenty minutes and you are to do nothing to put yourself forward."

"But she needs friends!" Gillian protested. "She said so herself, and the grand duchess said she ought to have more friends of her own age."

"I am totally uninterested in the duchess's views upon that or any other subject. And whatever the princess needs or doesn't need, I don't want you mixed up in the affairs of that household. And that's my final word on the subject." With that he turned blandly to Mrs. Periwinkle and asked her opinion of the play currently being presented at Drury Lane. She responded with undisguised relief, and Gillian was left to glare impotently at them both.

Neither of her companions made any effort to bring her into their conversation, so she was left to her own thoughts until they reached town. It was decided then to postpone their appearance at the Bettencourt ball, since it was already nearing ten o'clock, and the prince's guests would no doubt have left the dining table. It seemed no time at all after that before the carriage was drawing to a halt before the Pall Mall entrance to Carlton House.

The magnificent Ionic screen and well-lit Corinthian portico were nothing new to Gillian, for she had passed by the prince's primary residence often and had seen it lit up and teeming with colorful guests. But this would be the first time she herself would number among those guests, and excitement welled within her at the thought.

Her quarrel with Landover was forgotten instantly, and her eyes were sparkling as he handed her down from the carriage and gave instructions to his coachman to return in an hour. Following Landover's guidance, they passed quickly through the torchlit courtyard to the vestibule, then through a series of elegant drawing rooms, past the famous grand ballroom, to an exotic chamber that Gillian recognized from descriptions she had heard as the Chinese Room. Here they found his highness amidst a group of some twenty or thirty chattering guests. The presentation was quickly made, and Gillian soon found herself rising from a deep curtsy under the twinklingly appreciative gaze of the First Gentleman of Europe.

IV

As Gillian arose from her deep curtsy, she realized that the prince was eyeing her appraisingly, and she was promptly reminded of the grand duchess's warning. Determined not to be overset by his bold looks, she gazed at him straightly, her candid eyes wide with awe.

"This is such a wonderful house, sir! You must be ever so proud of it!"

" 'Tis well enough, Miss Harris." But he was beaming his approval of such admiration. "We seek continually to improve upon its perfection, however, and let me say that tonight your presence achieves that very purpose."

"Thank you, sir," Gillian replied, looking demurely down at her satin-covered toes.

"No need to blush, Miss Harris. No more than the truth, assure you." He turned to Landover. "Why have you been hiding such a light under your bushel, my lord? 'Tis to deny the rest of us poor mortals the blessings of basking in its glory. For shame, sir."

Landover gave a wry bow. "Pure laziness on my part, your highness. But I have been brought to understand my error, I assure you."

Gillian did blush this time, and the prince eyed both of them a bit doubtfully before once again giving her his full attention.

"Since you admire my house, Miss Harris, perhaps you will allow me the pleasure of showing you a bit more of it. I have lived here more than twenty years now, you know, and in that time I have achieved—if I might be pardoned for saying so— great things. My armory fills four entire rooms and includes a

Cellini sword as well as arms from every nation. Or perhaps the Plate Room." He beamed. "Some very fine King Charles plate and all manner of elegant things. Or perhaps you prefer to be amused by the antics of the gamblers in the Circular Drawing Room." He bent his head nearer hers and lowered his voice. "They play E.O. and *chemin de fer* there. Don't gamble myself, of course, but I do enjoy providing pleasure for others." He chuckled. "You won't credit it, but Lord Kenyon vowed he'd put Lady Bessborough and her friends in the pillory for their activities here. And do you know, some folk actually call this place 'the Pillory' as a result?"

He laughed, evidently thinking it all rather a good joke, and at the same time dropped a plump if princely arm around Gillian's waist as though to guide her whither he would.

"I'm sure we shall be delighted to see more of your glorious residence, your highness," piped up Mrs. Periwinkle enthusiastically. "The very pink of courtesy indeed."

The prince glanced doubtfully at Landover.

" 'Tis a quote from *Romeo and Juliet*, sir, but very apt. We should indeed be delighted to accompany you."

"Dash it, Landover," the prince glared in an angry aside, "I never meant to make a touring party of it. Surely your Mrs. Popwhistle there is dying for a *petit four* or a dish of tea. See to it, man. You're not the chit's guardian, after all!"

Landover leaned forward confidingly. "No, sir, that I am not—most thankfully. But you will certainly understand my predicament when I tell you that her guardian is a mere stripling, scarce dry behind the ears himself. Why, as a result of his rather haphazard surveillance, I have had to exert myself far beyond my normal practice. Already today, I've been forced to make my position clear to one young rake, so I think—with your permission—I shall continue to advertise my intention to keep Miss Harris well under my wing."

The prince continued to glare, but he had little choice other than to submit with as much grace as he could muster. Nonetheless, their tour of Carlton House was brief and uninspired. The moment they returned to the Chinese Room, the Regent indicated a nearby group surrounding Lady Hertford and took himself off, much in the manner of a sulky child.

The glint of amusement in Landover's eye deepened when

Mrs. Periwinkle turned anxiously toward him and exclaimed, "He is most put out, my lord! I trust our behavior tonight has not endangered your friendship!"

"Not to worry, my dear ma'am. One would scarce honor our relationship by such a term as 'friendship,' but his highness has far greater need for my purse than I have for royal favor. He'll soon come about."

"Your purse, Landover?" Even as the words tumbled out, Gillian realized that she had spoken out of turn. Such matters were no concern of hers. But instead of the setdown she knew she deserved, he smiled wryly and answered her.

"Indeed, Miss Harris. Even in the depths of Sussex, you are near enough to Brighton to have heard at least some of the gossip about Prinny's financial embarrassments."

"He is always dreadfully purse-pinched," Mrs. Periwinkle contributed.

"Well, of course I have heard things," Gillian replied, "but I thought that his greatest debts were paid off when he married Princess Caroline."

"My good child," Landover chuckled, 'that was nearly twenty years ago. Believe me when I tell you he has managed to accrue a good many more great debts in the meantime. There is that outlandish pavilion at Brighton, his horses, his treasures, and this place." He gestured. "An incredible drain upon anyone's pockets, believe me, and Prinny's are not all that well lined to begin with."

Gillian looked around again at the lavish furnishings, the elegant accessories, the magnificent artworks. "It must indeed be very expensive," she said slowly.

"You might well say so. Why, each night that the ballroom is used, the band costs one hundred and fifty guineas, while it costs another fifteen guineas per night just for the French chalk for the dance floor. And the ratcatchers' bills exceed those of the chimney sweeps, because the damned . . . ah, excuse me . . . the dratted place is infested with the vermin."

Gillian glanced quickly about her, half expecting to discover a pair of glittering, feral eyes examining her from under a nearby lacquered table, and was accordingly glad when Landover added that their carriage must be waiting. But she could not resist questioning him further, especially in view of the fact that he seemed more approachable now than before.

"But surely you do not pay such bills for him!" They were making their way toward the Pall Mall entrance, and she lowered her voice in order that it might not carry to other guests. At first, she thought he had not heard her, but he was merely waiting until they reached the semiprivacy of the vestibule.

"I do not pay those bills," he said slowly, "although I have been known to lend him money when he's been badly strapped. More often, however, I purchase antiques and artwork for which he expresses a fancy, and then I donate them to Carlton House."

"But why? Surely that is no way to help him learn economy."

"We may pity though not pardon him," murmured Mrs. Periwinkle. Then, realizing the other two had both turned to look at her, she added hastily, "His highness, of course, not you, Landover. His upbringing—so needlessly harsh—his family, so . . . so . . ." She spread her hands helplessly.

"Just so, ma'am, though I for one would not compare Prinny to Richard III. But I don't do what I do out of pity, you know." He paused, then smiled. "Prinny has a great many faults, but he also has wonderful taste and judgment when it comes to *objets d'art*. 'Tis my belief that the treasures he's been gathering for the British crown will be loved and cherished long after his own reign has faded into history."

They had reached the carriage, and Landover scarcely paused between phrases before he gave the coachman orders to take them to Bettencourt Hall. It was nearly midnight, but Gillian knew the ball would be in full swing. On evenings such as this one, when they moved from one entertainment to another, it was very often after three o'clock in the morning before she or her chaperone could lay their heads upon their pillows. The night was young.

Landover had changed the subject and was idly conversing with Mrs. Periwinkle. Gillian relaxed against the velvet squabs, listening to their voices—Mrs. Periwinkle's like water rippling over stones in a brook, Landover's slower, more solid, with a deep, melodious cadence that seemed to carry its vibrations to every corner of the carriage. It was a soothing voice, moving easily through the conversation with Mrs. Periwinkle's higher tones skipping and weaving over and about it. Gillian watched the light from the carriage lamps as it flickered over his face, her thoughts turning to their earlier conversation.

Clearly, he had not wanted to discuss his royal financial dealings any further, but the discussion, however brief, had shown her another facet of his personality. It seemed there might be more to Landover than the tyrannical despot she had thought him to be. He was certainly handsome enough, she mused now, watching the glow of golden light on the chiseled features opposite. His gaze shifted, and she was glad her own features were shadowed, for she could feel warmth invading her cheeks.

"You're very quiet, Miss Harris. Are you falling asleep?"

"Just relaxing, my lord. I find it easier to be gay if I rest between entertainments. I'm sorry if I seemed inattentive."

"Not at all," he replied politely. "But I think we have arrived."

They had indeed. A pair of flunkies stepped briskly forward to open the carriage door and let down the steps before handing first Mrs. Periwinkle and then Gillian to the carpeted flagway.

"An hour and a half, Jason," Landover ordered as he, too, descended.

"Very good, m'lord." The coachman touched his hat, then gave his team the office, and the well-sprung carriage rolled off down the cobbled street as the trio ascended the steps and entered the warm rotunda of Bettencourt Hall.

They were greeted enthusiastically by their host and hostess and soon made their way to the ballroom, pausing now and again to greet acquaintances. But no sooner had they entered the magnificent, flower-bedecked ballroom itself than Landover, directly behind Gillian, was heard to give a low chuckle. She glanced back curiously to discover that his eyes were twinkling merrily as with a little gesture of his head he directed her attention ahead and to their right. Her gaze immediately encountered the elegant though patently bored figure of Mr. Brummell.

Landover's hand on her elbow urged her toward him, and Gillian reached forward to tap Mrs. Periwinkle's arm in order to warn her that they were changing direction. Mrs. Periwinkle responded immediately and, catching sight of him, hurried to greet the Beau.

"Why, Mr. Brummell, how nice to see you again," she enthused. "But we quite thought we should be denied your further company tonight."

"Indeed, George," chuckled Landover. "What brings you here? And you, Alvanley—not a soul to call your own?"

Lord Alvanley cast his tormenter a speaking look, but the Beau was made of sterner stuff. "It seems Clarence promised her ladyship he'd look in for a moment or two," he confided sweetly, referring to the Duke of Clarence, one of the Prince Regent's five younger brothers. "He has promised not to remain longer than necessary, however, so we agreed to accompany him. Are you trapped for the duration?"

"Unlikely," chuckled Landover. " 'Tis too much of a crush to tempt us overlong. But I have been given to understand that my sister is somewhere in the midst of this rabble, and rather than submit to one of her scolds, I will attempt to pay my respects before taking departure. Ah," he added, his eyes still atwinkle, "I believe I am about to have the honor of presenting my second charge to you, George." He beckoned. "Sir Avery, may I claim your attention for a moment, if you please?"

Gillian, astonished to see her brother at such a party, watched wide-eyed as he approached with a rather weaving gait, accompanied by a beet-faced gentleman of his own age.

"How d'ye do?" he replied offhandedly when the introductions were made. "This is m' friend Willoby, Jasper Willoby, one of the Bettencourt cousins," he added, explaining their presence. "At least, he was m' friend till a moment ago." He lifted an owlish gaze to Brummell. "Wish y'd explain the rules of snuff-taking to 'im, sir. Tried to dip his fingers into my sort, doncha know, then went all huffy when I told 'im I'd have to cast the rest onto the fire if he contaminated it. Tell 'im."

A sudden, rather awful silence descended upon the group, Mrs. Periwinkle actually gasping with shock, while Lord Alvanley cast his eyes accusingly heavenward. Landover recovered first.

"You are foxed, sir," he said sternly to Sir Avery, "therefore, I shall not attempt to correct your atrocious manners here and now. However, I will require your presence—your clearheaded presence, if possible—in my study at ten o'clock tomorrow morning. I trust you will remember."

Sir Avery's wits seemed to sharpen momentarily, although he glanced at the others in some bewilderment. "Beg pardon, all. Your servant, my lord." And with a quick bow and an anxious tug at Mr. Willoby's elbow, he faded into the crowd.

"My apologies, George," Landover said brusquely. "It won't happen again."

Brummell's eyes had narrowed angrily at Sir Avery's comment about the snuff, and now he turned that dagger look upon Landover. "Your little hen is deuced pretty, Landover, but yon cock has more bottom than wit. I trust you'll drub some manners into his head."

"Your wish is my command, sir," Landover responded promptly, and Gillian was amazed to detect a note of ironic amusement in his voice. "Perhaps you would be so good as to suggest a word or two I might drop in his ear—just to get the point across, mind you."

The sardonic tone was not lost on the Beau, whose gaze glittered even more. But something in Landover's expression brought a reluctant smile to his lips. "Have a care, my lord. My day is not yet done. I could indeed supply you with a telling phrase or two; yet, methinks you'll do well enough on that score unaided. I've no doubt the lad's ears will ring ere you have done with him."

They parted company soon afterward, and Gillian's curiosity was well and truly piqued. At first opportunity, she drew Mrs. Periwinkle aside.

"Pray, ma'am, what was all that?"

Mrs. Periwinkle shook her head. "That dreadful boy! Surely, Mr. Brummell thinks it was a calculated insult."

"Because Avery refused his snuff to Mr. Willoby? But how on earth could such an action have anything to do with Mr. Brummell?"

"Well may you ask, child. But you are not conversant as I am with the babbling gossip of court circles. Not long since did Mr. Brummell make that same comment when the Bishop of Winchester helped himself to a pinch of his snuff. Indeed, Mr. Brummell actually called his servant and ordered him to pitch the rest on the fire, since it had been contaminated."

"A bishop! How rude of him!" Gillian was horrified.

"Hung himself in his own straps, too, I'm afraid," Mrs. Periwinkle added, "since Prinny himself was present at the time. It is said that he gave the Beau a royal wigging for his rudeness. Which is no doubt what Landover, naughty fellow, was referring to when he asked the Beau what he should say to Sir Avery."

"But I'm quite sure Avery never meant to insult Mr. Brummell!" Gillian exclaimed. "Why, the man is very nearly his hero. You know he is! Avery strives to dress, speak, even act like him. Oh!"

"Indeed," smiled Mrs. Periwinkle. "He has succeeded only too well in acting like him. But even Mr. Brummell was not allowed to behave so rudely with impunity." She frowned thoughtfully. "You know, my dear, Sir Avery could do no better than to match Mr. Brummell's elegance of attire, but to copy his social manner would be a grave mistake, to my way of thinking."

"Yes, indeed," Gillian agreed. "Why, Mr. Brummell makes a habit of rudeness."

Mrs. Periwinkle seemed perfectly ready to launch into a nice gossip on the subject, but Gillian's attention was claimed for the Scottish reel that was just beginning. Her partner was one of the young men whose acquaintance she had made within the past three weeks, and he was slightly intoxicated, which fact she thought might be partially to blame for his rather forward manner with her. He flirted; indeed, he leered. His grip on her arm when the pattern of the dance brought them together was familiar, even lingering. And when the moment came for them to whirl their way down the corridor made by the other couples, he literally lifted her from the floor.

"Oh, Mr. Wakely!" she gasped when she could catch her breath again. "You really are too physical, sir! Nothing but minuets for you after this!"

"Nonsense, Miss Harris," he breathed close to her face, brandy fumes wafting gently under her nose. "A brisk trot clears the head and exercises the heart. And, oh, my heart, Miss Harris!" He leered again.

"Will you introduce your friend, my dear?"

Gillian jumped at the sound of the harsh voice. Turning, she discovered Landover looming over her, his gimlet gaze impaling young Wakely.

"This is Mr. Wakely, Landover," she said, oddly breathless. "And this is the Marquis of Landover, sir."

"A marquis, eh?" Mr. Wakely beamed vacuously. "You in the running, too, my lord?"

"I beg your pardon." Landover spoke blightingly, but he might have spared himself the trouble. Wakely was far too insulated to notice his tone.

"The running," he explained carefully. "Y' know—the Harris Heiress stakes! Bein' a marquis gives you an edge, I daresay, but win, place, or show makes no never-mind to me. Don't need the guineas m'self. Well heeled. But the little filly's worth the race, whatever, doncha know."

Gillian stiffened with dismay and opened her mouth to correct Mr. Wakely's mistaken notions. But Landover spoke first.

"There are no stakes to be won, sir. Miss Harris is under my protection."

"What! Already? Quick work, my lord. And just to show there's no hard feelings, here's my hand on it." And to Gillian's outraged astonishment, he actually seemed to expect Landover to accept a congratulatory fist. Suddenly, the whole incident seemed ludicrous. She stifled a giggle.

"It is not as you seem to think, you young cur," Landover said angrily. "I am Miss Harris's trustee, not her . . . her . . ."

"He is not my lover, Mr. Wakely," Gillian put in helpfully. "Nor my betrothed. He has merely taken it into his head that I need looking after."

"That will do, Miss Harris." The tone was such that she subsided obediently. "Good evening, Wakely. I trust Miss Harris will not be annoyed by any further attentions from you."

This time his tone sliced through even the brandy. Young Mr. Wakely reddened perceptibly. "No, my lord. As you say, my lord. Not me, sir." He turned rather too abruptly upon his heel and stumbled against a corpulent gentleman following in the wake of a regal dame. "Beg pardon," muttered Mr. Wakely wretchedly. Then, bethinking himself of another detail, he turned back to Landover. "Want I should pass the word, my lord?"

"By all means," was the damping reply.

Gillian, her eye upon Mr. Wakely's careful progress, let a tiny chuckle escape as she turned back to Landover. The sound froze in her throat, however, when she encountered blazing fury in those hazel eyes.

"My lord?"

Her voice was tiny. She tried to clear her throat, but he took her hand, clamped it down upon his forearm, and drew her inexorably from the dance floor toward a group of chairs, temporarily vacant, against the nearest wall.

"Sit." She sat. At first he seemed about to deliver his lecture standing, but with a quick glance around the crowded ballroom, he thought better of it and took the chair to her left, growling, "That is exactly the sort of behavior I had hoped my presence would deter, Miss Harris."

"But how was I to know? He seemed all right when he asked me to dance, and I've danced with him often since I came to London. He's perfectly harmless, my lord."

"That remains to be seen," he retorted grimly. "As to how you should have known, that is the precise reason for having a chaperone. And don't try to flim-flam me by pretending Amelia Periwinkle approved Mr. Wakely for a partner. She would have noticed his condition straightaway."

"But she was right beside—" Belatedly, Gillian realized she had not so much as glanced at her companion before accepting Mr. Wakely's invitation. Her cheeks flamed, and she found it difficult to meet Landover's steady look.

"Just so. At least you do not prevaricate, Miss Harris. That must always be accounted in your favor. Nevertheless, henceforward, you shall dance with no one who has not been formally approved by Amelia Periwinkle or myself. Is that absolutely understood?"

"I am not a child, Landover," she grated between clenched teeth. "I can look after myself. I can even handle the Mr. Wakelys of this world, and I should vastly prefer to do so by myself. I cannot like having my every step overlooked."

"And the 'Harris Heiress stakes'? Can you handle those as well, my dear?" There had been a touch of sarcasm in the first few words, but at her stricken look, his tone gentled. Now he laid his hand comfortingly upon hers. "Do not look so distressed, child. And don't glare at me for calling you so. You may be of an age to become a matron lady, and you may have done a great many things in the past three weeks or even before that in Sussex, but you are still a child in experience. And it is my duty, whether either of us likes it or not, to protect you from yourself as well as from others who might do you harm."

"Who could do me harm, sir?" Gillian demanded in a last-ditch effort. "I am not a ninnyhammer. I do not hop into shabby coaches with strange men, nor do I meet would-be lovers at romantic rendezvous at midnight in the manner of a literary heroine."

"But you do go to Vauxhall Gardens with only a young jackstraw for protection," he retorted.

"We have already picked that bone, my lord!" she protested indignantly.

"So we have," he agreed ruefully, "and I for one detest having my past errors constantly flung in my face. I cry pardon. Forgive me?"

It quite took the wind out of her sails. It was as though she had girded for battle only to have her foe suddenly and without warning throw down his arms. "I forgive you," she replied gruffly, but she watched him warily, never having sparred with anyone quite like him before. She couldn't believe he had simply capitulated.

Nor had he. He patted her hand. "I shall want your word that you will make proper use of your chaperone, my dear. And once I have it, I think we should find my sister. She will be dashed unpleasant later if we fail to do the pretty."

"Can you not trust me, my lord? I would promise to be more careful."

"I know you would," he admitted. "But you are not yet up to snuff, and I admit candidly that this 'Harris Heiress' business worries me. I had heard nothing about it before, which means it has not yet reached White's betting book. But I dare not let it escalate. Once there are heavy wagers laid, anything might happen. On the other hand, if it is seen that you are under my strictest protection, it should scotch matters before they get out of hand."

Gillian stared at him in astonishment. "You can't mean that someone might attempt to abduct me!"

"I mean exactly that. It has happened before, and will no

doubt happen again. But not to you. Not if I have anything to say about it."

She could not believe that such a thing might be possible, but she could tell from the set of his jaw that further argument would be useless. Consequently, she allowed him to lead her to his sister. Mrs. Periwinkle had already joined Lady Harmoncourt, and the two were deep in conversation when Landover and Gillian approached.

"Landover, how nice to see you," her ladyship observed dryly, extending a plump, beringed hand in his general direction. He bowed over it obediently.

"Abigail, you are looking well. That gown suits you."

"It does, does it not," she agreed with a complacent look down the length of clinging emerald silk. "Claudette Moray did it. I expect her real name is Ethel Quince, or something equally common," she added in a caustic aside to Mrs. Periwinkle, "but she is handy with a needle, and her designs are all the rage just now. I must say," she went on with another glance downward, "she does know how to display one's assets to advantage."

It was true. Lady Harmoncourt was no longer the slender beauty who had taken London by storm at her coming-out, but she was by no means decrepit either. Her skin was still glowingly translucent, and a good deal of it was revealed by Mademoiselle Moray's creation. Her breasts were high, plump, and edged in Alençon lace. Her arms, still firm if a trifle rounder than they had been in those earlier, golden days, emerged triumphantly from tiny puffed sleeves that many of her contemporaries, in Gillian's opinion, might well have envied. And if the rest of her body was unable to compete, Mademoiselle Moray had disguised the fact admirably amidst cunning folds and draperies of the shimmering green silk. With her abundant chestnut hair piled atop her head and a magnificent emerald collar encircling her throat, Lady Harmoncourt presented an ideal advertisement for her dressmaker's expertise.

"Ah, here is Sybilla," her ladyship pronounced unnecessarily as an ethereal blonde in sprigged muslin approached, accompanied by a young gentleman who promptly made his bow and effaced himself. Sybilla curtsied to her uncle. "You will no doubt wish to dance with your niece, Landover," her ladyship pronounced grandly. "Give him your card, Sybilla."

"Oh, but . . ." The blonde, smiling shyly, seemed reluctant to relinquish her card. Glancing at it, Landover eyed his niece a bit searchingly. Her color heightened, and she looked nervously at her mother.

"Well, what are you waiting for, Benjamin?" Lady Harmoncourt demanded. "Her next partner will soon be along."

Landover smiled at Sybilla and returned the card. "Your daughter is too popular, ma'am. Johnny-Come-Lately can't sign where there is no space. I shall have to make do with Miss Harris's card. Hand it over, Miss Harris. The next dance is a waltz, and in my new role as protector-general, I cannot in good conscience allow you to engage in such low activity with anyone but myself."

Gillian obediently handed him her card, but not before she noted the look of gratitude cast him by his niece.

V

"Was her card really full?" Gillian asked as Landover swung her into the dance.

"No," he chuckled, "but I'm not so green as to fail to recognize wishful thinking when I come across it. There were two blank spaces, but our Lady Sybilla was clearly hoping for one particular name to occupy those spaces, and I fear it was not mine. I'd not be much of an uncle were I to dash such romantical hopes."

"Well, I've no notion who it might be," Gillian replied dampingly. "She's said nothing whatever to me about any special beau. I think you must be all about in your head, sir. She merely didn't wish to dance with you."

"Attempting to depress my pretensions, Miss Harris?" he gibed. "And what of yourself? Do you object to dancing with me?"

"Since you asked me to dance with you only to prevent my dancing with anyone else, the question is hardly a fair one," she retorted. He promptly whirled her into an intricate pattern of steps that necessitated her complete concentration, but when she could think again, she realized he had not pressed her for an answer, and that it was just as well for her own self-respect that he had not. For she thoroughly enjoyed dancing with him, although she would not have told him so for a wilderness of monkeys. He held her firmly and guided her steps with recognizable expertise, but it was not that alone which made the experience a pleasurable one. It was more that they seemed to fit, that she felt comfortable with him. Now that she came to think of it, even when he infuriated her, she still felt as though she had known him forever. It was not at all as though she had been scolded by a total stranger. And yet, before that morning, to all intents and purposes, that was precisely what Landover had been to her. It was all very odd, very odd indeed.

They parted company after that dance, and though she was aware of his gaze upon her from time to time, they did not meet again until their carriage was due. Consequently, Miss Harris returned to Landover House in perfect charity with her host. Unfortunately, that state of affairs was short-lived.

The following day, Landover presented himself in the drawing room with the first of her morning callers. He exerted himself to be genial, but nevertheless, his very presence could only cast a damper. And when she announced that an invitation had arrived as promised for her to drink tea with the Princess Charlotte the following day, Landover made it quite clear that he expected Mrs. Periwinkle to accompany her, despite the fact that the invitation had been addressed to Gillian alone.

"You're being positively Gothic, Landover!" she protested.

"Be that as it may, it is perfectly proper for your chaperone to accompany you, and I insist that she do so. I do not want you striking up an intimate friendship with Charlotte."

Gillian's reply to that was an exasperated and very unlady-like snort, but he was adamant, and so it was that the two ladies were ushered into the elegantly appointed drawing room at Warwick House the following day.

The princess professed herself delighted to see them both and behaved as naturally as any ordinary hostess. But Gillian was astonished by the number of ladies-in-waiting deemed necessary for the comfort of a royal princess and realized that even without Landover's warning, it would have been difficult to lay any real foundation for an intimate relationship. Nonetheless, she and Mrs. Periwinkle thoroughly enjoyed themselves. Gillian was particularly gratified, Landover's orders notwithstanding, when the princess took advantage of a moment while Mrs. Periwinkle's attention was diverted to plead with her to return another day, alone, so that they might enjoy a comfortable gossip together.

"Or perhaps we might meet at Catherine's hotel," she

suggested, stroking the elegant little crop-eared greyhound curled up at her side. "It would be much less formal."

"I should adore to, your highness," Gillian responded sincerely, smiling when the little white dog nudged the princess's hand with its nose, "but it might prove to be difficult. My trustee—Landover, you know—does not wish me to cultivate an acquaintance with her grace." The subject had not actually come up since the de Lievens' rout, but she doubted that Landover would give his blessing to any sort of meeting with the Grand Duchess Oldenburg.

Charlotte grinned conspiratorially. "I, too, am hemmed about by those who would seek to deny me simple pleasures, Miss Harris. But we shall contrive to confound them, you and I. I think you are not a faintheart, and I am only just learning to fight for what I want. We shall be friends, I believe, despite those who would order it otherwise."

With Mrs. Periwinkle's eye once more upon them, Gillian was spared the necessity of replying to this extraordinary statement, but she could not help feeling flattered by the princess's desire for her friendship. Besides, she liked Charlotte. One way or another, she decided, she would find a means to defy Landover's unfair restrictions.

Her determination became even stronger in the days that followed, when he continued to oversee her every move. It seemed almost as though she could do nothing without his presence. Even a morning ride in the park found him at her side in place of her groom. She could not, in good conscience, pretend she disliked his company; nonetheless, she would have preferred to have less of it. The final straw came one evening when, having honored three separate routs and a dinner party with their presence, Landover, Mrs. Periwinkle, and Gillian found themselves at Harmoncourt House as her ladyship's guests for a musical evening. Despite a collection of fine talent, the performers were nevertheless amateurs, and Gillian soon found herself fidgeting. Mrs. Periwinkle glanced at her reprovingly, and Landover picked that moment to lean forward apologetically.

"This is too much for me, ladies. I'm off to White's, but I shall send Jason back to collect you when this little affair has run its course. Pray for me that Abigail does not detect my absence until I am safely beyond recall." Gillian smiled, more in relief at his departure than at this near-sally. But the smile disappeared a moment later when Landover made it clear that he expected them to go straight home from Harmoncourt House.

"But we were going on to a late supper at Lady Heathcote's!" Gillian protested.

Landover chucked her under the chin. "They'll not miss you, child, and you can use the extra sleep. You'll soon have black smudges under those pretty eyes if you don't slow the pace a bit. Mind, ma'am," he added to Mrs. Periwinkle, "straight home." And he took his departure, leaving an indignantly sputtering Gillian in his wake.

"Of all the crack-brained, pompous—to call me 'child' and treat me as though I were ten years old!"

"Well, you did not act very grown-up, my dear," Mrs. Periwinkle chuckled, carefully adjusting a large purple ostrich feather in her headdress so as to deter its persistent attempts to tickle her nose.

Gillian opened her mouth to protest again, then subsided with a responding grin. "No, I suppose I did not," she admitted. "But his attitude would madden anyone. I cannot be held responsible for my behavior when he sticks to us like a limpet. But oh," she added as a buxom dame launched into an operatic aria with an exuberance that would have startled its composer, "how I wish we might have escaped with him!"

"Well, we could not," her companion replied matter-of-factly, "so we will be the pattern of all patience, if you please. Particularly since you promised dear Lady Sybilla you would remain to hear her play the harp."

Resigned, Gillian settled back in her chair and, by the time the last offering had been made, was only too glad to seek the comparatively blissful silence of Landover's comfortable carriage. Knowing it would be futile, she made no attempt to convince Mrs. Periwinkle that they might still attend the supper, admitting in fact, if only to herself, that it would be a relief to lay her head upon a pillow. But great was her astonishment when, having bidden her companion good night, she made her way to her own bedchamber only to discover her brother sprawled in the dressing chair, swigging down a liberal dose of Landover's brandy.

"Well, hello, Avery," she chuckled. "To what do I owe the pleasure? Although if you're foxed, I daresay it won't be much of a pleasure."

"Not foxed, m' dear," he replied, lifting his glass in a silent toast. "Not even half cast. Just drowning m' sorrow."

Gillian pulled pins from her hair. "Where's Ellen? Did you send her to bed?"

"Right. Told her late hours weren't good for her, that I'd maid you m'self if necessary. Hope it ain't, though. Not much of a dab at that sort of thing, y' know."

"Don't worry. I can manage." Reaching over his shoulder, she picked up her hairbrush and began to draw it rhythmically through the dusky tresses, watching her brother critically. She had scarcely laid eyes upon him since the Bettencourt ball and remembered that he had fallen afoul of Landover there. But while she debated the best means of introducing the subject, he saved her the trouble.

"Gotta do something about that damned fellow!"

"Landover?"

"Of course, Landover," he growled. "Who else? Who else would throw a fellow out of his own club even when he wasn't betting a sou? And who else would rob the dictionary blind just to flay a fellow to ribbons with his tongue? Who else? Answer me that! I defy you to name another but his bloody lordship, our precious trustee, the honorable Marquis of Landover!"

"Well, I know he was put out by your rudeness to Mr. Willoby—" she began cautiously.

"Put out! If that's all it was, I can dashed well assure you I don't want to meet the fellow when he's angry!"

"Oh dear." Gillian set down the hairbrush and began to remove her jewelry, reaching across him to put the pieces in her case. "Was he quite horrid?"

"I'd as lief forget the whole disagreeable scene, if it's all the same to you," replied Sir Avery with great dignity before taking another generous swig of the brandy. "Damned unpleasant fellow, that Landover."

"You say he pitched you out of one of the clubs?"

He grimaced. "White's. Stupid of me to go there, of course, but I thought it was safe enough since he seemed to be tied to your apronstrings for the evening. How was I to know he'd fight shy?"

"He got bored. I did, too, for that matter," Gillian confessed with a tiny, reminiscent smile. "But it's easier for a gentleman to slip away. Especially from his own sister's house."

"Like that, was it? What was the pitch?"

"Music. Amateur talent. They even asked me to exhibit my prowess on the pianoforte."

"Good Lord! No wonder he skipped!" Sir Avery responded with brotherly scorn, blithely unaware that his words might seem a trifle insulting to his sister. She shook her head with a mocking smile.

"Not so bad as that, my dear. I refused—politely, of course, but a refusal all the same. Most of the talent was unexceptionable. Sybilla played her harp very skillfully."

"By Jove, I must say I'd like to have seen that! She must have looked like an angel—all ethereal, doncha know."

Gillian shot him a searching look, but she was not so tactless as to suggest that he had lost his senses. She did hint rather gently that she could see to his name finding a place on any such future invitation list.

"No, dash it, Gill, that's carrying things too far! Didn't say I wanted to listen to a lot of caterwauling. Didn't even say I wanted to *listen* to Sybilla. Just said it ought to make a damned fine picture, that's all. No need to go making something more of it. Probably the brandy talking anyway. Probably she was insipid. The pale blonde beauties often are."

Gillian made no comment despite the fact that she could not think Sybilla Harmoncourt an insipid person. After a slight pause during which he seemed to be conferring silently with the dregs of his brandy, Sir Avery shifted his position and gazed at her more directly. "Thing is, Gill, we've got to do something. Can't go on being preached at and held on a damned leash like a couple of blinkin' puppies. It's embarrassing, that's what it is."

"Well, it is annoying. I'll give you that. But you did provoke him, Avery. Particularly if you went to White's after he expressly forbade it. And you were very rude to poor Mr. Willoby, after all."

He hunched a shoulder. "Said I didn't want to talk about

that. As to White's, I wasn't playing, just watching, having a drink with friends. No concern of Landover's. What that man needs is an Object in Life."

"He seems to have found one," Gillian said, picking up her brush again. "Do move to the window seat, Avery. I want to sit there." Obediently, he removed himself to sprawl inelegantly upon the French seat.

"If you mean us, I'd as lief he find another object. By Jove, Gill, the man ought to have a wife and a nursery to occupy his thoughts. He's past thirty, after all."

"But scarcely in his dotage. Nonetheless . . ." She paused, giving the seedling of an idea a moment to sprout if it was so inclined. "You know, Avery, Sybilla has mentioned any number of times that her mother wishes Landover would settle down with a proper wife. I think Lady Harmoncourt might even have dangled a few possibles under his nose. I doubt she's put much effort into it, though. Before now, that is." Her eyes began to twinkle suddenly, and her brother sat straighter, the few remaining drops in his glass temporarily forgotten.

"Dash it, Gillian, what maggot's bouncing in your bonebox now?"

She gazed at him thoughtfully, her hairbrush suspended midstroke. "Well, it seems to me that if Landover were busy courting, he'd have little or no time left to bother his head about us."

"By Jove!" Avery sat up even straighter. "You may have something there." He scratched his head. "Dashed if I can see how we'd manage it, though. Can't just thrust some poor chit into the man's arms and order him to court her, y' know."

Gillian chuckled at the vision produced by these words. She began brushing steadily again. "Of course not. Don't be silly. I really have no notion how we might manage it. But I daresay Lady Harmoncourt might know how to turn the trick if we approach her properly."

A light of respect dawned in his eyes. "By Jove, it might work at that! But mind, puss," he warned, "I won't appreciate it if this little scheme of yours lands us in the briars again. Just how do we approach her ladyship?"

She set the hairbrush down and leaned forward to examine

her neatly arched brows in the looking glass. "I don't know. I think I shall discuss the matter with Sybilla."

Sir Avery seemed to find nothing amiss in the notion of discussing their personal affairs with Lady Sybilla Harmoncourt and soon took himself off to bed, leaving his sister to ponder several interesting notions of her own. Accordingly, when MacElroy showed the Lady Sybilla into the morning room a half hour or so after Gillian had finished her breakfast the following morning, the visitor was greeted enthusiastically.

"Sybilla! I was just about to send you a message!"

"Did you want to see me?" The blonde girl moved to a chair near the window and sat gracefully, disposing a beaded reticule upon the parquetry table beside her. Her voice was light with a crystalline flavor. "Mama was going on and on about last evening, about how Mrs. Erskine-Smythe always screeches her high notes and how nice it would have been to have got Catalani, even if she is a bit past her prime, and I got sick of it, so I decided to pay you a call." She grinned. "Is Uncle driving you mad? Is that why you were going to send for me?"

Gillian chuckled. "It really isn't fair, Sybilla. You look like such a fleabrain, yet you're as sharp as can hold together."

"Then he *is* driving you mad." Lady Sybilla paid no attention to Gillian's comment on her mental agility. "I told Mama how it would be as soon as we heard he'd packed you up and moved you to Berkeley Square. And she agreed with me. Mama can be a slowtop about some matters, but where Uncle Benjamin is concerned, she's as quick as Mercury. I think myself that it will wear off eventually. He's bound to become bored with dancing attendance on you long before the Season ends. Particularly in view of the fact that the Allied Sovereigns are due to arrive next week. He will no doubt be involved in activities with which you will have nothing to do."

It was true. The whole city of London was gearing up for the forthcoming visit of Alexander of Russia and King Frederick of Prussia. There would be parades and parties, banquets and balls, all culminating in a grand masquerade at Burlington House, and Landover would no doubt be in the thick of things. But it would not be enough. Gillian shook her head as she said so.

"I wouldn't put it past the man to lock me up for the duration of their stay just to keep me out of his hair," she added bitterly.

Sybilla giggled. "I doubt he would go to such lengths. Think of the scandal!" She paused, wrinkling her pretty nose. "That is not to say, however, that he won't take it into his head to pack you off to the country instead."

"Then he will pack Avery off with me," Gillian stated roundly. "I'm not the only one suffering from an overabundance of his attentions." She saw Sybilla's eyes widen in dismay and felt a sense of satisfaction at the sight. "I may have a notion how to mend matters before that happens," she suggested gently, "but I shall need your help."

"Oh! Anything, Gillian. You know I shall be glad to do whatever I can. Provided, of course, that Mama does not get wind of it. I should no doubt be in for one of her most dreadful scolds if she knew I was plotting against Uncle Benjamin. She would not approve."

Gillian felt her spirits sinking, but she rallied valiantly. "She's got to know some of it," she said frankly. "We need her assistance."

"Oh, no! Gillian, she wouldn't! She hardly ever does—interfere with him, I mean. And only then if he makes her truly angry. But she wouldn't think it proper to take him to task over the way he treats you and Sir Avery. Why, she said herself that Avery—that is, Sir Avery—has been sailing too near the wind of late and needed taking down a peg or two." Lady Sybilla stopped speaking rather suddenly and looked self-consciously at her hands.

"And me?" Gillian asked softly. "What did she say about me, Sybby?"

Sybilla bit her lower lip, avoiding the gathering storm warnings in Gillian's eyes. "Just . . . just that you need a firm hand and that she was glad Landover seemed to be taking his responsibilities seriously for once." She did not add Lady Harmoncourt's expressed hope that Landover would introduce Miss Harris to the business end of a birch rod, but Gillian, being rather well acquainted with her ladyship by this time, had no doubt that the sentiment or one much like it had been vouchsafed at one point or another. Nonetheless, it would be unkind, not to mention counterproductive, to press Sybilla for further information on the subject. Therefore, firmly suppressing her resentment, she forced a tiny smile.

"His responsibilities? Perhaps she is right. But it does seem to me that he is overplaying the role. Does it not occur to her that he owes a greater responsibility to his own name than he does to us?"

Sybilla cocked her head. "What are you trying to say, Gillian?"

"He has a duty to secure the title. That's what I mean."

Blonde eyebrows arched a little higher. Then Sybilla smiled. "I see how it is. You'd like to divert his attention."

Gillian grinned. "I must say, you rarely have to have things explained down to the nits and grits. Do you think the notion has potential?"

There was a pause during which Lady Sybilla quite clearly subjected the matter to serious consideration. Gillian managed to keep still despite a nearly overwhelming desire to speak more forcibly to the question. At last Sybilla smiled.

"It is possible," she said. "I would have said no if you had just put the thing baldly, but your mentioning the succession has given me an idea. Landover's heir is a cousin of his, a sweet, limp-wristed fellow named Sylvan Darracott who spends most of his time fishing in Yorkshire. His title is actually Viscount Orison, but Uncle always calls him 'Sylvia' when he refers to him at all. And Mama cannot tolerate him upon any account."

"I think I can visualize the gentleman," Gillian said, grinning. "Was he not at Lady Jersey's ball the first week I was in London?"

"That's the fellow," Sybilla replied, her eyes atwinkle.

"Wearing a gold satin waistcoat and a watchchain clanking with fobs?"

"And the earring. I do hope you didn't miss the earring!"

"A pendant ruby in his right ear," responded Gillian promptly. "Good heavens, Sybby. You cannot mean to say that fellow's a Darracott! I know no one mentioned the fact to me."

"Well, he is, though I am not surprised no one thought to tell you. Thank heaven he only spends a week or so in town each year. He embarrasses Mama and annoys Uncle Benjamin. I mean, really, Gill, can you imagine him taking Uncle Ben's place as Landover? Why, Uncle rarely wears more than a signet ring!"

Gillian stared at her for a moment before the absurdity struck them both, and they dissolved in giggles.

"Is this a private joke, or may one share the merriment?"

They had not heard him come in, but it was clear from Landover's smile that he had heard nothing incriminating. Sybilla's giggles ceased abruptly, and she glanced from Landover to Gillian and back again in pretty confusion. Gillian could not stifle her mirth so easily, and her eyes were still twinkling when she answered him.

"Sybilla was just informing me that I have had the honor of meeting your heir, sir."

"I see. Well, if you have been discussing Orison's deficiencies, I can understand your laughter, though it borders on impertinence, miss."

Her eyes twinkled wickedly. "Orison, my lord? I was given to understand that you generally call him—"

"Gillian!" Sybilla protested in dismay.

Landover shot his niece a look that boded ill for her future, and Sybilla flushed, looking away uncomfortably. But Gillian was having none of that.

"How unfair of you, my lord, to blame Sybby! If it was something she should not have repeated to me, then it was something you ought never to have said yourself in the first place. For shame, sir, to try to frighten her like that!"

Sybilla stared at her in shock, but Gillian ignored her, forcing herself to meet Landover's stern look instead. His grim expression softened suddenly, and a rueful smile touched his lips. "Perhaps you are right, Miss Harris. The blame is mine." He glanced around the room, and his gaze came to light upon a pile of notes resting haphazardly at her elbow. He seemed glad to change the subject and gestured toward them. "Today's post?"

"Yes, sir." Then, as she recalled one note among the others, Gillian reached out a guilty, protective hand to cover them only to snatch it back as soon as she realized how the action would look. "Nothing of grave importance, my lord," she said calmly.

But Landover missed nothing. "Let me see them."

His steady gaze caught hers, and she could not look away,

though she was very conscious of Sybilla's presence. Hoping he would remember that they were not alone, she reached out blindly for the stack of invitations and handed them up to him. One fluttered from the pack and drifted to the floor, but Landover ignored it as the elegant crest atop one invitation caught his attention. He laid the others absentmindedly upon a table while he perused this interesting item. In the ensuing silence, Gillian could feel the warmth invading her cheeks. She scarcely dared to breathe normally lest she recall his attention to herself. But he finished reading the elaborate script soon enough and looked up at her over the top. His eyebrows lifted slightly.

"I need scarcely ask what sort of answer you have returned to this impertinence."

"Impertinence, Landover? I feared you would not approve, but how can you call an invitation to visit a grand duchess an impertinence?"

"Don't quibble, miss. 'Tis not the invitation, and well you know it. 'Tis the suggestion that you evade your chaperone—that's the impertinence."

Gillian wrinkled her nose. "Evade my—" But then she remembered. Her grace had not phrased it so bluntly, of course, but the fact that the afternoon was to be an informal one had been strongly emphasized, despite a similar emphasis on the fact that the Princess Charlotte would be present. It was clear that Gillian was meant to come alone. She couldn't deny it. She swallowed carefully. "Perhaps you are right, sir, though I hadn't thought of it in those terms. I am perfectly certain that I shall come to no harm in such company. However, if you insist upon it, I shall naturally ask Cousin Amelia to accompany me."

"You are not going," he said flatly.

"What!"

"You heard me. And we shall not debate the matter." He glanced pointedly at his niece.

"But how dare you!" Gillian cried, ignoring the look. "And what on earth shall I write to her grace that will not be taken as an insult?"

"Leave that to me. I know precisely how to respond to this. You need not be troubled further by it." And with that, he turned upon his heel, the offending scrap of vellum clenched in his fist, and left the two young women to stare at one another in astonishment.

"Merciful heavens," breathed Lady Sybilla. "Whoever would have thought he'd arouse himself to such exertion?"

"Exertion, my rosy aunt!" exclaimed Gillian indignantly. "This is nothing but another example of his highhandedness. Why, he nearly forbade my attendance at the de Lievens' rout merely because the grand duchess meant to be present, and he came very near to making me refuse an invitation to drink tea with the Princess Charlotte herself! 'Tis all of a piece!"

"The Princess Charlotte!"

"Indeed, and if I have not misread the invitation, she will be at the Pulteney tomorrow, too. But Landover mislikes the connection."

"Surely he cannot dislike the princess!"

"No, of course not. He just doesn't want me involved with her, lest I get caught in the middle between her highness and the Regent."

"A rather exalted middle to be caught in, I should think," Sybilla observed dryly. "You'd think he'd be flattered that you've drawn royal attention."

"Well, he's not!" Gillian snapped. Then she sighed, casting an apologetic look at her friend. "I'm sorry, Sybilla. It isn't your fault, and there's no reason you should have to suffer my bad temper. But perhaps you can understand a little better just what Avery and I must put up with from his infernal lordship."

Sybilla giggled. "Indeed I do! Why, it would drive anyone mad. I thought Mama was a nuisance, forever reading my letters, lecturing me on my behavior, and screening my friends. But I'm not nearly so confined as you seem to be. I came here alone today, after all. Of course, my maid came with me, but she doesn't really count. No doubt she is belowstairs right now exchanging all the latest 'crim cons' with your Ellen. But that is a very good thing, of course. For how else should we keep up with all that goes on in the world?"

"Very true," Gillian chuckled, her spirits heightened considerably. "The *Times* and the *Gazette* will never surpass the servants' grapevine for pertinent news of the day. But what

on earth are we going to do about Landover?" she added with a
deep sigh.

Sybilla smiled at her. "I shall speak to Mama for you. I
think I know how the thing may be accomplished. After all,
she cannot wish for Orison to step into Uncle's shoes. And
perhaps if I prevaricate a bit—let it be known that whilst here I
was given to understand that Uncle *might* be in the market for
a wife . . ." She let the final thought hover tantalizingly.

"Your mother would never leave the choosing entirely to his
lordship," Gillian grinned.

"No, indeed," Sybilla agreed. "She would be certain he
would choose someone entirely unsuitable. However, that approach might be too vague. She exerts far more influence over
him when she loses her temper, for he abhors a row. I don't
think she has properly considered Sylvan Darracott. Perhaps a
nudge in that direction will set her off." Sybilla had been
thinking aloud, but now she gathered up her reticule and
looked directly at Gillian. "I shall have to consider the matter.
Shall we see you at the Deering ball tonight?"

"Yes, I believe so."

"Good. I shall attempt to speak to Mama before then."

When Sybilla had gone, Gillian sat back in her chair and
contemplated the morning's events. All in all, she decided, it
had not been a bad day's work. If anyone could succeed in
diverting Landover from his self-appointed task, she was convinced it was his sister. And if anyone could motivate her
ladyship to such a task, it was Sybilla. She must trust Sybilla
to get the ball rolling.

In the meantime, she had her own tasks to attend to, and
first of all, courtesy demanded that she reply to the invitations
in the morning's post. She would need to consult Mrs. Periwinkle before accepting any, but there was one note she decided to
write herself before going in search of that lady. No matter
what Landover chose to write to the grand duchess, Gillian was
determined that Princess Charlotte, at least, should know that
she had had nothing to say about declining that particular
invitation, and that she personally hoped to further their slight
acquaintance. The note was sent off with a sympathetic footman before she went looking for Mrs. Periwinkle.

At the Deering ball, Landover seemed to hover over her, so

there was little opportunity for private speech with Lady Sybilla, but Gillian did manage to intercept a nod encouraging enough to lead her to believe Sybilla had spoken with her mother. The following morning she found her hopes justified, for she descended the grand stair just in time to see MacElroy showing Lady Harmoncourt into Landover's study.

Her ladyship moved with regal grace, like a ship in full sail; however, she did not wait for the butler's departure before announcing stridently that she had come to discuss a matter of vast importance. ". . . in effect, my dear brother, I wish to discuss that mooncalf Orison!"

MacElroy shut the door carefully upon these promising words and, after a twinkling exchange of looks with Gillian, who was halfway down the main stair, disappeared through the green baize door. Gillian would have dearly loved to eavesdrop upon the conversation presently progressing in the study, but she didn't dare. She had already begged off accompanying Mrs. Periwinkle to visit the Berry sisters, acquaintances from their Curzon Street days, by insisting that she had letters to write to friends in Sussex. Now that Landover was clearly occupied, there seemed no reason she should not put another plan into effect.

"Miss?" She looked up to see Ellen leaning over the gallery rail. "Be we going now, Miss Gillian?"

"Yes, come along," Gillian replied, keeping her voice low. It was nothing more than a small bid for freedom. She would face the consequences, if any, later. She had no intention of doing anything outrageous; she merely wanted to go shopping by herself. Since removing to Berkeley Square, she'd scarcely had a moment to call her own. As soon as she and Ellen reached the flagway, Gillian took a deep breath of fresh air. It was a fine morning for a walk to Bond Street.

But they had scarcely reached Bruton Street before an elegantly appointed light carriage drew to a halt alongside them. A liveried footman leaped to the pavement and approached Gillian with a bow.

VI

"Miss Harris?" he inquired politely

"Why . . . why, yes, I am Miss Harris," she replied. She glanced at the elegant equipage doubtfully.

"Begging yer pardon, miss, but her highness said I was t' deliver this. The coach has been waiting more than an hour on the chance you might appear alone."

Gillian searched his face carefully before she accepted the note. He was young, with a fresh-scrubbed, open countenance, and she could not imagine his being part of any nefarious scheme to abduct her. A glance at the coachman showed him to be an elderly man who carried himself with great dignity. Their livery seemed to be what she remembered from Warwick House, but she couldn't be certain. Nevertheless, even if they were agents in the Harris Heiress stakes, they could hardly snatch her up, along with her no doubt shrieking maid, right here in broad daylight. She unfolded the message.

The Princess Charlotte hoped that Miss Harris would not let any gentleman, no matter how well intentioned, stand in the way of friendship. If she had contrived to slip away from Landover House, as she must have done in order to be reading the missive, her highness hoped very much that she would defy authority a bit further and join her at the Pulteney Hotel, if only for half an hour.

Gillian grinned at the footman. Why not? "We might as well be hung for a sheep as a lamb, Ellen. Come along."

"Oh, Miss Gillian, I hope you know what you're doing," Ellen whispered as the young footman helped them into the carriage. "His lordship'll be fit to be tied!"

Gillian firmly repressed all thought of his lordship's temper. With any luck, he'd never know about the visit. But she could not deceive herself with that notion for any length of time. Long before the carriage drew up at the entrance to the Pulteney, she had resigned herself to an inevitable, uncomfortable few moments with Landover. But it would be worth it. She would show him he could not dictate her every move. She would pick her own friends.

The young footman showed them directly upstairs to the luxurious suite occupied by the grand duchess, but it was Charlotte herself who greeted them.

"You have managed it! How wonderful! But will there be trouble, Miss Harris?"

"Nothing I cannot handle, your highness," Gillian replied airily as she made her curtsy.

"It is good to hear you say so, Miss Harris," commented the duchess, entering through a door at Gillian's right. "Jeanelle!" she called. A pretty maidservant hurried in from yet another room. "Take Miss Harris's woman to the servants' quarters, Jeanelle. Then you may see to our refreshment."

"Oui, madame." The maid bobbed a curtsy and gestured to Ellen, who followed her out in a daze. Gillian smiled.

"Poor Ellen. She's expecting fireworks when we get home and cannot decide whether to enjoy herself in the meantime or not."

"And you, Miss Harris, shall you enjoy?" The grand duchess smiled charmingly.

"Yes, your grace, I shall. What may happen later is of no concern to me until it happens." She hesitated, then grinned. "I do hope Landover's note was not too rude."

"Ah bah," replied the duchess with a Gallic shrug. "Englishmen have not the trick of rudeness. 'Twas not even of a sufficiency to demand recall, and 'tis of little consequence anyway, since you are here. We shall drink tea together, and then I shall leave you two young ladies to become better acquainted with one another. Is that not an excellent notion?"

They agreed to it, and Gillian noted with interest that the duchess made a perfectly charming hostess. There were none of the pithy remarks she had made at the de Lieven rout, and for this Gillian was grateful, since she would have had no notion how to respond. It occurred to her that the Princess Charlotte, no matter how much she disliked her father, might find it difficult to listen to a steady stream of contempt for him. He was, after all, her father. She gave the duchess full marks for good sense.

There was no lack of conversation. The duchess had had a letter from her brother, the Tsar, informing her that he expected to land at Dover the following Monday. He was to be met there by the Duke of Clarence.

" 'Tis a pity that my exalted brother should be met by a buffoon with a head like a pineapple," observed the duchess.

Charlotte giggled. "Really, Catherine, you should not speak so. Of my five royal uncles, only he and my dearest Sussex are truly kind to me, you know."

"He wipes his nose with his finger," retorted the duchess flatly. That seemed to dispose of Clarence, but even the duchess seemed to have nothing particularly negative to say about the gentle Duke of Sussex. "What do you hear these days from Orange?" she asked glibly.

Charlotte's face fell. "He still wants to take me to Holland. I daresay Papa would be only too happy to see the back of me."

"But surely you will live in England!" Gillian protested. Charlotte was the crown princess. No one should try to separate her from her people.

Charlotte smiled a trifle sadly. "Be assured, Miss Harris, I have already refused to go, although I daresay that will not be the last of the issue."

"I have told you before, *chérie*, that things will work out for the best," said the duchess gently. "Even if you decide you cannot stomach marriage to the so estimable William of Orange. They cannot think him so great a personnage if they house him with his tailor in Clifford Street, instead of at Carlton House or St. James's."

"Well, he has clammy hands, and I think he is very dull," pronounced Charlotte. "I do not care where he stays. At first, I thought being a married lady would be very nice because I thought I should have more freedom, but now it seems that will not be so. I wish to be a young girl like other young girls, if only for a short space of time, and besides, William is so ugly that I am sometimes obliged to turn my head away when he is speaking."

"Her majesty is holding another Drawing Room tomorrow," Gillian said quickly, knowing she should not be hearing such things and hoping to change the subject to a more acceptable one. "Are you to be presented at last?"

Charlotte nodded. "But again my mother has been ordered to stay at home, so I am tempted to refuse as I did before."

"Nonsense, my dear," chuckled the grand duchess. "I am to sponsor you instead. That will put the smile on the other side of your royal papa's pudding face!" Charlotte grinned at her, her good humor restored.

A few moments later, when the duchess had left them alone to exchange, as she put it coyly, "girlish confidences," Charlotte chuckled. "I could almost feel sorry for Papa if he weren't such a beast. Catherine puts him in a constant taking. The first time I visited her here, I was accompanied by seven of my ladies. Catherine said she couldn't tolerate the din and sent every one of them home again. Papa nearly had an apoplectic seizure."

"I'm surprised he didn't forbid a second visit," Gillian commented.

"Oh, he did. Shouted it, in fact. But, for once, he cannot stop me, because he daren't offend the Tsar. So Catherine pretty nearly has her own way about things. I come here whenever I like, and only my dearest Notti—Miss Cornelia Knight, you know, who has been with me for years—attends me. But even she retires to a smaller sitting room whilst I'm here, and I'm certain she likes the respite quite as much as I do."

Gillian thoroughly enjoyed the next half hour. The two young women found they shared a good deal in common, particularly their mutual dislike of continually being curbed and restrained. Gillian told her highness about the Harris Heiress stakes and was pleased that Charlotte found the whole notion as absurd as she did herself. But Charlotte's understanding was acute nonetheless.

"It is difficult when one has something men want, whether 'tis a crown or a fortune. How can we know, my dear Miss Harris, which one of them might like us for ourselves alone? I should like very much to meet a man like that," she added wistfully.

"Perhaps his grace of Orange will prove to be just such a man, your highness," suggested Gillian gently.

"Pooh! That stick! I should like to see it," Charlotte scoffed. "William of Orange wants only one thing, and that is power. He wishes to be King of England, but I become daily more certain that I do not wish to share my throne with such a man."

When it was time to leave, the princess insisted that Gillian take her carriage, and Gillian could think of no polite way to refuse. But any hope of concealing her visit from Landover was dashed the moment the carriage drew up in front of the house, for as the young footman helped her to alight, she glanced toward the study window to see the marquis himself glaring down at her. There could be no mistaking his expression. Landover was in a blazing fury. Gillian looked helplessly at Ellen when the girl jumped down beside her.

"Oh, Miss Gillian!" the maid wailed. "The cat's among the pigeons now, right enough!"

Gillian nodded. She could not believe for a moment that Landover wouldn't recognize the Warwick House livery, but perhaps she might still conceal her visit to the Pulteney Hotel. "You go straight up to Mrs. Periwinkle, Ellen, if she has returned. Offer my apologies, and say it is unlikely I shall be able to join her for luncheon but that I shall speak to her later." Ellen cast her a speaking look, and Gillian sighed. She would be lucky if she was in shape to speak to anyone later. Landover was no longer at the window, but the one glimpse she had had of him convinced her that it would be a mercy if he didn't beat her.

He was standing on the threshold of the study when they entered, but he stood aside, making it clear that he meant Gillian to precede him into the room. At that moment, MacElroy entered the hall through the green baize door, and with a glance at him and another at Landover, she turned her eyes toward the grand staircase and squared her shoulders.

"I shouldn't advise it." The words were spoken softly, but there was a savage undertone that told her he would brook no further defiance. Wistfully, she watched Ellen hurrying up the stairs to the gallery, and by the time she turned back, MacElroy had disappeared, and she was left to face the marquis alone. He still stood just as he had stood before. Glaring defiantly, she brushed past him into the study, waiting for the click of the door latch before she turned to confront him.

"Would you like to tell me where you've been, or shall I guess?" he growled.

"I don't care if you guess or not!" she flared. "I've been with the Princess Charlotte, and that is scarcely a thing to be ashamed of!"

"In other words, you deliberately defied my orders and went to the Pulteney Hotel!" he snapped. "Alone at that."

"And what if I did?" Gillian shouted, throwing caution to the wind. "I had a perfectly splendid time, and I have not been seduced, abducted, or morally corrupted!" Arms akimbo, she would have said a good deal more, but Landover advanced purposefully, causing her to draw back a step or two with a small gasp of dismay. Her arms dropped to her sides.

He towered over her. "What happened there is of little concern to me at the moment, Miss Harris. But you need a good lesson in obedience. I will not tolerate defiance, and the sooner you learn that, the better it will be for all of us."

She turned away, unable to cope with his anger head on. "You've no right to dictate to me like this, Landover," she muttered. "I must and will have the right to go where I like and to choose my own friends." But her breath caught in her throat on the final words when his hands clamped painfully down upon her shoulders. He spun her around again.

"You made a damned fool of me," he grated wrathfully, shaking her. "To go to that scheming woman after I had written to tell her you would not come! How dare you speak to me of rights, when you show not the slightest sense of civilized courtesy! Your precious duchess is no doubt laughing up her sleeve right now, thanks to you." He was still shaking her, his fingers bruising her shoulders, and Gillian feared her bones would soon begin to rattle. His words penetrated, but she couldn't think straight until the shaking became less violent. Then, as her thoughts fell into order again, she realized that he believed she had deliberately set out to defy him, to make him a laughingstock. But when she opened her mouth to refute this notion, he spoke again in a nearly weary tone. "You are quite spoiled, Miss Harris, and have been allowed to chart your own course far too long, but perhaps a month or so spent kicking your heels in Sussex will help bring you to your senses. I dislike having to—"

"No!" She wrenched from his grasp, given extra strength through sheer fury. "No, you'll not send me away! You'll not humiliate me like that!" He reached for her again, but she eluded his grasp at first, and when he did succeed in grabbing one of her arms, she launched herself at him, pummeling him with her fists, swinging blindly. But suddenly, it was over, and she cried out as his grip snapped painfully around her wrists, holding her away, and at the same time forcing her almost to her knees. She looked up at him miserably, but the look of intent on his face brought fear welling to the surface, and she cried out again, this time in fright. "Oh, please, no! Please, my lord. It was not what you think! The princess sent her carriage for me! Please, don't." The last came as a mere whisper, but her words had an effect. The pressure on her wrists eased, and he helped her to her feet.

"Don't what, Miss Harris? What did you fear I would do?"

Gathering the shreds of her dignity, Gillian tried to rub feeling back into her numbed wrists and realized that her knees were quaking. She subsided into one of the Kent chairs with a sigh of relief, but her voice still trembled slightly. "I . . . I thought you meant to beat me." She glanced up hesitantly. "I am not generally such a coward, my lord, but you are so big, and you looked so fierce."

"I think you deserve to be beaten for this morning's work," he said grimly, "but I do not have that right. If it had been your brother whose orders you defied so outrageously, I daresay you'd smart mightily for it, my girl."

She could not deny it. Looking up at him from under her lashes, she said quietly, "It was not as you thought, sir. I truly did not intend to go to the Pulteney when I left the house this morning."

Landover sighed and pulled the other Kent chair closer to hers. "Go on," he said as he sat down. "I am listening, but it had better be good. You said something about the princess's carriage."

So she told him. Sensibly, she made no effort to conceal the fact that she had refused to accompany Mrs. Periwinkle to the Berry sisters' house in order to indulge in a private shopping spree, but she went to great lengths to prove to Landover how unexceptionable her visit to the Pulteney had been. He wasn't particularly receptive.

"I cannot approve any association with the Duchess of Oldenburg. That woman is not to be trusted."

"She was perfectly charming, sir. She said nothing to which anyone—even you—might object."

"She is a manipulator. No doubt she is using the princess for her own ends and would not hesitate to use you as well, could she but think of a way to do so."

"Nonsense! She truly likes the princess. I have seen them together, and you have not!" Her voice had begun to rise, but Landover quelled her temper with a gesture and a mocking smile.

"Easy, child. Stay off the high ropes. You cannot afford to antagonize me further. It is not impossible that the duchess truly likes her highness. The Princess Charlotte is a most likable young lady. Nevertheless, the Grand Duchess of Oldenburg is mistress of a world you know nothing about. She is dangerous, Gillian, and I want your promise you will have nothing further to do with her."

"Very well," she replied grudgingly, "but I cannot make such a promise with regard to her highness, so pray do not ask it of me."

"Perhaps we can effect a compromise," he agreed with a smile. "I would prefer that you steer clear of the royal menage altogether, but I really have no valid objection to your friendship with the princess. It is not what I like, and I must urge you to be most circumspect, but if you are careful, I will withdraw my objections."

"Then I," returned Miss Harris grandly, "will be only too happy to give my solemn promise to avoid her grace." Then a thought occurred to her, and she looked at him with a shy smile. "You will not send me home?"

"For the moment, we will agree that I was perhaps a trifle hasty. However," he added on a warning note, "you are not off the hook entirely. There remains the small matter of your departure from the house this morning."

"I am sorry for that, sir," Gillian said meekly.

But Landover wasn't fooled for a moment. "Are you?"

She looked up, prepared to insist upon it, but discovered when she looked into his eyes that she could not lie to him. Flustered, she looked away again. "I am not used to such constraint, my lord."

"No doubt, but if you wish to remain in London, you will submit, my girl," he declared implacably. "Do you know that my first thought when I discovered you were not with Amelia Periwinkle was that you had been abducted? It was not a pleasant thought. Fortunately, you returned before I had begun a concerted search."

"The Harris Heiress stakes," she muttered bitterly.

"Exactly. But besides disobeying me, you deceived your cousin, and that was not well done of you. For that, if for nothing else, you deserve to be punished."

Gillian bit her lower lip. He was right. Her behavior had been childish. She looked at him, and her voice was small. "What will you do?"

"I don't know," he replied candidly. "Have you any suggestions?"

She swallowed carefully. "It is Wednesday, so I suppose you could forbid my going to Almack's tonight. I should be unhappy to miss the assembly, but perhaps you would not consider that sufficient punishment."

His reaction astonished her. "Oh, no you don't!" he retorted, his eyes alight with sudden amusement. "I don't doubt for a moment that you would consider it a punishment, but it would be a far worse one for me, and I've done nothing at all to deserve it!"

"My lord?" Her face was blank with confusion.

He chuckled. "No, of course not, how should you know what I'm talking about? We are dining at Harmoncourt House before the assembly, and I wish you to be there."

"I did not know we were to dine out."

"If you had not slipped out this morning," he pointed out, "you would know. My sister descended upon me at an ungodly hour to inform me that it is time I set up my nursery."

"Surely not, my lord!" Gillian gurgled.

He grinned at her. "I left out the wife part. That comes first, of course. Abigail intends to introduce me to a suitable damsel this very evening."

"Do you always submit to her dictation, my lord?" She could barely conceal her delight at the news.

"Well, not always," he conceded, "but I daresay she's right this time. She chose to fling Orison in my teeth." He paused suddenly, shooting her a rather searching look. Gillian shifted a bit in her chair, self-consciously smoothing her skirt.

"Orison, sir? Your cousin?"

"And heir. Odd that you and Sybilla were discussing him only yesterday, is it not? Abigail says he's getting notions above his station. Haven't noticed it myself, but I daresay she's got the right of it. Abigail's a very noticing female. Anyway, it is time I settled down, I suppose, so I've no objection if she wants to trot a few possibles across the track; however, I'd just as soon not be abandoned entirely to this chit's tender mercies, so you will not stay at home tonight."

Gillian found, to her amazement, that his attitude annoyed her. She should be grateful for his acquiescence, she scolded herself. Instead she merely thought him arrogant and rather poor-spirited besides. She rose to her feet.

"If we are to dine at Harmoncourt House, I must wash my hair earlier than I had intended, sir. Pray, will you excuse me now?"

He said nothing, but when she turned to go, he stood and placed a gentle hand upon her shoulder. "One moment, Miss Harris."

She turned back to him, intensely aware of his nearness and strangely pleased when he placed his other hand on the opposite shoulder. "Sir?"

He looked down into her eyes, and she felt her pulse quicken. Color crept into her cheeks. "We are leaving a loose end or two, are we not?" His voice was as gentle as his touch, and she could think of nothing to say. "Perhaps it is just as well," he went on when she lowered her lashes and did not speak. "Next time you are tempted to misbehave, perhaps you will remember that the dibs are not in tune and will resist the temptation."

"I . . . I'll try, sir."

"I shall accept nothing but perfection, Miss Harris. You will no doubt become a paragon of propriety."

"Oh dear," she murmured.

He squeezed one shoulder and nudged her toward the door. "It won't be so bad as all that, you know. You may even enjoy it."

She wrinkled her nose in disbelief, but he only chuckled. A moment later, as she climbed the stairs, she realized how close a call she had had, and for a moment, her knees threatened to betray her. But then she remembered that Lady Harmoncourt had entered the lists, and her heart began to sing again. Soon she would be free of his constant surveillance, free to be herself again. Oddly, the notion seemed to lack some of its earlier flavor.

Mrs. Periwinkle was waiting for her in her bedchamber and gave her an appraising glance before waving her hand toward a table where a plate rested, temptingly piled with cold slivered beef, cheese, bread and butter, and fruit.

"I thought you might need sustenance, my dear."

"Oh, thank you, ma'am. I'm starving!" Gillian looked fondly at the thin little woman, elegant today in puce sarcenet with a pink satin cap. "Ellen must have told you what happened. I'm dreadfully sorry if I caused you any worry. I should not have behaved so selfishly."

"Indeed. A bit tetchy and wayward of you, my dear, but I collect Landover was not too harsh."

"He was furious at first," Gillian replied, taking a seat at the table and piling beef and cheese onto a slice of buttered bread. "He very nearly sent me back to Sussex."

"Oh, my dear! But only 'very nearly'?"

"Yes. He came round. But it was a near miss, I promise you."

" 'Sweet mercy is nobility's true badge,' " quoth Mrs. Periwinkle solemnly.

Gillian grinned. "This is hardly a comedy of errors, my dear ma'am. Where is Avery?"

"Off sulking somewhere, no doubt," stated her companion with just a trace of uncharacteristic exasperation. Gillian stared at her, and Mrs. Periwinkle shrugged. "Perhaps I should not say such things, but he has been living life like a drunken sailor on a mast. 'Tis no wonder Landover called him to book.

But now he says he has no turn for dancing or doing the polite and don't see why he should be made to play the fool."

Light dawned. "Landover has ordered him to accompany us to Almack's tonight, and Avery doesn't wish to go." Mrs. Periwinkle nodded. "Well, I shall have a word with him," Gillian said, smiling. "He cannot have thought properly."

Accordingly, once she had finished her repast, she went to find her brother. A few words from her with regard to Lady Harmoncourt's intentions soon put Sir Avery in a better frame of mind, and once he discovered that they were to dine at Harmoncourt House before going on to Almack's—a detail Landover had quite forgotten to mention to him—he began to look forward to the evening ahead.

The dinner was a very fine one, and the placement of guests gave Gillian an excellent opportunity to study Lady Sharon Clevenger, the damsel provided for Landover's inspection, since they sat opposite one another. Lady Sharon was an elegant piece of goods, Gillian decided. Her sea-green evening dress showed good taste, her manners were polished, and she had no difficulty holding her own in conversation with Landover. And as if all that were not enough, Lady Sharon was a beauty, with a slim, willowy figure, aquamarine eyes, and a mane of magnificent red hair.

When they went on to Almack's, Gillian was a good deal in Lady Sharon's company, since the party tended to stay together. As a beginning, it seemed promising. Landover clearly seemed to pay more attention to Lady Sharon than to Gillian. He did not so much as ask the latter to dance, but this was explained by Lady Sybilla when the two had a moment to discuss the success of their little scheme.

"Mama was only too glad to bring Sharon Clevenger to his notice," Sybilla confided. "Besides dragging Orison in, she also told him people were beginning to talk about his intentions toward you. So that ought to keep him out of your hair a bit."

Gillian wasn't sure if that was the cause or not, but she couldn't deny that during the following week, Landover stayed very much out of her hair. On Monday, as promised, Tsar Alexander and King Frederick landed at Dover, and on Tuesday evening, Landover attended a magnificent banquet at Carlton House in their honor. Gillian saw him at breakfast the following morning.

"Was it wonderful?" she asked. "We got tired of waiting for the procession, so Cousin Amelia and I came home."

Landover chuckled. "The banquet was marvelous, but only one of the guests of honor showed up. You didn't see the procession because the Tsar never joined it. He slipped into London on his own. Then he chose to dine privately with his sister at the Pulteney instead of attending the dinner at Carlton House. Prinny's nose is sadly out of joint."

"Oh dear!"

"There is worse news. Alexander has declined to stay at St. James's. He has taken over the principal apartments at the Pulteney instead, and I am told that Mr. Escudier, the manager, has pulled out all the stops."

"What of King Frederick?"

Landover grinned, helping himself to toast from the silver rack. "Oh, he will stay at Clarence House as planned, but all the fine satinwood furniture Prinny ordered especially for his suite has been removed. His majesty is the spartan sort. He will sleep on nothing but a straw palliasse, and he has ordered a plain table and looking glass, with one common chair to be substituted for all the finery."

Gillian stared at him. "You're joking!"

"Not a bit of it. He likes to be thought a soldier first, king second."

"How absurd!" Jeremy refilled her teacup, and she smiled up at him gratefully, then turned back to find Landover eyeing her speculatively. "Yes?"

He shook his head. "Just wondering if you've been behaving yourself," he confessed. "I've been busy."

She knew it. Since the arrival of the foreign visitors, she had scarcely seen him, and for days before, much of his time had been claimed by the Regent, who wished to discuss last-minute plans and details with anyone who would listen. She had, however, caught a glimpse of him at two or three of the events she had attended during the week. On each occasion, Lady Sharon Clevenger had been tantalizingly near at hand. An imp of mischief danced in Gillian's eye as she grinned at him now.

"How is Lady Sharon?"

He grinned back. "Delightful. Very submissive and obedient—a refreshing change for me, you will allow."

Sparks routed the imp of mischief. "You've had no complaints of my behavior, sir!"

"Very true," he agreed sweetly, "but experience warns me 'tis merely the calm before the storm."

"Ooh!" Gillian could think of nothing further to say that might answer the purpose, although several demolishing rebuttals would occur to her once she reached the peace and quiet of her bedchamber. At the moment, however, she merely arose from the table with as much chilly hauteur as she could muster and flounced from the room, sped along by Landover's chuckles.

As a consequence, when she received a message from the Princess Charlotte asking that she call at Warwick House, she canceled her other plans straightaway, informing Mrs. Periwinkle that she would see her later in the afternoon. Several people were joining them at Landover House for supper that evening before going on to the weekly assembly, and Gillian meant to have plenty of time to prepare herself.

Mrs. Periwinkle frowned. "Are you certain you don't want me to accompany you?"

"No, no, don't trouble yourself, my dear ma'am. Landover has waived all objections to my visiting her highness, and I'm perfectly certain you would enjoy a morning to yourself, indulging in a comfortable coze with an old friend or two. You cannot pretend that you haven't denied yourself such pleasures on my account."

Blithely ignoring the fact that Landover had not precisely rescinded his order that Mrs. Periwinkle accompany her wherever she went, Gillian called Ellen and ordered a carriage to drive her to Warwick House. Thus it was that when Princess Charlotte confided a wish that Miss Harris accompany her upon a visit to her mother, the Princess of Wales, there was none to say yea or nay. But with Landover's comments fresh in her mind, Gillian had no hesitation in agreeing to the outing. She did mention the necessity of an early return, however, and received a royally infectious grin in reply.

"Not to worry, my dear Miss Harris. 'Tis an illicit visit for both of us. My respected father strictly curtails intercourse between dear Mama and myself, and he will descend upon me

like the Furies if he discovers I have defied him." Gillian made
a move to protest, but her highness silenced her with a graceful
gesture. " 'Tis of no consequence, I assure you. Papa is by far
too much occupied with the business of currying imperial favor
to bother his head about us. There is the Tsar's levee at my
Uncle Cumberland's house at one o'clock, and then the King of
Prussia's levee at Clarence House. Then between five and six
this evening is Grandmama's court, where he must introduce
them both. Afterward, they will all dine at Carlton House. I
shall no doubt have to attend the dinner and possibly the court,
but no one will bother about me before that, so I shall surprise
Mama."

The journey to Connaught House assumed the outlines of a
royal progress. Gillian, the princess, and Miss Knight rode in
one carriage, followed by another containing several ladies-in-
waiting and surrounded by outriders.

Connaught House was an elegant residence standing in well-
kept gardens near the corner where Bayswater Road met the
Edgware Road, and Gillian thought it a charming place. She
was not so impressed by the Princess of Wales, however.
Having expected an older version of Charlotte, she was rather
put off by the plump, guttural-voiced woman who greeted them.
There could be no doubt that the Princess Caroline welcomed
her daughter's visit, but Gillian could see none of the signs of
maternal love that she associated with her own dear mother.
The Princess of Wales seemed only to complain of her lot—in
particular, to complain of the fact that the Queen had ordered
her to avoid all the June drawing rooms on account of the fact
that the Regent meant to grace them with his presence.

"To be forbidden even *mein* own daughter's presentation,"
she moaned wretchedly. " 'Tis an abomination, don't you agree,
Miss Harris?"

Noting Gillian's reluctance to take sides on an issue about
which she knew very little, Charlotte spoke up more quickly
than usual.

"I missed you dreadfully, madam, but her grace of Oldenburg
was very kind, and it quite upset Papa to have to be civil to
her—or to me, for that matter," she chuckled.

Her highness nodded. "She is a very clever woman, that
duchess," she said to Gillian. "Knows the world and mankind

well. My daughter could not be in better hands." Her sudden, wry smile gave her a more noticeable resemblance to her daughter. "Besides, they are a great deal together, which makes the Regent look outrageous."

There being no acceptable reply, Gillian was once again grateful to the younger princess when she changed the subject abruptly to discuss forthcoming events such as the Ascot races, the Opera, and the Burlington House masquerade, as well as the upcoming Guildhall Banquet. The latter was an annual dinner given by the City of London to honor the prime of the English nobility and was particularly intriguing to women in that it was always an all-male affair.

Although the visit lasted barely an hour, Gillian was extremely grateful when Princess Charlotte signaled for their departure. On the way back to Warwick House, the princess maintained a lively chatter, so it was not until she was alone in her own carriage that Gillian paused to reflect upon Landover's probable reaction to her visit to the Princess of Wales.

It proved not to be a matter of immediate concern, however, for she discovered upon her return that he was out, and she would have to hurry if she meant to be ready when their guests began to arrive.

The first to arrive was the Harmoncourt contingent. Lady Sybilla greeted Gillian enthusiastically and stayed speaking with her for some moments, though her eye tended to shift rather often to the hearthstones, where Sir Avery stood, Malaga glass in hand, conversing idly with Lord Harmoncourt, an affable, plumpish gentleman with a perpetual twinkle in his eye.

"It's going splendidly, is it not?" Sybilla observed with a grin, dragging her gaze back to Gillian's amused countenance.

"Yes, Avery is growing accustomed to doing the fancy," Gillian replied wickedly. "I expect it is because he has discovered how well he looks in knee breeches."

Lady Sybilla flushed delicately. " 'Tis Landover and Lady Sharon I meant, Gillian, and well you know it. I am sure Sir Avery's activities are of no consequence to me."

Gillian smiled but forbore to tease her friend, and at that moment, MacElroy opened the doors of the salon to announce the arrival of Lady Sharon and her mama, the Countess Edgware, a stout dame solidly encased in corsets and wielding a gold-rimmed lorgnette like a lethal weapon. Lady Sharon, in a becoming russet-silk robe trimmed with gilt fringe, paused on the threshold with an air of pretty shyness and surveyed the room much, thought Gillian with strong disaffection, as though she were assessing the value of its contents. Then, catching sight of Landover and Mrs. Periwinkle, the redhead rushed forward holding out her dainty, white-gloved hands.

"Mrs. Periwinkle!" she gushed. "Dear Mrs. Periwinkle! How nice to see you again. And Landover." She laid a possessive hand upon his arm. "What a marvelous house, my lord." The marquis smiled down at her.

"Fatuous idiot!" muttered Miss Harris wrathfully.

"What's that you say?" drawled a familiar voice at her shoulder. She started, then glared.

"It won't do, Avery! That redheaded witch is impossible!"

VII

Sir Avery stared down at his sister with a mixture of amusement and exasperation. "It's doing just fine, Gill," he said pointedly. "Landover hasn't had a moment to scold in a week, and that chit's had a good deal to do with the fact."

"But she's unsuitable, Avery! Can't you see that? Just watch her. Though she stands perfectly still, it's as though she's gloating over gold coins clinking through her fingers."

"Can't see it m'self," he refuted, "but whether you're right or not makes no never-mind to me, just so long as the chit keeps his mind off me." His eyes widened suddenly, and there was a surprising stiffness in his next words, spoken past Gillian's shoulder. "Good evening, sir." She turned to find Mr. Brummell approaching them.

"Good evening, children." He gestured toward the rest of the company. "Nice pleasant group you've got here. Surprised the Clevenger chit's still hanging about, but I daresay Landover is encouraging her to humor his sister. Must want to humor her mighty bad if he's willing to have that Edgware dragon in his house. Still, a far superior group to the mob gathering just now at Carlton House."

Gillian dimpled. "A rather august gathering, however, Mr. Brummell. It surprises me that you would choose to honor us instead."

"You'd not be surprised if you knew what sort of morning I had, my dear Miss Harris. Prinny descended upon me before I had finished my breakfast, babbled on about the insults he's suffered from his charming visitors, and positively hovered whilst I ruined I don't know how many neckcloths. He *would* keep nattering on whilst I attempted to achieve the proper crease, you know."

"Nattering, sir?" Gillian noted her brother's flushed cheeks and realized this must be the first time he had encountered the Beau since his unfortunate blunder at the Bettencourt ball, but her comment was enough to encourage Brummell's confidences.

"Indeed. What with the two levees, a Queen's Court, and a state dinner all in one day, he was at his wit's end about his wardrobe, so I am in favor again for the moment. There was little I could do for him, of course. No one can convince him to tone down his style, and with that fat carcase of his forever creaking about in Cumberland corsets, there is nothing he could wear that would not call attention to itself. I did my poor best. Nonetheless, I had a sufficiency of his company for one day, so I shall not grace his dinner tonight. I only hope," he added, "that his flair for the unique has kept him from ordering a river of carp flowing down the center of the tables as he did for the Carlton House fete several years ago." He lapsed into reminiscent silence, and Gillian, conscious of Sir Avery shifting from foot to foot at her side, wracked her brain for some brilliant comment to keep the conversational ball rolling.

Sir Avery cleared his throat uncomfortably. "Mr. Brummell," he said, speaking with care and struggling manfully to meet the Beau eye to eye, "I owe you an apology for my unfortunate behavior when last we met. There can be no excuse for . . . for—well, just no excuse at all, sir. I'm sorry."

"Well said, young fellow," murmured Brummell with a tiny smile. "We all have our moments, and no doubt Landover made you regret yours." Avery's color deepened, and Brummell's smile grew wider. "Perhaps I ought to have been flattered instead of taking such a pet. Generally have better control of myself, I assure you."

Avery returned the smile gratefully, and just then MacElroy announced dinner. Lady Harmoncourt graciously declined her brother's arm and nodded for him to take Lady Sharon in instead. Landover bowed, and Lady Sharon accepted his arm with a gentle air of submission that nearly caused Gillian to snort aloud, but she caught her brother's stern gaze and subsided.

Dinner itself was uneventful. Conversation seemed to focus, as expected, upon the antics of the visiting sovereigns, particularly upon the Tsar, who, like his sister, made no attempt to disguise his contempt for the Regent.

Gillian overheard Lady Edgware remark that Alexander had already refused to dance with Lady Hertford, the Regent's mistress. "He's got a nice eye for the female figure," she added complacently, "but he supposedly said Lady Hertford is too old. Prinny didn't like that much, I daresay."

Gillian, aware of Landover's watchful eye, stifled a grin and returned her attentions to the delicacies on her plate, which included a mouthwatering fricandeau of veal, as well as a ragout of celery with wine. She particularly enjoyed the second-course sweet, an elegant strawberry ice provided by Gunter's, the fashionable caterer located just across the square. But after dinner, while the ladies were gathering their wraps in preparation for the departure to Almack's, she overheard a remark that sent her temper soaring again.

They were in a small sitting room off the green saloon, and most of the others had moved back to the saloon itself, when Gillian overheard Lady Sharon speaking to Sybilla in an undertone that nevertheless carried easily to her own sharp ears.

"I'm ever so grateful to your mama, Sybby dearest," the redhead said sweetly. "If I play my cards well, my mama says there's no reason I cannot be the next Marchioness of Landover." She grinned smugly. "He must be worth forty thousand a year. How will you like having me for your aunt?"

Whatever Sybilla might have responded was stifled when she caught Gillian's eye, and her expression must have warned Lady Sharon. The redheaded girl turned with a light blush but recovered quickly, and drawing herself up, she looked down her nose at Gillian and passed disdainfully by without so much as a word. Gillian looked at Sybilla.

"She's awful."

"Indeed she is," agreed Sybilla heartily, "but you must agree she answers the purpose."

"Mr. Brummell says Landover is merely humoring your mother."

"Perhaps. Although there is already talk. If he keeps squiring her about and allowing her to drool over him as though he were a platter of Gunter's best eclairs, he will have to offer for her. And that will certainly solve your problem, for you'll be back in your little house in Curzon Street before the cat can wink her eye."

Gillian tried to convince herself that that was precisely what she wanted, but the vision of Landover saddled for life with a woman who wanted only his fortune and title was a bit too much—a high price for him to pay for her freedom.

She gave the matter some thought as she rode in a carriage with her brother, Mrs. Periwinkle, and Mr. Brummell to Almack's, but she could think of no acceptable way to stop what she had begun. It was not until after the second set of country dances that the glimmer of an idea occurred to her. A strand of hair had escaped her elegant coif, and she excused herself to a nearby withdrawing room to repair the damage. No sooner had she swung the door shut behind her, however, than she realized she was not alone. Her brother and his friend Mr. Willoby turned suddenly, guiltily, to see who had entered. Sir Avery expelled a breath of undisguised relief.

"Dash it, Gillian, you've no notion how you startled us. Thought it must be Landover, looking for me to do the pretty."

"Well, it's not. He's occupied with his current interest." She shot him a searching look. "Why on earth are you skulking about in here anyway?"

"Not skulking," he insisted, gathering his dignity. Mr. Willoby, managing to look the picture of guilt, said not a word. Sir Avery hemmed and hawed a bit, but when he realized Gillian wouldn't leave without an explanation, he capitulated. Her eyes widened when he produced a silver flask from behind his back.

"Wherever did you find that?"

"Didn't. Brought it with me in the waistband of these dashed breeches. Can't dance with it, though, so we hid it in the potted plant yonder." He seemed to take her unblinking silence as a sign of disapproval. "Dash it, Gill, can't expect a fellow to muddle through an evening like this one fortified only by orgeat and ratafia. Not possible, assure you!" Mr. Willoby nodded in solemn agreement, and Gillian chuckled, turning away toward a nearby looking glass to fix her hair.

"Very well, gentlemen. I shan't cry rope on you, but it will be bellows to mend with you, Avery, if Landover happens to smell gin on your breath."

"Not gin," he said cagily. "Took a lesson from our august visitors. 'Tis Russian vodka. They say you can't smell a thing. But it does pack a wallop. I'll say that for it. Very potent stuff. Puts the uninitiated under the table before they can say Jack Robinson. Not to worry, though. I'll steer clear of his lordship." He secreted the flask once more in the plant and slipped out with Willoby, leaving Gillian alone with her thoughts.

There was no *acceptable* way to rid Landover of the Lady Sharon, but perhaps— She stifled the thought as unworthy of her, but it continued to nag, and when she noted Lady Sharon in cozy conversation with Lady Cowper and observed the red-headed damsel give a coyly proprietary nod in Landover's direction, she began plotting more seriously.

It was Landover himself who provided her with the opportunity she needed. She and Lady Sharon had both been returned by their respective partners to Lady Harmoncourt and Mrs. Periwinkle, whose chairs were quite near the pertinent withdrawing room, and Gillian's partner, Lord Darrow, offered to acquire refreshment for them both. No sooner had he returned with the crystal punch cups filled with orgeat, however, than Landover strolled over to remind Lady Sharon that his name was down for the waltz just beginning. He glanced at her cup.

"Of course, if you would prefer to sit this one out—"

"Don't be silly, Landover," interrupted his sister. "Of course she don't wish to sit out when she could be dancing with you. Run along, Sharon dear. Just set your cup on the side table yonder. It will still be there when Landover brings you back."

Lady Sharon obeyed with alacrity, and the melting look she threw Landover as he swung her onto the floor was more than Gillian could tolerate.

"I think my hair is coming down again," she said quickly to Mrs. Periwinkle, and before that lady could deny it, she had slipped into the withdrawing room. Lord Darrow had already excused himself with a flattering air of reluctance to find his next partner, and since it had not yet been approved for Gillian to dance the waltz in that most conservative of clubs, she knew no partner would come looking for her. Drawing a deep breath, she hurried to the potted plant and hefted the silver flask. Plenty for her purpose. Spilling more than half of her drink into the plant, she replaced it with vodka from the flask and hurried back out into the ballroom.

It took but a moment's glance to assure her that no one was paying her any heed before she deftly exchanged the cup in her hand for the one waiting innocently on the side table. Hoping Lady Sharon wouldn't notice how much the color of her drink had faded in her absence, she returned to her place to await her partner for the next dance.

She contained herself with difficulty when Landover and Lady Sharon returned, but she could not help an oblique glance or two to see if her ladyship would remember her drink. She need not have worried. With a smile, Landover himself picked up the punch cup and handed it to her. Lady Sharon smiled her gratitude and took a sip. Gillian held her breath, but there was no outcry. Lady Sharon took a second, deeper sip. Then, as she observed her next partner approaching, she turned toward the side table as though to set the cup down again. Gillian sighed. But her spirits leaped again when Lady Sharon, with rather unmannerly haste, gulped down the rest of her drink, and turned, laughing, to take her partner's arm.

Gillian looked up suddenly to find Landover standing over her. She quailed momentarily, thinking that somehow he knew what she had done.

"My dance, I think, Miss Harris." He held out a hand to her, and swallowing carefully, she put hers into it and allowed him to lead her into a nearby set. As luck would have it, it was the same one joined by Lady Sharon and her partner. Gillian caught the other girl's eye, and Lady Sharon glared, then unaccountably giggled.

As the dance progressed, the redhead seemed to move more and more enthusiastically through the pattern of steps, verbally encouraging the others to greater energy. When at last the music faded, she came up breathlessly to stand, weaving a bit, in front of Landover. Her partner, crimson with embarrassment, made a halfhearted attempt to lead her from the floor, but she waved him away with a vague, disoriented gesture and leaned intimately toward the marquis.

"Did you enjoy the dance, my lord?" she asked with a giggle that lurched rather unexpectedly into a hiccough.

Landover's eyes narrowed in puzzlement. "I did. Shall we return to our party now?"

But Lady Sharon ignored the polite suggestion. She tossed her head flirtatiously and nearly stumbled as a result. "No hurry, my lord. The musicians are resting." She smiled at Gillian, who was watching her in fascination. "How nice for you, Miss Harris, that Landover extends the field of his duties as your trustee to such pleasurable ends. I hope you don't expect him to extend them further than this, however."

Gillian gasped and darted a look at Landover. His lips had thinned to a hard line, and his jaw was stiff with anger, but he maintained careful control over his voice. "People are beginning to stare, my lady, wondering why we stand like fenceposts. Let us return to your mother." He placed a hand firmly on her upper arm, and Lady Sharon immediately leaned against him, gazing adoringly up into his stern face.

"How considerate you are, Landover," she crooned. "How thoughtful. What a lovely husband you will make, to be sure. And, of course," she slurred musingly, "there's all that lovely money. Just how much lovely money have you got, my dear?" There was a pregnant silence. Then, suddenly, her ladyship seemed to hear the echo of her own words and to feel the strong aura of disapproval they had engendered. The adoring look faded to one of shock just before her eyes glazed over entirely. She might well have crumpled to the floor at his feet had Landover, acting swiftly and with commendable presence of mind, not managed to scoop her into his arms. He strode quickly away with his burden, making only the brief statement that her ladyship had been taken ill.

"Ill, my aching back," commented one wag near Gillian. "That wench is drunk as a lord."

Word seemed to flit from one end of the room to the other, and Gillian saw Lady Edgware, a deep scowl on her plump face and that lethal lorgnette poised as though she'd like to strike someone, hurrying in Landover's wake. Gillian went to join the others in her party but kept silent as they exchanged indignant comments with one another. Once she thought her brother looked at her a bit searchingly, but then he turned away again to reply to something Sybilla said to him, and Gillian could not be sure.

Landover returned some moments later. He smiled at his sister. "Her mother has taken her home, and there's little doubt the poor wretch is in for the trimming of her life. 'Tis a pity, too, for I'm as certain as can be that it wasn't her fault."

"Well, you certainly cannot be expected to offer for her now, Landover," Lady Harmoncourt said indignantly, "though who would have thought that sweet child would have said such vulgar things to you—for we heard all about it, I can tell you, and I've not a doubt in the world that everyone else has heard by now as well. 'Tis clear enough she was under the influence, not that that excuses her, of course. But where do you suppose she got the drink?"

"Some prankster, no doubt," replied Landover. "Her cup was left sitting there in the open, you know. 'Tis possible that whoever did it didn't even know whose it was. Any number of these young cubs have flasks in their pockets. You know that as well as I do, Abigail."

And there the matter was left to rest, but Gillian didn't breathe easily until she had reached the sanctuary of her own bedchamber, where she slipped off her dress and wrapped a fleecy robe around herself to let Ellen brush her hair. They were chatting desultorily about Gillian's evening when suddenly the bedchamber door was thrust open without ceremony, and Sir Avery stood glaring upon the threshold. He gestured briefly toward the maid.

"Send her away, Gillian. I want a word with you."

Ellen gasped indignantly at such an intrusion, but Gillian realized there would be no denying him. "It is all right, Ellen," she said quietly. "I can manage now. Go on to bed."

"Yes, miss." She eyed Sir Avery askance. "Are you quite sure, Miss Gillian?"

"Quite sure. Good night."

Her brother advanced toward her, scarcely waiting until the maid had shut the door before he pounced. "Just how much of that vodka did you give her?" he demanded.

"About half a cup," Gillian responded, watching him warily.

"Good Lord, Gillian!" he expostulated. "How did you dare? I've a good mind to haul you straight off to Landover. I suppose you realize that poor girl's reputation is utterly ruined! She won't be able to show her face in town for months."

"Fiddlesticks," Gillian retorted. "She may choose to absent herself for a week or two, but it will be little worse than a nine-day wonder, especially in view of everything else that's occurring right now. No one else knows for certain that she was not merely stricken ill."

"Be that as it may," her brother returned angrily. "I've a good mind to put you across my knee or, at the very least, to make you confess the whole to his lordship, for you had no business to do such a thing."

Since he seemed truly displeased, she was conscious of a small tremor of fear, but she repressed it, facing him squarely. "That girl had it coming, Avery. Her behavior was despicable, and she condemned herself with words straight from her own mouth. I couldn't have planned it better had I written a script and forced her to read from it."

"But she would never have said such things if you hadn't got her tipsy."

"Fiddlesticks. She wouldn't have said them then if she hadn't been thinking them all along. I am not going to pretend that I'm proud of what I did, but I'm not sorry for it either. She would have made Landover a dreadful wife!"

"You might have let him decide that, my girl. Dash it, he hadn't even offered for the chit yet!"

She shrugged.

"Well, I still think you ought to tell him what you did," Sir Avery repeated stubbornly. "Dash it, Gill, I had to leave my silver flask behind in that dratted plant for fear he'd find it on me and think I was the guilty party. You cannot do such things without being willing to take the consequences."

"Very well, Avery." She stood up purposefully. "Is he downstairs, or must you fetch him for me?"

"What?" He seemed completely taken aback.

"Landover. Where is he? I shall confess to him right now. He will no doubt make good his threat to pack me off to Sussex, but at least I'll have your charming company on the way."

"What do you mean?" he asked suspiciously.

"Well, I shall certainly have to tell him where I got the vodka, shan't I, and he is scarcely like to approve of the source."

"Here now, Gill, let's don't be hasty!" he asserted, back-pedaling rapidly. "Perhaps I ought to have thought about this more carefully. Can't deny the chit had a lesson coming. No doubt it will all blow over soon."

He blustered a bit more but soon took himself off, leaving his sister to breathe a sigh of relief. She sat down again, casting a rueful glance at her reflection in the looking glass. "She did deserve it," she whispered softly to the face staring into her own. But even saying the words aloud did not ease the remorse she was feeling. Somehow the fact that Sir Avery knew what she had done made her even more ashamed of herself than she had been before. Lady Sharon didn't deserve to become a marchioness, but she had done little to deserve such a severe setdown. While she finished preparing for bed, Gillian did her best to convince herself that there had been no other way to accomplish the purpose, but when she climbed into the high bed, a whisper of doubt remained to prick at her conscience.

The next few days were busy ones, what with the Ascot races, a dinner at Carlton House, and various activities arranged for the entertainment of the visiting sovereigns, but Lady Harmoncourt did not allow grass to grow under her feet. She soon had a replacement for the disappointing Lady Sharon in the person of the Honorable Miss Clara FitzWilliam.

Miss FitzWilliam was a slender, flaxen-haired beauty in her second season, noted for her choosiness. Despite her reputation, however, it seemed possible that she might consider the wealthy marquis a suitable mate. At any rate, when Gillian was introduced to her at a supper preceding a gala night at the Covent Garden Opera, Miss FitzWilliam seemed perfectly content to have Landover as her escort. Gillian's own escort for the evening was Lord Darrow, and the other two places in Landover's box were occupied by Mrs. Periwinkle and the Honorable Mrs. Robinson, Clara's chaperone for the evening. The Harmoncourt box, adjoining Landover's, contained Lord and Lady Harmoncourt, their daughter Sybilla, a pretty young friend of hers, and Sir Avery Harris, as well as his friend Mr. Willoby. The latter confided to Gillian over the partition that opera wasn't really his dish, but that Sir Avery had insisted he lend his support to the occasion.

The opera house was full to overflowing. In the pit, several people actually fainted, and many young bucks were weaving long before the curtain went up and the singing of "God Save the King" was begun. The Regent was accompanied in his box by the Tsar and the Duchess Oldenburg as well as the King of Prussia, and all joined a large portion of the audience in singing the chorus.

The applause was tremendous, but just as the sovereigns were seated, there was a fresh burst, and heads began to turn toward the box opposite the Regent's. "By Jove!" muttered Darrow. " 'Tis the Princess of Wales!" And sure enough, there she was, glittering with diamonds and sporting an outrageous black wig. Gillian thought there must be diamonds everywhere, and just as she realized she was staring, the Tsar of Russia rose from his seat and bowed. The King of Prussia quickly followed his example, and the Regent, perforce, bowed also.

"A moment of triumph for her highness," chuckled Landover, but the chuckle ceased abruptly when the princess, upon taking her seat, noticed Gillian and nodded to her regally. Gillian had no choice but to return the nod. "I did not know you claimed the princess's acquaintance, Miss Harris." His tone was harsh.

"I have met her briefly, my lord," replied Gillian carefully, not daring to meet his eye. "I can only be flattered that she should remember the occasion."

Mrs. Robinson, a rather fluffy soul, chose this moment to observe that she thought it a great pity the Regent and his wife were not upon better terms. "Why, I have heard it said," she went on in her fluting voice, "that these foreigners mean to negotiate a reconciliation between them."

"Why on earth should they do that, ma'am?" asked Gillian, gratefully diverted.

"Why, to strengthen Prinny's popularity, my dear."

"Quite right, if true," observed Mrs. Periwinkle. " 'For how can tyrants safely govern home, unless they purchase great alliance?' And Prinny will make a much sounder ally if he is more popular with his own people."

"I heard he was actually hissed going home from Clarence House today," confided Miss FitzWilliam in tones that indicated such a thing could never happen to so superior a being as herself.

"Dear me!" Mrs. Robinson clicked her tongue. "So embarrassing for him."

" 'Tis a pity he and the Tsar don't get along better than they do," added Mrs. Periwinkle.

"Indeed, yes," agreed her friend, "but the Emperor of Russia is, I am told, rather flippant in his conversation sometimes, which Prinny cannot like. Why, just the other day, Alexander lectured the Regent on toleration, and Prinny replied that it might be very well in his imperial majesty's dominions to admit people of all degrees into offices and power, but that if he was thoroughly acquainted with our constitution and habits, he would know that it could not be. I give Prinny full credit for so wise and spirited an answer."

Gillian's gaze encountered Landover's at last, and she had all she could do to keep from dissolving into laughter at the absurdity of the Tsar of Russia lecturing anyone, but particularly the head of a constitutional monarchy, on the subject of toleration. By the twinkle in his eye, she knew Landover to be similarly afflicted, but fortunately the curtain going up on the first act saved anyone from having to reply to Mrs. Robinson.

At the first interlude, Landover suggested to Miss FitzWilliam that she might like to accompany him to pay their respects to the Regent. She accepted at once, favoring him with a brilliant smile. Gillian sighed.

"Would you care to stroll a bit, Miss Harris?" Darrow inquired. "We'll not trouble the Regent, but I confess I'd not mind stretching my legs a bit."

She agreed, and they walked out into the corridor together, nodding and greeting a friend or acquaintance as they met them.

"I noticed your merriment at Mrs. Robinson's observation," Lord Darrow murmured when Gillian remained silent for a few minutes. She looked up at him quickly, her color rising, but then she returned his infectious grin.

"I am afraid she's a bit of an eccentric, but Miss FitzWilliam seems to be nice."

"Oh, Clara's well enough," Darrow shrugged. "She's a cousin of mine, you know." Gillian stared, and he seemed suddenly defensive. "Well, I can't help it, can I? Never could see what all the fuss was about. Known the chit from the cradle, after all."

"Is there fuss?"

"Lord, yes! Since the day she emerged from the schoolroom. It's not as though she were an heiress, either, although my uncle will see she's dowered well enough. But what it is that keeps the young fools bowing and scraping is more than I can tell you."

"Well, you must admit she's very beautiful."

"Is she? Hadn't noticed. Not my style," he added with a pointed look. Gillian only blinked at him, and he seemed to search for something further to say. "Guess she's maybe thinking a marquis is better than a measly viscount. Never know, though. Fearfully fickle wench, when all's said and done." They reached the end of the corridor and turned back only to be stopped by an elderly gentleman who wished to exchange a few brief pleasantries with Darrow.

"Which viscount?" Gillian asked as soon as they were moving again. Darrow glanced down at her in puzzlement for a moment before he reconnected with her train of thought.

"Linden," he replied. "Son of the Earl of Fairleigh. Going to be an earl one day himself, of course, but Clara will no doubt prefer being a marchioness to being a mere countess. Thing is, I think Linden is in love with her, so she'd best have a care. She tends to toss her head a lot when he's in the vicinity, but I think she's rather fond of him, too, despite her baser instincts."

"Why should she have a care?"

"Linden's got a reputation as a rake, and he's certainly got a bit of the devil in him," Darrow replied. "I just think he's likely to become dangerous if she continues to taunt him, that's all."

Gillian fell silent, digesting the information he had given her. If Miss FitzWilliam only wanted Landover because his title made him a superior catch to her other suitors, then she was quite as contemptible as Lady Sharon.

She watched the other girl when they all returned to the box and noted that there was little warmth in the brilliant smiles she lavished on her escort. She noted also, however, that Landover seemed to be regarding Gillian herself through narrowed eyes. Somehow she had managed to incur his displeasure again, but she couldn't imagine how she had done it this time. It was not until they had returned to Landover House that she found out. When she and Mrs. Periwinkle began to climb the stairs ahead of him, he suddenly spoke her name brusquely. Gillian turned.

"I wish to speak with you," he said. "In the study."

"Surely not at this hour, Landover!" protested Mrs. Periwinkle. "The girl needs her sleep. Tomorrow she will be up even later than this, what with the Marquis of Stafford's dinner and the Earl of Cholmondeley's ball!"

"Nevertheless, I would speak with Miss Harris now," he said firmly. "I shall not keep her overlong."

Gillian glanced at her companion, hoping Mrs. Periwinkle would think of a way to postpone what looked like being another uncomfortable interview. But the older lady merely shrugged.

"Have a good night then, my dear. I shall see you in the morning."

Gillian replied suitably, then turned with reluctance to follow Landover into the study. "What have I done now, my lord?" she asked as he shut the door.

"It has to do with your so-called 'brief' meeting with her highness of Wales," he answered grimly.

"Oh, that."

"Indeed. You might have mentioned that you had paid her a morning call."

"Well, it wasn't exactly like that, you know." She looked up at him candidly, but her nerves seemed a little on end. Particularly when he moved toward her. "I . . . I didn't precisely pay her a morning call."

"I know exactly what you did," he retorted. "I have had it straight from the horse's mouth."

"The horse's m— Surely you don't mean her highness's!" He shook his head, but she noted with relief that her misunderstanding had afforded him a touch of amusement. "Then who?" Landover continued to regard her, but quizzically now as though daring her to use her head. Suddenly she realized what he meant. "Good gracious! Not the Regent! He knows?"

"He knows."

"But he has forbidden the Princess Charlotte to visit Connaught House. Was he livid?"

"He was not pleased. He, too, noted her highness's nod to you and demanded to know if I have been encouraging the connection. I informed him quite frankly that I have not." He placed both hands upon her shoulders, and for a moment she feared he meant to shake her again. But his hands were gentle, and there was a disturbing warmth in his eyes when she gazed contritely up at him. "It would have been helpful, child," he said quietly, "if you had informed me of the visit yourself."

VIII

Gillian trembled, affected more by his gentle distress than she would have been by his anger. Her shoulders seemed to burn where his hands touched them, and her breath caught raggedly in her throat.

"I'm sorry," she muttered, looking now at his broad chest, at the snowy white shirtfront, then at the intricate neckcloth. When he said nothing, she let her gaze continue upward to that firm chin, to the narrow lips parted slightly over even teeth, then to the straight nose and finally the deep-set, hazel eyes. What she encountered there nearly stopped her breath entirely. He was watching her intently, although there was no sign of anger. She wasn't precisely certain what she saw, but it was disturbing. She caught her lower lip between her teeth, then swallowed carefully. "I ought to have told you, I suppose."

"Yes." His voice was very low.

"But I must confess I was a little afraid to do so, and the princess said no one would know."

"Prinny always knows. He has spies in her household."

"Spies!"

"Of course. She is his daughter, and she is not a particularly obedient daughter." Amusement crept into his eye again, and Gillian responded with twitching lips.

"I see."

"No doubt." His tone was ironic, but he lifted his hands from her shoulders with an excess of care. "It is part of the reason I was reluctant to allow your friendship with the princess."

"You feared she would teach me to be disobedient?"

He chuckled appreciatively. "No, you little minx, the thought didn't so much as cross my mind, oddly enough. I doubt anyone could give you lessons on that subject." He hesitated for a moment, an odd expression on his face, then stepped back, speaking more firmly. "In future, I would appreciate it if you would avoid visits of that nature. If the Princess Charlotte is the sort of friend you insist she is, then she will understand. She cannot wish for you to incur Prinny's displeasure." He looked directly into her eyes, that enigmatic expression still lurking behind the surface sternness. "Or mine," he added softly.

Her hands were trembling. Firmly, she pressed them against her skirt, but no matter how she tried, she could not continue to meet that steady gaze. "I . . . I will speak with her highness, my lord," she muttered. "May I have your permission to retire now?"

In answer, he stepped past her and opened the door, saying nothing until she had put her foot upon the bottom stair. "Miss Harris."

She turned, one gloved hand upon the polished rail. "Sir?"

"Pleasant dreams." Then, before she could reply, he turned back into the study, leaving her to stare at the huge door when he had shut it gently behind him.

Gillian stood for a moment, gathering her wits, trying to understand the man she had just been with. One moment, he seemed almost friendly, the next, censorious. And just as she thought she had gained the confidence necessary to deal with him, he had reduced her, with seemingly little effort on his own part, to the status of a naughty child. It was incomprehensible.

With a sigh, she turned back up the stairs, half expecting to find Mrs. Periwinkle awaiting her in her bedchamber. But there was no one there except Ellen, who seemed quick to read her mood and to realize her mistress would not welcome idle chatter. So it was that Gillian was quickly tucked into bed and the candles extinguished. Despite a lingering sense of confusion and disorientation, however, she soon drifted into slumber.

When she awoke the following morning, the sun splashed golden rivers across the blue carpet, bringing a smile to her face. It looked like being a beautiful day. And she had no special plans until the evening. Remembering that the royal sovereigns were to embark at nine from the Whitehall Stairs for a trip by water to Woolwich, it occurred to her that the Princess Charlotte might very likely welcome a visit. It would be as good a time as any to have the little talk Landover had suggested.

Gillian smiled to herself. More a command than a suggestion, if one were to be precise. But once she had had her chocolate, she slipped on a dressing gown and went in search of Mrs. Periwinkle. It had seemed obvious that private conversation with the Princess at Warwick House would require some advance planning.

"So, if you please, Cousin Amelia," she was saying a few moments later, "if you could induce Miss Knight to show you the gardens or something, it would enable me to speak plainly with her highness."

" 'An honest tale speeds best being plainly told,' " agreed that lady with a smile. "I shall do my possible, my dear. I confess I had feared to find you not so cheerful this morning. Do these smiles indicate that Landover treated you gently? It was her highness of Wales who stirred his wrath, was it not?"

Gillian nodded with a grimace. "He still treats me like a child!"

"Then you should be grateful, my dear. 'Men ne'er spend their fury on a child,' as the bard so shrewdly wrote. I admit I am glad to see you submit to his wishes instead of flouting them. Much more comfortable for us all."

With a sigh and a tiny smile, Gillian confessed that she'd rather flout Landover's decrees. "It is just something about the man, cousin. He brings out the worst in me, makes me want to fly out at him, to enflame him to anger. But then, sometimes, his anger makes me feel small, childish and selfish, makes me dislike myself. The visit to Connaught House was not my doing, yet he made me feel as though it were, as though I had somehow betrayed his trust by not making the princess stay at home."

"And could you have done so?"

"No." She glanced up to find Mrs. Periwinkle's eyes twinkling. "Well, I couldn't have stopped her going," she insisted defensively. There was a silence. Gillian shrugged. "But I daresay I needn't have gone with her."

"Honestly said," applauded Mrs. Periwinkle. "And now that

you have acknowledged the fault, I shall apply balm to that wriggling conscience of yours. I have been part and parcel of this world for more years than I care to count, my dear, and I tell you most truthfully that it takes a very strong soul to deny a royal request. And don't make the mistake of believing it will be any the easier now. No doubt her highness will agree to help you avoid Landover's displeasure, but that is not to say she will not request your company the next time the notion strikes her to do so. She has not been trained to think of others first, you know."

Gillian nodded. "But how am I to deal with that when the time arises, ma'am? Shall I be strong enough then, do you think, to deny such a request?"

Mrs. Periwinkle shrugged elaborately. "You must follow your own conscience, my dear. Decide which is more important to your happiness, to submit to Landover or to Charlotte." And with scarcely a pause to allow contemplation, she turned the subject to the important matter of Gillian's dress for the upcoming Burlington House masquerade. Gillian suggested that she might like to go as Helen of Troy.

"A domino and a loo masque will suffice, my dear," her mentor said firmly. "One does not wish to be thought demimondish."

"Cousin Amelia!"

"Pish tush. Stop being missish, Gillian. You know perfectly well that half of the females at a do like this one will be lightskirts and birds of Paradise. If that Harriette Wilson and her sisters do not show up, you may call me a monkey."

Gillian's eyes widened. Harriette Wilson was one of the most infamous courtesans in London! And she, Gillian, might actually stand up in the same set with her. It suddenly occurred to her that the masquerade was going to be quite an event, and considering his reaction to the last one she had attended, she would not be surprised if Landover suddenly took it into his head to forbid her attendance.

What with worrying about that possibility and thinking about other matters, it was not until after breakfast, when she was in her own bedchamber making final preparations for her visit to Warwick House, that Gillian found herself thinking again about Mrs. Periwinkle's advice regarding the Princess Charlotte.

It was really the first time the older lady had offered advice, she realized. Oh, she had suggested details of fashion and dress and had made observations about various people and situations. She had even outlined certain concrete rules of behavior, such as no waltzing at Almack's or galloping in Hyde Park, but those were rules laid down by others. This was different. This was the sort of advice Gillian might have got from her own mother, had that dear lady survived long enough to offer it.

But it was not like Cousin Amelia to offer such advice. Then, with a niggling discomfort, Gillian realized that she had never asked her before. Rather had she treated her cousin like a sort of glorified paid companion. She had even, if the truth be admitted, treated her a little patronizingly. It had certainly never occurred to her that Cousin Amelia might care about her, might even *wish* to help her make her way in the complicated world of high society. It had all simply been a state of affairs not to be analyzed, merely to be accepted, and not always, she admitted unhappily, accepted graciously.

By the time she joined her companion in the landaulet for the journey to Warwick House, Gillian had determined to turn over a new leaf. She would become a paragon, just as Landover wished. She would do nothing to upset dear Cousin Amelia. She would show Landover he need not worry about her embarrassing him with the Regent. She would be strong.

It was not nearly as difficult as she had expected to have private discussion with the princess, who urged her dearest Miss Knight to show Mrs. Periwinkle over the famous gardens and then, with the influential Notti safely out of the way, promptly dismissed her other ladies-in-waiting. But just as Gillian was congratulating herself upon a successful strategy, the princess made it clear that she had her own reasons for ensuring their privacy. To Gillian's careful explanation of Landover's desire that she not visit Connaught House again, the princess returned quick agreement.

"But of course, my dear Gillian. It would never do for my father to forbid your visits to me. And he has threatened to do so, thinking you urged me to visit my poor mama."

"Good gracious!"

"Not to worry," grinned Charlotte. "I explained the matter,

and he knows enough to believe me. Yet, now he has spoken to Landover, who has spoken to you, so it would be most foolhardy to do such a thing again. And we, we are not fools, my dear Gillian."

"No indeed, your highness."

"But it is not of Mama that I wish to speak." The princess clasped her hands together and peered into Gillian's eyes. "I have met the most wonderful young man."

"Young man, your highness? But surely—"

"Ah, you think of Orange, do you not?" Gillian nodded. "Well, I think of him less and less. There are several others to take my mind off him, after all. But Leopold, ah, now there is a man!"

"Leopold?" Gillian had a sudden horror that the princess might have fallen for one of her grooms.

"Prince Leopold of Saxe-Coburg." The name purred from her lips. Her expressive blue eyes lit with pleasure, and she made a little gesture with her hands. "He is . . . how can I describe him? He is beautiful. We are kindred spirits. He is the sort of man I have always wished to know."

"But who is he, highness? I confess I have not heard his name before this."

"He is a member of Alexander's entourage. I met him at Catherine's hotel."

"Is he staying at the Pulteney, then?"

"No." Charlotte seemed to hesitate, then went on bitterly, "He has been poked away over a greengrocer's in the High Street of Marylebone. But that is nothing to the purpose," she added quickly. "After all, his highness of Orange occupies an attic in Clifford Street, hardly an auspicious address for the man my father would see a future King of England."

Gillian could see no good to be accomplished by pointing out the fact that since William of Orange was staying with his own tailor, the Clifford Street address, attic or not, was still far superior to an unknown grocer's in Marylebone, so she merely asked if Prince Leopold was very handsome.

Charlotte's sigh spoke volumes. "Did I say he is beautiful? And my dearest, most delightful Catherine says he bears a most distinguished record for war service. She made particular mention of his famous cavalry charge at the battle of Leipzig, where he took several thousand prisoners, and for which he was rewarded with the Order of Marie Thérèse. I care little for that, of course, except that it means he is brave as well as beautiful, but I can tell you, my dear Gillian, that in his uniform he is magnificent!"

Later, in their carriage, Gillian confided a portion of Charlotte's artless conversation to her companion. Mrs. Periwinkle snorted. "In his uniform! I've no patience with uniforms. Oh, I've no doubt Prince Leopold looks exceedingly well in his, but to my mind, young impressionable girls like the Princess Charlotte ought never to be allowed to meet handsome young men in uniform. All that glitter and dash blinds them to the fellow underneath. And that one! I can tell you I hope she isn't thinking Prinny will allow her to replace Orange with Saxe-Coburg, for he won't. Not in a thousand years!"

"But why not, ma'am? After all, they are both princes."

"Don't you be fooled by a title, my dear. I've heard of your Prince Leopold. He's a pauper, the third son of a ruling duke. His eldest brother will inherit, the second will join the church, and Leopold must make his way as best he can. I've no doubt of his war record, nor of his figure in uniform, but his income is barely two hundred a year, while as to status and rank, he has none—hence the greengrocer's attic. And Charlotte has mice in hers if she thinks to have him for her king. That I can promise you."

Silence fell while Gillian digested all that Mrs. Periwinkle had told her. She could not be surprised that the older lady had Prince Leopold's statistics right on the tip of her tongue. With her connections, she could no doubt recite the pedigree and income of nearly every eligible nobleman in Europe.

Her companion frowned suddenly. "I wonder if this has been her grace of Oldenburg's game all along. The Tsar has got another sister back in Russia, after all, and though 'tis said she's as plain as ditchwater and well past the age mark as well, if Orange is looking for royal connections, he could do worse. And if Charlotte does send him packing—"

"Could she do that, ma'am?"

Mrs. Periwinkle shrugged. "I should have thought not. After all, Prinny is her father and can dispose of her any way he chooses. Yet, perhaps it will depend upon who is able to influence him most. He does wish for popularity, and he does seek the Tsar's approval. I can tell you this much, my dear—I would not risk a wager on the outcome of all this nonsense."

Gillian chuckled, but her mind was busy the rest of the day. She had much food for thought what with trying to understand Landover's behavior and, in her own small way, to unravel the more basic intrigues that seemed to be afoot amongst the visiting sovereigns, as well as to wonder what effect these might have upon the future of England's crown princess. Of course, she could not begin to fathom the latter intricacies, but it made for interesting fantasies at least, especially in view of the fact that Landover had promised she would actually meet Alexander and the King of Prussia at the Marquis of Stafford's dinner that very night.

They did not arrive at Stafford House until nearly eight o'clock, the dinner having been planned for a late hour in order that the sovereigns might have time to rest a bit after their return from Woolwich. Gillian had dressed with care in an exquisite puff-sleeved, low-scooped gown of white silk, daintily embroidered with silver lilies at the hem and nipped in under her breasts with silver ribbons. She wore a collar of pearls, and her dark hair was confined at the top of her head in a twist woven with silver ribbons and seed pearls. Dainty pearl drops in her ears, a simple silver filigree bracelet over one white glove, and satin pearl-rosetted slippers completed her outfit. The look in Landover's eyes as she descended the grand staircase told her her selection was a success. Even Sir Avery seemed suitably impressed.

For once, they would not be part of a larger party, although they would meet the Harmoncourt contingent as well as other friends later at the Cholmondeley ball. But for the dinner itself, they would, as Mrs. Periwinkle put it, be attending *en famille*.

In the carriage, Gillian was particularly conscious of Landover's presence. Memories of the night before, when she had expected to be scolded and had met instead with gentleness, seemed to hover between them. She felt unaccountably tongue-tied and was grateful for Mrs. Periwinkle's spirited chatter. Suddenly, she realized that her companion was recounting Princess Charlotte's confidences about Prince Leopold. Flushing, she glanced at Landover, fearing he might not approve of her

having passed such things on to Cousin Amelia. But he seemed
to have got the idea that the information had come to the older
lady firsthand.

He smiled, saying lightly, "It seems her highness is no more
immune to infatuation than any other young girl. You will no
doubt agree, ma'am, that it would be kindest to say naught of
this to anyone 'else, since nothing can come of it. Her highness
could only be hurt by such rumors."

"Of course, Landover. You know you may trust me. I only
mention it to you because I felt you should know what was
going on." She glanced pointedly at Gillian.

"And I appreciate that, ma'am." He, too, turned to Gillian.
"You will heed me, miss, and say nothing to anyone. Such
tittle-tattle can only do mischief. You, too, sir."

Sir Avery nodded, but Gillian's eyes snapped. She nearly
gave Landover a piece of her mind for daring to think she
would indulge in idle gossip about the princess. But remembering her resolution, she swallowed the angry words threatening
to spill from her lips and merely said, "Of course, my lord."

He seemed suddenly amused, and his eyes were still twinkling when he helped her from the carriage to the carpeted
flagway. Gillian pursed her lips, not daring to meet his eye lest
she lose her temper after all. Landover bent his head near to
hers.

"Afraid I should send you home if you speak your mind,
miss?"

Her eyes flew wide, but she gritted her teeth. "I do not indulge
in petty gossip, my lord."

"Nor do I in petty revenge, child. 'Twould take more than
sharp words to make me send you home tonight, looking as
beautiful as you do. 'Twould be to deny me the pleasure of the
congratulations I shall receive for having you on my arm."

His words caught her entirely off guard, and her mouth
dropped open in astonishment. She realized soon enough that
she must look utterly besotted and snapped it shut again. But
her expression remained one of wonder.

"Do you truly think me beautiful, sir?"

He grinned at her. "I'd be an idiot to deny it, when every
other gentleman in the place will no doubt be showering you

with compliments. But, yes, Miss Harris, I do. Of course, your smile is much more compatible with the elegance of your gown than that scowl you've been wearing. Take a small bit of advice and cultivate the smile." Sparks lit her eyes, and he grinned again. "Will you take my arm?"

She did not so much place her small hand as slap it down upon his forearm, but he bore up valiantly, without so much as a grimace of pain. Nevertheless, Gillian restrained an impulse to pinch him, fearing his tolerance might diminish a bit at such Turkish treatment.

For the next half hour she nursed a glass of ratafia as she accompanied Landover on a social round of the grand saloon at Stafford House. She met several people of note, including Marshal Blucher, that hero of the Peninsular Wars whose popularity far outweighed the Regent's or, for that matter, the visiting sovereigns'. He seemed jolly enough, she thought, although his present claim to fame seemed to be a penchant for drinking himself under the table at most of the entertainments provided for the visitors.

The guests of honor finally arrived, and the moment Gillian had been waiting for followed soon after when the prince beckoned Landover forward and asked that he present her. She made her deepest curtsy, thinking that both rulers seemed rather aloof, although she agreed with all she had heard about the Tsar's good looks. When she looked up, she found his eye upon her in a rather disconcertingly speculative way. She blushed, and the Regent chuckled.

"A rare beauty, is she not, your excellency?" A gentleman just behind the Tsar spoke briefly in his ear, and Alexander nodded with a delighted smile. Gillian glanced helplessly at Landover.

"I think you have taken my charge's breath away, sire, with your compliments," he said smoothly, "but we must not monopolize your time. I see that Stafford has given the signal for dinner to be served."

Alexander had been conferring again with his interpreter, ignoring Landover entirely, and now he turned pointedly to Gillian. "We shall meet again," he said with stilted formality.

Gillian, not knowing what to say to this, merely curtsied,

giving Landover's arm an unconscious squeeze at the same time. Once they were safely out of earshot, he chuckled.

"Too thick for your blood, Miss Harris?"

"He makes my flesh creep. I'd not be Russian right now for a wilderness of monkeys."

"You like monkeys?"

She stared at him, but he looked so innocent that she couldn't help laughing. "You know perfectly well what I mean, Landover. He looked at me as though he had only to snap his fingers to have me served up for his supper."

"Very likely that's how it's done back home, but Prinny will warn him off, I promise you."

"To think I should be grateful for your protection," she sighed.

"Are you?"

"Indeed yes! For tonight at any rate," she qualified, grinning impishly.

"Baggage."

Dinner was announced a moment later, and Gillian soon found herself sitting between Marshal Blucher and an elderly gentleman who appeared to be quite deaf. The Regent sat a few places up and on the opposite side of the table, between the Grand Duchess Oldenburg and the Countess de Lieven. For the most part, conversation drifted along as it always did at such affairs, in a constant hum, but as the second course was being served, there came a sudden lull, and the grand duchess's voice carried easily when she spoke in her deliberate way directly to the Regent.

"Why do you keep your daughter under lock and key, your highness? Why does she go nowhere with you?" All eyes turned toward them, and Gillian, her sweetbreads in claret momentarily forgotten, noted that the Countess de Lieven had lost her usual rosy color.

"My daughter is too young, madam, to go into the world," replied the Regent icily.

"But she is not too young for you to have fixed upon a husband for her."

"She will not marry for two years."

"I hope that then she will manage to make up to herself for

her present imprisonment." Gillian and several others gasped in dismay at these knife-edged words.

Prinny shot his tormentor a fulminating glare. "When she is married, madam," he retorted crushingly, "she will do as her husband pleases; for the present, she does as I wish."

The duchess stared back at him unblinkingly, then said with malicious gentleness, "Your highness, between husband and wife, there can be only one will."

The Regent turned away and said loudly to Dorothea de Lieven, "This is intolerable."

Immediately, Gillian heard Mrs. Periwinkle's lilting voice and Landover's lower one as both began speaking to their dinner partners. A rush of conversation started that soon settled into the normal drone, but Gillian, though she pretended to return her attention to the delicious sweetbreads, watched obliquely as the Countess de Lieven exerted herself to smooth things over. It was said that the countess knew well how to amuse him; however, the savory had been served before the Regent was heard to laugh again.

In the days that followed, the duchess's behavior grew more and more outrageous. Gillian saw little of the royal visitors, but the Countess de Lieven came to unburden herself to her dear friend Mrs. Periwinkle and gave not a snap of her fingers for Gillian's exceedingly interested presence.

"For I can tell you, Amelia, I am well-nigh distraught. I know not how I shall survive the next few days till their departure, but I can promise you no one will be more grateful than I to see the backs of them all!"

Mrs. Periwinkle called her "dearest Dasha" and made soothing noises, but Madame de Lieven was unimpressed. "No, no, you can have no notion what it's been like. It was not so bad when they all went up to Oxford—the morning after Stafford's dinner, you know—except that she wore that stupid straw bonnet with the dangling feather—vastly unbecoming but already the rage. They call it the Oldenburg poke. Disgusting. Where was I? Oh, Oxford. Well, they all ignored poor Prinny when he tried to lecture them on the history of the city. Of course, Catherine is the only one of the lot who speaks much English, but she pretended he wasn't even there. Flirted with one of the dons instead."

"Very rude, but no doubt gratifying to the don," observed Mrs. Periwinkle. Gillian chuckled, and even Madame de Lieven smiled.

"No doubt." She sighed, accepting a *petit four* from a silver plate and nodding to a suggestion that she might like more tea. "This is the most relaxing half hour I've spent in a week. It has been one ghastly affair after another—the Oxford ball, dinner at Lord Castlereagh's—you can imagine what that was like— Lady Hertford's ball . . ." She shuddered delicately. "And then, my God, then the Guildhall Banquet!"

"Even we heard a rumor or two about that," Mrs. Periwinkle smiled.

Gillian nodded. Landover had attended the banquet. The royal guests had been met at Temple Bar by the Lord Mayor, Sheriffs, and Aldermen mounted on horses, robed and bedizened, arrayed in cocked hats and gold lace. The Tsar and the King of Prussia had been welcomed as usual with jubilant yells, the Regent with groans and shouts of "Your wife! Where's your wife?" Unpleasant enough, Gillian thought, but there had been worse to come.

"Why that dreadful woman insists upon accompanying her brother everywhere I cannot imagine!" the countess said roundly. "That dinner is meant to be attended by men only, and her presence certainly would not have been tolerated back home. But no, here she must be catered to. I was the only other female, Amelia, and I can tell you, I scarcely knew where to look for embarrassment. Prinny was in a rage because he had to give up his seat to her; the Tsar was bored by the whole affair. Only his majesty of Prussia was the least congenial. But Catherine was particularly difficult."

"We heard she covered her ears when the band played 'Rule Britannia,' " said Mrs. Periwinkle.

"Said she had the headache," scorned their guest, "that she would be sick if the noise did not stop. So Prinny stopped it. Our civic hosts were in an uproar, to say the least, and I received an anonymous note to the effect that if she refused to allow the National Anthem, they could not be responsible for the royal table. I passed it on to her, but she was very ungracious, just said, 'Let them bawl then!' Then she closed her eyes as though she were in great pain and grimaced to the end. The Prime Minister came up to me afterward and said, 'When folks don't know how to behave, they would do better to stay at home, and your duchess has chosen, against all usage, to go to men's dinners.' *My* duchess!" the countess wailed. "I can tell you, Amelia, I was ready to sink!"

Gillian absorbed every detail, scarcely able to contain herself until she could share her knowledge with the princess, who might not have heard everything yet. How would she respond to such a report about her precious Catherine?

As it happened, however, it was not until the following Monday, the very day scheduled for the magnificent Burlington House masquerade, that she was able to visit Warwick House, and by then the princess had other matters upon her mind. She greeted Gillian in agitation, waving two sheets of closely written foolscap at her.

"He goes too far!" she cried. "Just look at this!"

Gillian took the paper, which proved to be a list of names, headed by that of the Prince of Orange. "What is this, madam?"

"A list of those to be invited to my wedding!"

"Your wedding! But his highness said himself that it would not take place for two years. I heard him myself less than a week ago."

"He has discovered about my dearest Leopold, I think. But whatever the cause, he has put forward the date to September and says he will send for the Dutch royal family at once. My esteemed grandmama, the Queen, is already making arrangements to obtain her wedding clothes. But that is not all. Study the list, Gillian."

Obediently, she scanned the list of names. Her own was not there, but Landover's was, and there were a good many other familiar titles. It was not until she turned to the second page that she understood the princess's agitation. The Princess Caroline of Wales' name had been boldly scratched off the list.

"Your own mother will not be allowed to attend!"

Charlotte nodded, but then her eyes narrowed, and she held out her hand imperiously. Gillian gave her the papers, and Charlotte laid them upon a nearby table, picked up a quill, and drew two bold lines through the name heading the list. Refolding the pages carefully, she called to one of her ladies. "See that this is delivered to his royal highness at once." The woman curtsied and disappeared. Charlotte turned back to Gillian with a satisfied grin. "That will show him!"

IX

Word that the bridegroom's name had been deleted from the royal wedding list spread quickly, giving rise to all manner of rumors. It was a well-known fact that the princess had received a Sunday-afternoon call from the Tsar and the grand duchess, so it was not exactly wonderful that many persons thought such rude behavior must be at their instigation.

The princess made no secret of her actions; therefore, many of the guests at the magnificent masquerade given by White's Club at Burlington House that night indulged themselves in idle speculation, but they were doomed to disappointment. The Prince Regent was in high spirits and made no reference whatsoever to the incident.

Gillian worried until the very last moment that Landover might forbid her attendance, but she need not have bothered her head about it. A party had been organized by Lady Harmoncourt and Lady FitzWilliam, Clara's mother, and everyone was to meet at the FitzWilliams' elegant home for dinner before going on to the masquerade.

Gillian was delighted to discover that Lord Darrow had been included in the party, and she greeted him warmly. "Good evening, sir. But you are not in fancy dress either! I had hoped to see you as a pirate again."

He grimaced and looked quickly around to see if anyone had overheard her. "I'd as lief you'd not bring that up, Miss Harris. And as a matter of fact," he added, eyeing her rose-pink satin domino and dainty, lace-edged loo masque with a teasing glint of mockery, "I daresay you'd as soon I not ask why you are dressed so demurely upon this occasion."

Gillian blushed rosily. The one matter that had not been discussed after her first experience at a masqued ball had been her dress. And what Landover might have had to say on the subject had he been privileged to see the daffodil taffeta confection she had worn that night did not bear thinking of.

Darrow grinned at her expression. "Would you believe me if I tell you I liked the yellow bit of fluff a dashed sight better than the admittedly elegant gown you're wearing tonight? This color becomes you well enough, but there was a certain something about the other."

"Oh, I'd believe you, my lord," she laughed. "The 'certain something' is called impropriety. That gown was wickedly improper, as you well know, and I quite agree that the less said about the other ball, the better. Where is your cousin?"

"Waiting to make her entrance, I daresay. No doubt she wants to impress Landover."

Gillian sighed. For the past week, while the Countess de Lieven had been plagued by the Grand Duchess Oldenburg, she had been plagued by Miss Clara FitzWilliam. The girl seemed utterly ubiquitous. Whenever Lady Sybilla came to call, she was accompanied by the flaxen-haired beauty, and like as not Landover would make an appearance. He always seemed perfectly at ease, and Gillian could not see that his interest in Miss FitzWilliam had abated in the slightest. If he did not go out of his way to shower her with attention, neither did he avoid her, and Gillian was convinced that between Lady Harmoncourt and Clara herself, the marquis would soon find himself whisked, willy-nilly, to the altar.

"I don't think he should offer for her," she said frankly to her companion.

"He'll be a damned fool if he does," responded Darrow with cousinly candor. "And if he thinks to have her fluttering about him afterward as she does now, he'll soon find he's mistaken his mark. She'll spend her time thinking how nice it is to be a marchioness instead."

"Well, I fear he'll be forced to offer soon if nothing occurs to stop it, and I for one can think of no way to put him off."

"Only one person I know of could stop it, but since it would mean cutting Landover out, I doubt he would."

"One person?"

"Aye. Linden. I told you about him. Remember?" Gillian nodded. "Well, with the least encouragement, I daresay he'd ride off with Clara across the saddlebow, but she won't even bat her lashes at him. He left his card this afternoon whilst I was at my uncle's house, but she wouldn't even see him. Told the butler to say she wasn't home, then said she was, not two minutes later, to a second caller. Linden can't even have got out the front door. Must have been fit to be tied."

"Well, it certainly was rude of her," said Gillian thoughtfully, "but it does sound as though she meant to agitate him."

"She's lucky he didn't barge upstairs and shake her till her bones rattled," chuckled Darrow, much as though he might have enjoyed such a scene. "Here comes the wench now."

Gillian turned in time to witness a vision descending the staircase. Miss Clara was dressed as a fairy princess in a gown of celestial blue, spangled with scalloping strings of silver stars. Her loo masque was mounted on a wand topped by a larger star, and her lovely hair was worn in long curls and bound with a silver fillet that resembled a tiara. Silver sandals twinkled on her tiny feet as she tripped down the stairs. She held out one white-gloved hand to Landover.

"My lord, I give you greeting," she said in her clear treble voice. "Does my costume meet with your approval?"

Landover took the outstretched hand and brushed it with his lips. "You are delightful, my dear. The knowledge that we have you and they do not will turn our visiting sovereigns green with envy."

"How nice," she giggled, holding a demure hand to her lips, "but perhaps," she confided with a twitch of her wand, "I shall choose to turn them into frogs, you know." At that moment, dinner was announced. "Shall we, my lord?" He smiled, and she placed her dainty hand upon his arm.

Darrow chuckled. "She's bewitched him all right."

Gillian glared at him. "I'd have expected Landover to show better sense!" she snapped. She recovered her composure quickly enough and was even able to restrain her disgust at Landover's behavior during dinner. The man seemed totally unaware that he was being reeled in by a determined angler. It was really too ridiculous, as though he were too lazy or too uncaring even to attempt to evade the lures being cast his way.

By the time their party had reached Burlington House, she was thoroughly fed up with him, but upon entering the huge ballroom even Landover was temporarily forgotten. Upwards of four thousand people had chosen to attend the final ball in honor of the visiting sovereigns. The whole of Burlington House was teeming with costumed humanity, and it resembled the masque at Vauxhall far more than any other ball Gillian had attended. Girls shrieked from the galleries where they were chased headlong by young men bellowing, "Tally ho!" and many couples seemed to be indulging in the sort of hand to body combat that would be better suited to a bedchamber than a ballroom. One gentleman, dressed as a seventeenth-century cavalier, actually plunged his hand down a shepherdess's bodice just as Gillian passed by. She felt both ears and cheeks burning and knew her face must be the color of a ripe tomato. Glancing back, she saw Landover grinning at her and quickly faced forward again. How dared he smirk!

They greeted the Dukes of Devonshire and Leinster, cohosts for the gala event, then made their way to the Prince Regent and his party. At least, most of his party. Frederick of Prussia stood on one side of him, with the grand duchess, magnificent in plunging red satin, on the other. Others, including the de Lievens, hovered in close attendance, but the Tsar was nowhere in sight.

"Out hunting," explained the Regent with a chuckle. "I believe his imperial majesty means to seduce as many of our lovely young Englishwomen as possible tonight." The duchess favored him with a frigid glare but said nothing, and Prinny only grinned, enjoying her displeasure for once. He turned to Gillian, saying with ponderous humor, "Perhaps, Miss Harris, if I were to promise to keep you out of Alexander's clutches, you would honor me with a dance?"

"Of course, your highness," Gillian dimpled. "Although, 'tis I who should be honored."

He insisted that it be the very next dance, and so it was that she found herself partnered in a lively quadrille with the Regent trying to outdo the other gentlemen in the antics of the dance. She enjoyed herself hugely. Everyone was watching her, and even though she disapproved of him and thought he treated his wife and daughter abominably, she could not deny the royal charm and enthusiasm. The prince always made her feel beautiful, witty, and desirable. Such a man could not possibly be rotten to the core.

She found her party easily when the dance was done and noted immediately that Landover was leading Clara FitzWilliam onto the dance floor for a set of country dances. Gillian enjoyed a dance with Lord Darrow and one with Sir Avery before a dark-haired stranger, nearly as tall as Landover, with piercing black eyes and bristling eyebrows that arched like a raven's wings, stepped up and quite nearly demanded the favor of a dance.

"We have not been introduced, sir," she responded saucily while taking good care to hold her masque in place. The gentleman was unmasked and wore ordinary evening dress.

" 'Tis the great advantage of a masqued ball, mademoiselle," he replied in a dulcet baritone. "Introductions are not required. Come."

He held out a commanding hand, and obediently she placed her own in it and let him guide her onto the floor. It was a waltz, but there were no restrictions tonight, and as he placed his arm firmly around her waist, she caught sight of Landover leading the fairy princess onto the floor yet again. Gillian stiffened, and her partner's gaze followed hers. A sharp intake of breath caused her to look up at him. The dark eyes smoldered under narrowing lids, and she gave a little gasp.

"You are Viscount Linden!"

His arm tightened. "What makes you think so, Miss Harris?"

"You know me!" She thought quickly, then added in a sighing voice, "I daresay you only asked me to dance in order to make Miss FitzWilliam jealous."

"Don't be daft," he muttered. "She wouldn't care a straw."

Gillian chuckled, letting him sweep her into a complicated series of steps, enjoying herself. "Men are all so blind," she said sweetly a moment later.

He glared down at her. "What are you trying to say, Miss Harris?"

"Only that every sign indicates that Miss FitzWilliam welcomes your attentions, my lord."

"Tommyrot! She lookes for wealth and title."

"You have both, sir."

"I am not a marquis, nor does my income compete with King Midas's."

"But you love her, and I think she loves you. In that regard, Landover must lose on two counts." She sighed again. "He merely wants a conformable, decorative wife, after all. Any one of a number would do."

She could have sworn she heard his teeth gnash together and mentally hugged herself. This was going rather well.

"You honestly think she loves me?" He seemed to have difficulty thrusting the words out.

"Indeed, my lord," Gillian smiled. "I have it on excellent authority that she teases you in hopes that you will master her. I daresay that given half a chance, she would gladly play Matilda to your William. In truth, sir, and I speak as a woman, had she wished to send you about your business, she would have done so graciously and not as though she were flinging down a gauntlet."

"You would liken me to William the Conqueror," Linden observed with a musing smile that showed he rather liked the notion. "But he is said to have won his Matilda with a horsewhip."

"Exactly so," Gillian replied demurely. "I heard what took place this very day when you would have paid her a simple morning call. That was a calculated insult, my lord, as calculated as Matilda's slurs against the Conqueror's birth. I'd wager Miss FitzWilliam was astonished and even a trifle disappointed that you allowed it."

He nearly missed a step, and his eyes glittered as he gazed speculatively down at Gillian. "I shouldn't have allowed it. You are quite right, Miss Harris. I daresay that should such an occasion come to pass a second time, I shall, thanks to this little talk, react quite differently."

By the time he returned her to her party, Gillian's eyes were sparkling, and she was well pleased with the work she had done. She could not help but wonder, however, how long it would be before Vicount Linden would make his move and whether or not he would carry the day. After all, a girl like Clara FitzWilliam would be nearly as well protected as she was herself, and the thought of a gentleman, even one of Linden's stamp, successfully forcing his way past MacElroy and the Landover footmen was nearly ludicrous.

So deep in thought was she that she scarcely paid any heed to the unknown gentleman who partnered her through the next set, responding to his conversational gambits in monosyllables. Thus, she was annoyed but not particularly surprised when, at the end of the dance, she found herself abandoned on the far side of the huge ballroom, a good distance from her own party. In resignation, she began to make her way back, soon discovering that the deed was not so simple as the thought.

The crush of people was astonishing, and without a gentleman beside her to clear a path by brute force if necessary, Gillian suddenly felt as though she were adrift in a sea of elbows, armpits, and bosoms. It was not the first time she had wished for greater height, but matters became even a trifle frightening when she began to suspect she might even be going in the wrong direction. The orchestra struck up for the next dance, and the surge of humanity became more confusing as some couples moved toward the dance floor and others pressed back to make way for them.

Suddenly she came plump up against a rock-hard body encased in a glitteringly bemedaled uniform. Two strong hands grasped her shouders as she glanced up in dismay. "Excellency!"

"Miss Harris." A small space seemed to clear around them as if by magic, and the Tsar dropped his hands. His eyes gleamed as his gaze swept her from the top of her dark curls to the tips of her satin slippers. Gillian dipped a low curtsy, but Alexander reached forward gallantly and drew her to her feet, smiling in pleasurable anticipation. "We dance."

The seductive look in his eyes frightened her, and she remembered the Regent's earlier compliments, but she could not imagine how one said, "No, thank you" to the Emperor of all the Russias. She opened her mouth, but no words came out, and the people around them, now recognizing Alexander, were beginning to stare.

"Ah, Miss Harris, here you are at last. I have been searching for you these past ten minutes. This is my dance, I believe." Landover's suave, familiar voice came from behind Gillian and affected her much in the way that an approaching Yorkist cavalry call might have affected the King's forces at Bosworth Field. "How do you do, your Majesty?" Landover went on with a bow as she turned toward him gratefully. "Are you in need of a partner? Here, Harriette! Here's a treat for you."

He beckoned imperiously to a smart, saucy-looking girl with laughing black eyes and glossy curls nearly as dark as her own. The girl was accompanied by a delicately fair, rather wide-hipped youth in black satin breeches and a light blue silk shirt.

To Gillian's amazement, when the "youth" turned in response to Landover's command, "he" was quite clearly seen to be a beautiful young woman in boy's clothes. Gillian blushed, then looked uncertainly at Landover. He ignored her, but the fair-haired beauty did not approach them. She merely smiled and waved two fingers at Landover before fading back into the crush.

"Well, my lord?" The dark-haired young woman spoke in a sultry voice and gave Landover a teasing smile, while at the same time shooting Gillian a slanting look.

"Well yourself, Harriette." He grinned at the Tsar. "Excellency, may I have the honor to present this lovely creature to your notice. She is Miss Harriette Wilson, and she would be most pleased to dance with you."

Miss Wilson grinned but swept the Tsar a deep curtsy. As he had done with Gillian, however, Alexander reached forward and drew her to her feet. Miss Wilson lowered her lashes demurely. "We dance," announced Alexander firmly. He glanced as an afterthought at Landover. "Our thanks."

Landover gave a slight, mocking bow to the Tsar's back, and Gillian stared at him in astonishment. "How did you dare to introduce the Tsar of Russia to a common courtesan!"

"There is nothing the least bit common about Harriette Wilson, my dear child, and I can safely promise you that there is no one in London to whom Alexander would prefer an introduction tonight."

"You did not introduce her to me!"

"No, I did not!"

Gillian chuckled, making no demur when he took her hand and firmly placed it in the crook of his arm. Suddenly, it seemed much easier for her to make her way through the constantly shifting mass of people. "Who was that person with her?" she asked, looking up at him. "I thought at first it was a rather chubby gentleman."

"Julia Johnstone, another of Harriette's sisterhood. They came as brother and sister, though I must say they seem to have got their roles mixed. Julia's got at least five children, and hasn't the slightest claim to a boyish figure, whilst Harriette is a good deal slimmer and has, besides, the manners of an obstreperous schoolboy."

Gillian chuckled again and gave his arm an impulsive little squeeze. "I haven't thanked you, have I? I was imagining myself served up for an imperial savory, and I can tell you quite frankly, Landover, that I have never been more grateful to hear your voice."

"We'll see if you still feel that way ten minutes hence," he retorted. She glanced up again quickly, surprised by the grim note in his voice. "I've a good deal to say to you, miss. We'll begin with an explanation from you of where you had got to before you crossed his majesty's lecherous path."

Gillian made a *moue*. "My partner vanished after the last set, and we had somehow managed to get to the far side of the room. I thought I'd never get through the crowd."

"Who the devil was your partner?"

"I haven't the slightest idea. Never saw him before. But I daresay he was no gentleman. Although," she added with disarming frankness, "it was not altogether his fault. I was rather rude. I expect it put him off."

Landover's lips twitched, but he managed to retain the stern note. "I've no doubt you were rude if you say you were, but perhaps you would care to explain a trifle more fully."

"I was distracted, actually," she replied on an airy note. "I was thinking about other matters and did not precisely attend to him when he spoke. I've noticed gentlemen prefer an attentive audience."

Landover was not distracted, however. "What other matters?" Gillian, after a brief, dismayed glance at him, blushed to the roots of her hair and clamped her lips shut. There was certainly no way she was going to tell him she had been savoring her potential success at rescuing him from the designing schemes of Miss Clara FitzWilliam. "No? You wish to say nothing? Well, I have a bit more to say, I'm afraid."

And he proceeded to make good his promise while he guided her back to their party. First, he informed her flatly that, masqued ball or no, she was to let Mrs. Periwinkle have the final word on her partners if he was not himself at hand, that furthermore it was her business to see that her partners did not merely fade away but returned her to her chaperone, that so on and so on and so on. Gillian merely bowed her head before the muttering storm, knowing it would be useless to protest. But as they emerged from the thickest part of the crowd, she saw Miss Clara FitzWilliam slip into an anteroom, closely followed by her companion, Mrs. Robinson. Miss FitzWilliam was holding a string of silver stars that seemed to have detached themselves from the blue fairy gown, so the matter was self-explanatory. What caught and held Gillian's interest, however, was the sight of a tall, dark gentleman with raven's-wing eyebrows lounging artlessly against the wall not ten feet from the door through which the two ladies had passed.

Smoldering dark eyes turned first one way, then the other; then, with a purposeful stride, Viscount Linden made his way to the anteroom door. Here he paused again, glancing about quickly before slipping inside and shutting the door behind him.

"Miss Harris! I'll swear you've not been attending to one word I've said to you!"

Gillian gulped and turned to face him, discovering another set of smoldering eyes rather closer than was compatible with her comfort.

"Oh, I was listening, sir," she insisted contritely. "It was prodigiously foolish of me not to take better care, and I shan't do it again, so please forgive me." And she held out her hand, gazing at him limpidly.

His responding smile had a tendency to mock her. "I ought to quiz you, young lady, for I'm as certain as can be that you didn't hear half of what I said, but to do so after such a generous and—might I add—unexpected apology would not only be foolhardy but churlish. I trust I am rarely accused of either trait. More important, however, I've no wish to quarrel with you tonight."

"Thank you, my lord," she replied, genuinely grateful. She tucked her hand in his again. "And thank you for rescuing me." He patted her hand, gazing down at her with an enigmatic gleam in his eye.

"Landover! Oh, my lord, how glad I am to find you! You must come at once." Mrs. Robinson, seemingly appearing out of thin air, grabbed his arm in agitation.

"What seems to be the trouble, ma'am?" Landover returned calmly in an effort to soothe the little woman's ruffled feathers.

"It is Clara, my lord. She's being assaulted by that dreadful man!"

"Where?" demanded the marquis in a much harsher tone.

Gillian drew a sudden breath. What if Landover felt obligated to fight a duel with Linden? It was a notion that had not previously occurred to her. She had thought only to nudge Viscount Linden into doing what he so clearly wanted to do anyway; she had not paused to think how Landover might react. Mrs. Robinson pointed now to the anteroom and fluttered along beside him as he strode determinedly forward. Gillian hastened after them, not wanting to miss a thing and straining her ears to hear as Mrs. Robinson breathlessly twittered out the details.

"It is that dreadful rake Linden, my lord. If I've warned dearest Clara once, I've warned her a thousand times. 'Have nothing to do with him,' I said. 'He's a rake,' I told her. 'A dangerous man.' But some idiot during the last set yanked a string of those lovely stars from poor Clara's gown, and we retired to the anteroom to effect a repair. No sooner had we got inside, though, than that brute nipped in behind us and demanded words with Clara. She was mighty angry, I can tell you, but he just walked bang up to her and said she'd been behaving badly and he meant to put a stop to it. Well, I wasn't surprised at all when she slapped him for his rudeness, but you could have tipped me over with a feather when he slapped her back. Just as calm as you please, mind you, but the blow nearly knocked poor Clara plumb off her feet. Needless to say, my lord, that's when I fled to get help."

"And a very good thing, too," approved Landover as they reached the anteroom door. "But perhaps you ought to remain here now with Miss Harris whilst I see what can be done."

Mrs. Robinson seemed perfectly willing to let Landover attend to the matter, but Gillian was not about to be set aside while he walked into a trap of her creating. Determined to do her possible to prevent the duel she had by now convinced herself was imminent, she slipped into the anteroom right behind him and thus was witness to a scene that neither of them had expected.

Miss Clara FitzWilliam was enfolded in the strong arms of Viscount Linden, but she did not seem the least averse to her position. In fact, she was returning his kisses with what Gillian could only describe later to Lady Sybilla as "passionate abandon." Landover cleared his throat loudly, and the two sprang involuntarily apart. Miss FitzWilliam, a wicked bruise forming at her delicate jawline, flushed guiltily.

"Oh, Landover!" she cried, stepping toward him. "'Twas not what you think, my lord. 'Twas merely—"

"Enough, Clara!" admonished Linden sharply, taking a firm grip on her upper arm and ruthlessly pulling her back to stand beside him. "It was exactly what you thought, my lord. I love this unprincipled baggage, and I believe she loves me. At any rate, I intend to marry her just as soon as things can be properly arranged, but if you've a desire to debate the matter, I urge you to name the time and place."

"No!" Gillian cried, springing forward as though to fling herself between them. Linden's meaning could not be mistaken. Even Clara seemed taken aback, and she stared at Linden as though she had never really seen him before. But Landover caught Gillian's arm and drew her closer to himself.

"Be still, child. There will be no 'debate.' I cheerfully leave the field to so determined a warrior. I think they will deal admirably together, and I wish them only happiness. Shall we leave them to take up the discussion we so rudely interrupted?"

Silently, she let him lead her from the room, and as silently did she listen while he explained to Mrs. Robinson, anxiously awaiting them just outside the door, that rather than an assault, she had witnessed the onset of a proposal of marriage and therefore a scene of quite unexceptionable behavior.

"Landover," Gillian said, recovering her equanimity with a delighted chuckle once Mrs. Robinson had gone away, "slapping each other is scarcely the accepted prologue to a civilized courting ritual."

"No? Well, I had to say something to the poor little widgeon.

27

The sun shone bright Tuesday morning, in an almost impossible run of good weather in Philly, but Judy was too psyched to care. She couldn't see the blue sky for the TV and still cameras, tape recorders held high, and klieg lights. She couldn't breathe the fresh air for the reporters exhaling coffee in her face. It was a Starbucks contact high.

Judy plowed in her navy suit and lucky pumps through the press outside the Criminal Justice Center, with Pigeon Tony wedged between her and Frank. For the first time, she not only tolerated the reporters, she welcomed them. She felt safer for all of them with 384 witnesses on the scene, and the media was key to Judy's new and improved plan.

"Ms. Carrier, any comment about Kevin McRea's disappearance?" "Judy, over here! What do you say to reports that Marco Coluzzi was trying to buy McRea Excavation?" "Ms. Carrier, do you believe Kevin McRea has met with foul play?"

"No comment," she shouted. She threaded her way to the courthouse entrance, putting on a professional mask to hide her glee at their questions. Obviously her late-night telephone calls, placed anonymously to any newspaper that would pick up, had worked like a charm. She had planted the story about Marco Coluzzi's attempted purchase of McRea Excavation, and eager reporters had investigated the facts and gotten sources to confirm. It had been a year or two since a Philly paper had won a Pulitzer and nobody was forgetting it.

"Ms. Carrier, do you care to comment on Marco Coluzzi's

X

Gillian stared at him in dismay, wondering if he could somehow have discovered her activities, knowing he would not
approve at all if he had, and fearing his next words. But he
only grinned wider and moved toward his sister.

"Best get it over with, I suppose. She won't be pleased, but I
think Linden will deal better with Clara than I should have
done."

Gillian gave an inward sigh of relief and held her tongue
while Landover described the past quarter hour to his sister.
Sir Avery was standing with Lady Sybilla, enjoying a cup of
wine punch but easily able to hear Landover's words, and at
one point in the tale he glanced rather sharply at his sister.
Gillian felt the telltale color creeping into her cheeks, but at
least this time Avery would find nothing to condemn. It was
scarcely a reprehensible thing to bring two lovers together.
Nevertheless, she experienced another surge of relief when,
after a slight narrowing of his eyes, Sir Avery turned back
to the girl at his side. Really, thought Gillian, her mind
still on matchmaking, the two would be well suited to each
other.

Sir Avery was certainly beginning to show signs of an attachment to the lovely Sybilla, and the lady did not seem totally
blind to his virtues either. But there was an easy camaraderie
between them that seemed to be at odds with courtship as
Gillian romantically expected it to be. Viscount Linden's rough-
and-ready methods were a good deal more in keeping with her
notions than Sir Avery's, if indeed the latter was even interested in forming a permanent attachment. Perhaps—she eyed

the pair speculatively—perhaps she might be able to nudge things along a bit.

But no, she dismissed the notion almost as soon as it occurred to her. Sir Avery would never countenance her interference. Her ears actually tingled at the thought of his probable reaction to any matchmaking by her on his behalf. Far better to let matters take their own course, even if he muffed it.

Following this course of thought, she began to wonder why Landover tolerated his sister's busy interest in his future. Lady Harmoncourt was presently bemoaning Clara FitzWilliam's poor judgment in preferring a mere viscount to a so well-endowed marquis, but Gillian could easily interpret the speculative gleam in her ladyship's eyes as they scanned the crowded ballroom. Clara FitzWilliam was already a dead issue. Lady Harmoncourt was looking for another prospect to present to her brother.

Why did he put up with it? Gillian glanced up at him. He, too, was watching her ladyship, but the expression in his eye was one of tolerant amusement. Did he think it was a game? she wondered. She remembered Lady Sybilla describing him earlier as lazy and likely to take the course of least resistance. She herself had seen little sign of laziness, however, and although he made a great fuss about fearing his sister's temper, Gillian shrewdly suspected that he exaggerated his fears in order to indulge the lady. But surely, he must realize that the game this time was a dangerous one. So far, thanks to her, nothing had come to a head, but he could not go on behaving as he had been with impunity. Sooner or later, if he continued to let Lady Harmoncourt lead him by the nose, he would be standing at the altar watching his bride walk down the aisle. Which was, of course, exactly what Gillian wanted, was it not? She sighed at the thought. Of course it was, since he would then be too busy to interfere with her. But only if the girl walking toward him would make him a suitable wife. And so far, the qualities Lady Harmoncourt deemed essential were not the same ones that Gillian herself would have sought for Landover's marchioness.

The right girl for him, in her opinion, would be kind and gentle, willing to put his interests ahead of her own, submissive to his will, and completely uninterested in matters of title and wealth. She sighed again. Surely an impossible task, to discover such a paragon. But arrogant and dictatorial though he was, interfere though he constantly did in the affairs of others, still did he deserve a wife who would be cherished years after the wedding, not some shrew who would spend his money as though his pockets were bottomless, and flaunt her title as marchioness rather than basking in that of wife.

She realized he was looking at her, and the color crept into her cheeks again.

"I fear we have missed our dance, Miss Harris."

She rallied. "I shall endeavor to bear up, my lord."

He smiled at her, and the rest of the evening passed quickly in a blur of partners. Linden appeared briefly with Miss FitzWilliam blushing demurely at his side, but as he informed the company at large, they came only to collect Lady FitzWilliam and Mrs. Robinson before departing.

"This affair is becoming entirely too rowdy for such an innocent as Clara," he pronounced firmly. "We'll bid farewell." He turned to the marquis and held out a hand. "You've been dashed decent about all this, Landover, and I appreciate it. I've told Clara I'll speak to her father in the morning. You may look for the announcement immediately in the *Gazette*."

Clara blushed more deeply, not daring to look at Landover, but he merely grinned at the erstwhile rake. "I meant what I said earlier, Linden. You'll suit each other down to the ground. Good night."

Immediately after the official unmasking, Lord Harmoncourt announced that he, too, had had enough, and Sir Avery very kindly offered to help him escort his ladies home. Following closely upon their heels, Landover's party paused to pay their respects to Mr. Brummell, who lounged in one corner with Lords Alvanley and Petersham to bear him company. The Beau smiled at them. "Nice to meet friends amongst all this rabble."

Landover returned the smile with a dry one of his own. "You'd be astonished at whom you might meet, George, if you would but bestir yourself to mix with the company."

"Too true, my lord," replied the Beau as, with a droll but speaking grimace, he waved a languid hand in the direction of the royal party. "But only a fool would attempt to compete with the big guns this night. I am content, sir, to linger here amongst the peasants."

Petersham bridled at such a reference, but Alvanley chuckled. "Hold hard, my lord. Surely you recognize bait when you hear it. He seeks to stir coals and will be disappointed only an your embers stay banked."

Petersham subsided with a rueful grin and helped himself to a pinch of snuff with the flair of an expert. Gillian had heard it said that he had a separate snuffbox for each day of the year, but she was singularly unimpressed. She had not thought kindly of the eccentric earl since the night he had betrayed her visit to Vauxhall. Brummell shook his head now in mock despair.

"They take the fun out of sharpening one's wit, Landover. Truly they do."

"Don't expect sympathy from us, George. We're leaving."

It was not as easy as that, of course, for they still had to make their way through the seemingly undiminished mob to the main entrance. Then it still remained for one of the numerous linkboys to fetch their carriage, but at last Landover, Gillian, and Mrs. Periwinkle were able to relax against the plush squabs of the comfortable, crested coach. Mrs. Periwinkle sighed deeply as the carriage rolled away from Burlington House and down the now silent stretch of Piccadilly.

"That was quite a do," she said appreciatively. "Prinny will be well pleased, I think." When neither of her companions vouchsafed a response, another thought struck her. "Ought we to have stayed until the Regent and his guests departed, Landover?"

He chuckled. "My dear Amelia, it is nearly two o'clock in the morning, and I'd wager it will be three at least before they even *find* the Tsar. No one will notice our departure or care a hoot if they do. But if it will make your mind easy, I'll promise to tell his highness that Miss Harris was taken ill. He'll never be so ungallant as to blame us for taking her home."

"Well," declared Gillian roundly, "I trust the circumstance will not arise, for I'd hate to be the subject of such a plumper. I am not such a poor spirit, sir."

Once home, Gillian's head had scarcely touched the pillow before she drifted into deep slumber that lasted well into the next morning. It was a lazy day spent paying and receiving calls, and it ended with an evening concert of sacred music at Carlton House. The following morning, the visiting sovereigns, accompanied by the Prince Regent and a noble retinue, including the Marquis of Landover and the Earl of Harmoncourt, left London for Portsmouth, where there would be five days of farewell activities, including a Grand Naval Review, before the visitors set sail from Dover.

Gillian and Mrs. Periwinkle accompanied Lady Harmoncourt and Sybilla to Almack's that evening, but freed of Landover's constant vigil, Sir Avery begged off, leaving the ladies without a male escort. Lady Harmoncourt and Mrs. Periwinkle saw nothing amiss in this defection, but Sybilla confided to Gillian that Almack's was becoming rather *ennuyeux*.

Gillian agreed, and when Lady Harmoncourt announced that since the sovereigns' departure would mean a lull in the social activities in town, she meant to pay a long-overdue visit to her sister-in-law Daisy in Bath, it was an easy matter to convince Mrs. Periwinkle and Gillian to accompany her.

They left early the next morning, and once again, Sir Avery declined to grant escort. Gillian knew that since Landover intended to deal with some minor business on the Harris estates after the sovereigns' departure and meant for his secretary to meet him in Sussex, he had arranged for Sir Avery to receive his quarterly allowance a few days ahead of time. Therefore, she assumed that her brother would renew his acquaintance with his tailor and bootmaker and revert to his former habits, at least until the marquis returned. So she could not be surprised that the prospect of a week in Bath failed to tempt him.

Sybilla's Aunt Daisy proved to be a kindly lady, and her house in Laura Place was large enough to accommodate them all easily. What with the assemblies and card parties, visits to the Pump Room and the Abbey, and shopping in Milsom Street, there were certainly enough activities to occupy two young ladies, but oddly enough, both seemed to find the visit sadly flat and looked forward to their return to the metropolis. Thus it was with a touch more dismay than might properly have been expected that they greeted the information, the afternoon before their scheduled departure, that Aunt Daisy had taken to her bed with an unknown complaint.

Her doctor was speedily summoned, and after much head-shaking and thumbing of side-whiskers, that learned gentleman diagnosed a mild attack of the ague, prescribing bedrest and herbal doses to be taken four times daily, alternately to be accompanied by mustard footbaths and hot tansy tea.

Lady Harmoncourt was clearly impressed by the doctor's expertise but noted in an aside to Mrs. Periwinkle, after his departure, that if all else failed, Dr. James's Powders were always to be relied upon in such cases.

"And calves'-foot jelly," observed Mrs. Periwinkle, nodding her agreement. "I have always set great store by the efficacy of calves'-foot jelly."

Gillian and Sybilla sighed in discontented unison. Clearly, neither Lady Harmoncourt nor Mrs. Periwinkle meant to leave Aunt Daisy until she was at least well on the road to full recovery. It took several days, and all four ladies were exhausted enough to agree that a break in the return journey to London was a necessity. Therefore, it was not until the second Wednesday after their departure that the Harmoncourts' heavy traveling coach lumbered back into Berkeley Square.

Gillian was still tired, but when Mrs. Periwinkle kindly suggested that she might prefer an early retirement to a visit to Almack's that evening, she speedily disabused her of the notion. She and Sybilla had discussed the matter at length.

"We have been out of touch long enough, ma'am, and I look forward to seeing all our friends again as soon as may be. A nap will put me right as a trivet, and I promise I shall not fade before the evening is done."

Landover had returned some days previously and greeted them cheerfully at dinner. The news that both he and Sir Avery meant to accompany them sent Gillian's spirits soaring. It had been very dull without a man in their party, she told herself. It would be far more comfortable to have two of them.

As it happened, they actually had three, for Lord Darrow presented himself soon after their arrival and seemed disposed to linger. Nonchalantly scribbling his name after three of the entries on Gillian's dance card, he then took Sybilla's and scrawled "Darrow" twice.

Landover, taking Gillian's card next, glanced down, raised his eyebrows, and cast the younger man a rather speculative look. Gillian had been about to remonstrate with Darrow and insist that he limit himself to the acceptable two dances, but Landover's attitude dissuaded her, and she decided that if he took issue over the matter, she would insist upon that third dance. She must and would show his lordship that her sojourn in Bath had done nothing to make her more amenable to his arbitrary rule. She would behave herself in most matters, but she would insist upon making her own decisions whether he liked it or not.

He glanced at her a bit narrowly; however, he made no comment, and Miss Harris was astonished to feel a surge of disappointment. But after all, she told herself firmly, it was only that he had denied her an opportunity to put him in his place. It could not possibly be anything else. Not possibly.

She threw herself into the evening with enthusiasm. So gay was she that even her brother made comment.

"You must have been well-nigh stifled in Bath, my dear, to be so gay as this tonight. Lady Sybilla, too. It is as though you are both tasting freedom after being caged."

"Nonsense," Gillian laughed, hoping to disconcert him. "Sybby and I had a prodigiously exciting time. You can have no notion how lively it is in Bath. Sybby, especially, left a good many beaux bewailing their sorrow at her leaving."

"Indeed." His tone seemed a shade on the chilly side, and Gillian chuckled silently to herself.

"Indeed, sir. Did you think we would be wallflowers?"

"Of course not," he retorted gruffly. "Didn't think about it at all. Far too busy myself."

His tone belied his words, but much as she would have liked to pursue the matter, Gillian wisely fell silent. He would not thank her for her interest.

A short time later, Sir Avery could be seen dancing with a petite brunette when a relaxed and smiling Countess de Lieven approached to greet Gillian and Mrs. Periwinkle. The latter told her that she was in excellent looks, to which she responded with a nearly girlish grin. "So my husband has said several times tonight. Things have certainly grown more peaceful since our royal visitors took their departure." The three of them chatted amiably until Gillian's next partner arrived to claim her hand.

Her first two dances with Lord Darrow were the lively sort that make intelligent conversation impossible; therefore, she was not surprised when he approached her for the third time to be informed that he wished to sit out.

"There is much I would discuss with you, Miss Harris."

"Of course, my lord. I confess I shall be grateful for the respite." She assumed he would wish to exchange news and opinions of Miss FitzWilliam's betrothal to Viscount Linden, but when she would have taken a seat near Mrs. Periwinkle, Darrow guided her firmly toward the familiar little withdrawing room instead. She went obediently enough, becoming disconcerted only when he closed the door behind them.

"My lord, 'tis not seemly," she said quietly. "You should leave it open."

"I do not wish to be disturbed," he replied, striding toward her. "But do not worry about your reputation, my dear. I'll see to everything." He smiled tenderly. "Ah, Gillian, how I have missed you! Had I known you meant to be away so long, I swear I'd have followed you to Bath." And to her astonishment, he moved to take her in his arms.

"My lord!" she exclaimed, stepping hastily backward. "Whatever are you saying?"

He grinned at her discomposure. "Do not dissemble, my love. You have driven me near to distraction, but I know you care for me, and I can wait no longer. I want you for my own." He moved forward again, and this time her astonishment held her motionless while he put one arm gently around her shoulders and, with his other hand, tilted her chin up and lowered his lips to hers. She had never really been kissed before, except of course for that rather chaste experience with young Featherstonhaugh at the Bedford House ball. But the sensation was not an unpleasant one. Darrow's lips were soft against hers, and although she had wondered from time to time how it was that noses did not get in the way when lovers kissed, it seemed to be quite an easy matter indeed. He raised his head and looked down at her, his eyes filled with warmth. "That was very nice."

"Yes, my lord," she whispered.

"We'll try it again to see if we improve with practice." She did not deny him, and he bent his head once more to hers. The hand that had held her chin moved to caress her curls and then the nape of her neck. The arm around her shoulders dropped to her waist, urging her closer. His lips moved more deliberately against hers, then sought her eyelids, the tip of her nose, and the hollow behind each dainty ear before returning to the primary target. His hands began to roam more freely, stirring new sensations deep within her.

The experience fascinated her, for Gillian had never known such feelings could exist. Her nerves seemed to tingle with life of their own wherever he caressed her. Darrow was handsome, gentle, and charming. She had not previously considered him as a potential husband, of course, but the notion was not an unpleasant one, not if he could stir such wondrous feelings as these. Lord knew, she could do a great deal worse. She did not hear the door open.

"What the devil goes on here!"

Gillian flung herself from Darrow's embrace and turned guiltily to face Landover, only to quail involuntarily at the ragged fury in his expression. She could not remember ever having seen him so angry. Behind her, Darrow squared his shoulders manfully.

"If you please, my lord—"

But Landover did not please. His voice was deadly. "Get out." He had let the door swing to behind him, but now he reached back and held it open pointedly, his heated gaze never leaving Gillian's face.

Darrow spoke desperately. "My lord, I wish to—"

"I care not a whit for your wishes, man. Begone from here whilst you can still go unaided." Then with a tremendous effort, he seemed to collect himself. Taking a deep breath, he said more calmly, "Do not, for God's sake, be so foolish as to tempt me to violence, Darrow. Whatever you wish to say to me can be said at my house before eleven o'clock tomorrow morning, by which time I trust I shall have managed to bridle my temper."

"Sir," declared the younger man staunchly, "I cannot leave Miss Harris like this."

"Damn it, you young idiot, get out of here!" His eyes shifted briefly from Gillian, and whatever expression it was that Darrow saw in them was sufficient to stifle any further words he might have uttered. He passed by Gillian and out the open door without a backward look. Landover shut the door.

"You go too far, Miss Harris," he growled, turning back to her angrily.

The look in his eye caused Gillian's breath to catch in her throat, but she faced him determinedly. "It was not what you thought, Landover."

"It was exactly what I thought. I am not blind, miss, nor am I a fool."

"He loves me," she replied simply.

"Does he, by God?" he sneered. "And you? You were scarcely struggling, my dear. Do you love Darrow?"

Gillian hesitated. Did she love him? She glanced up at Landover, and the mocking gleam in his eye made her attempt to put her thoughts into words.

"I do not know about love, my lord, except for the rather silly stuff I've read in books. I only know that what took place just now was very pleasant."

"Was it indeed?" he retorted, the words low in his throat. "And you think to mistake those feelings for love, do you? Well, Miss Harris, I can prove you wrong, and your behavior tonight has been such that I shall deem it both a duty and a pleasure to do so."

The gleam of mockery had changed to something else that made Gillian take a hasty, involuntary step backward, but he was too quick for her. His fingers closed painfully around her upper arm just below the lace edging of the delicately puffed sleeves, and in the blink of an eye, she found her soft body crushed against his harder one.

When she struggled, he held her easily with one hand while he forced her head up with the other. But unlike her earlier experience, Landover's kiss was no gentle caress. His lips were hard against hers, the pressure bruising, demanding. His hand dropped to her shoulder, squeezing it, no doubt leaving more bruises, but then his fingers slid under the lace trimming at the upper edge of her bodice, and his touch seemed to set fire to her skin. She trembled and, without conscious thought, her lips began to move against his.

At once, he responded. His lips seemed to soften just the slightest bit, and then, to her amazement, she felt the tip of his tongue against her teeth, pressing gently at first, then more urgently. She clamped her lips together protectively, but at the same moment, his thumb slipped down over the silkken bodice to caress the tip of her breast. She gasped at the tremors that pulsated through her body, and his tongue gained entrance immediately, exploring the soft inside of her mouth with a thoroughness that sent her every nerve clamoring for more.

Gillian decided without hesitation that Landover must be far more experienced than Darrow. What else could explain the fact that what had been a pleasant, rather interesting experience before was now a soul-searching business that effectively separated body from mind? She had no control over herself. She had known from the first with Darrow that she could stop the interlude whenever the fancy struck her to do so. But with Landover, now, it was not even a matter of stopping him—though she doubted she could do so—but of stopping herself. She felt a strong sense of shame at her own weakness, but even that was not sufficient, for she could not ignore the heady, stirring impulses. Something deep inside her responded naturally to his every stimulus. She scarcely noticed when his hand slipped inside her bodice and began to caress her naked breasts. She only moaned at the ecstasy of the new sensations.

Landover straightened, setting her firmly back upon her heels, and Gillian stared at him, disoriented and wide-eyed with bewilderment.

"That should suffice," he said grimly. "Fix your gown, Miss Harris. It has got a bit mussed, I'm afraid."

Glaring with both anger and mortification as she realized what he had done, Gillian hitched her bodice into place again. "H-how dare you use me so!"

"Easily, my dear," he retorted harshly. "You more than asked for it. Now perhaps you will think twice before heeding the suggestions of your body, for you have discovered, I think, that it will betray you with greater haste than would your deadliest enemy."

"Why, you . . . you—" Words failed her, and drawing back her arm she let fly with the full force of that little, traitorous body behind it, but the blow never landed. Landover parried it easily, catching her wrist in an iron grip that would leave yet another bruise. She flinched as much from his glittering expression as from the physical pain.

"Be grateful you did not succeed," he growled. "I should not have been content merely to return the favor, and I daresay you've suffered enough at my hands tonight without the added humiliation of finding yourself across my knee with a blistered backside."

Gillian flushed, stepping quickly away from him. "You'd not dare!" she blustered. "You said yourself you have not the right to do such a thing."

"Do not tempt me overmuch," he warned, running his fingers through his hair and absently smoothing his neckcloth. He took a deep breath in an obvious effort to calm his temper. "That young cub will make an offer tomorrow, you know," he said next in what sounded to be a nearly normal tone. "What would you have me reply to him?"

She stared at him in amazement. She had forgotten all about Darrow, and it had certainly never occurred to her that he would truly offer for her now. She searched Landover's grim, unyielding countenance for a hint that he was merely attempting to cause her further distress. But she saw nothing there other than increasing impatience.

"Well?" His tone goaded her, and her own temper flared again. He wanted an answer, did he? Her eyes flashed, and she fairly spat her reply at him.

"You may tell his lordship that I shall be deeply honored to be his wife!"

There was a throbbing silence, and the echo of her words came winging back to haunt her. She had just agreed to marry Lord Darrow! The thought was somehow rather appalling, but not a whisper of her doubt showed as she faced her tormentor defiantly.

Landover let out a long breath, but the rigid control he was exerting over his temper was nearly tangible, and Gillian knew he was even angrier with her than he had been earlier. She forced herself not to look away. When he spoke, his tone was icy.

"Your day is done, Miss Harris. I shall call for the carriage whilst you inform Amelia Periwinkle that you wish to make an early night of it."

"But I do not, my lord," she replied, striving to match the chill in his tone. "There are still a number of names on my dance—"

"Enough." There was none of that biting anger now, only weariness. "I'll not debate the matter with you, but I promise that if you do not cease this childishness, I shall treat it—just as I treated your other behavior—as it deserves. If you are wise, you will do as you are bid, which is to go home at once and go to bed. We shall discuss this other business more thoroughly tomorrow after I have met with Lord Darrow."

His tone brooked no further argument, and she fell silent, nibbling her lower lip in frustration. Landover gazed at her briefly, then, apparently satisfied by what he saw, turned on his heel and left the room. Watching him go, Gillian swallowed sudden tears of humiliation. But she would not give in to them. Instead, she gritted her teeth and stepped to an oval looking glass to smooth her hair before setting out in search of Mrs. Periwinkle.

XI

The following morning brought overcast skies, and Gillian could only think that the weather matched her own mood. She had her chocolate in bed as usual and glanced through the morning post; however, thinking it would be wiser not to encounter Landover before he had met with Lord Darrow, she decided to do without breakfast.

What on earth had possessed her? It was as though another person had stepped into her body and replied to Landover's question. But she had no wish to marry Lord Darrow. He was a charming, gentle man, and he both entertained and amused her, traits she knew many women would give a great deal to find in a husband. But much as she liked him, she was certain now that she did not love him, and although she knew love was rarely a quality looked for in marriage, she had rather romantically hoped to find it in her own.

There was still time, of course, if she was willing to humble herself to the point of admitting to Landover that she had made a mistake. The very thought stiffened her backbone. Never would she do such a thing! She had rather marry Darrow. But then she remembered the way she had felt in his arms and, disconcertingly, the way she had felt only a few moments later in Landover's. Truly, one's body was a treacherous thing. That she could feel merely pleasant in the arms of a man she was seriously considering as a potential husband and mad with unbridled passion in the arms of a man she detested—well, it was terribly confusing, to say the least. But one thing was certain. She would regard all men a bit differently henceforward. She had been too trustingly friendly before, which was no doubt what had led Darrow to think she held a *tendresse* for him. But now that she knew her body would kindle even to the caresses of a man who could only irritate and annoy her, she would be a great deal more careful. Whether she married Darrow or not, Gillian knew she had learned a valuable lesson.

Worried when she did not put in an appearance at the breakfast table, Mrs. Periwinkle soon came to discover if she was ill. Today, the elderly lady wore lavender silk and another of her outrageous matching wigs. Gillian repressed a fond smile.

"I'm perfectly well, ma'am, I assure you. 'Tis merely that Landover and I have had a bit of a falling-out, and I thought it best to let his temper cool a trifle before . . . well, you know."

"There! I knew there was something in the wind. Something occurred at Almack's to set the two of you at odds," pronounced her companion triumphantly. "Though I did not wish to trouble you for answers last night, it would have required a featherbrain, which I am not, thank heaven, not to notice that you were out of sorts. And Landover was in the devil's own temper at breakfast this morning, believe me." She smoothed a wrinkle from the lavender silk skirt. "I daresay you were wise to remain abovestairs." Her curiosity was rife, but she made a valiant effort to leash it, waving a hand at the pile of notes on the table near Gillian's chair. "Is that the post?"

"Indeed, but 'tis meager, to say the least. There is a note from the Princess Charlotte desiring to know when I mean to call, but everyone else seems to have fallen into a slump. Perhaps we ought to organize a card party or a Venetian breakfast or something."

"Perhaps," replied Mrs. Periwinkle, but her heart was clearly not in it. There was a small pause while she regarded her charge with compassionate eyes. Then she said gently, "My dear, Landover may be full of sound and fury at the moment, but he is a man of evenhanded justice all the same, so I doubt the outcome of all this will be as bad as you seem to expect. I've no wish to pry, of course, but perhaps it would help to tell me about it."

Gillian examined her fingertips. "I don't really wish to discuss the matter, ma'am, although I should probably tell you

that Lord Darrow is calling upon Landover this morning to . . .
to—"

"To make an offer! Never say so, my dear. Why, he is a
charming young man, and you could do a deal worse. Will you
have him?"

"I . . . I have said I will."

Mrs. Periwinkle burst into a bright smile and nearly fell
upon her in delight, but Gillian's wooden countenance stopped
her in her tracks. "Oh, my dear," she said kindly, "you are
already having second thoughts."

"I never had any first thoughts," moaned Gillian. "I spoke
out of pure temper and because I knew it would annoy Landover."

"I see." Mrs. Periwinkle grew thoughtful but said little more
and, wisely, did not press Gillian for details. No doubt sensing
that the girl would prefer solitude to idle chatter, she soon
mentioned an engagement, settled her wig, and took herself
off.

Gillian moved to the French seat in the window bay and
gazed miserably out into the square. The lack of sunlight gave
everything a dismal, monochromatic look. Very depressing,
she thought, and very likely accountable for her present mood.
She forced herself to focus on colorless flowers, on gray-green
grass, on individual leaves of dreary-looking trees. A nurse-
maid pushed an infant carriage through the gray garden, her
charge so carefully wrapped up against the dangerous elements
that Gillian could see nothing more than a heap of blankets. A
stray dog lifted its leg against a wrought-iron area fence. A carriage
drew up at the main door of Gunter's, across the square. A
perch phaeton entered from Bruton Street and swung around to
a stop below her window.

Gillian sat up straighter. Lord Darrow's tiger leaped to the
horses' heads. But this time, his lordship got down slowly,
hesitated on the flagway, and seeming to find his neckcloth too
tight, tugged at it once or twice, then squared his shoulders and
started up the steps.

Gillian jumped up and flew to her dressing table. Her dress,
a simple sprigged muslin with a wide, bright green sash, was
fine. Her complexion might have been rosier, but she pinched
her cheeks and decided it would do. Her hair . . . well, it
would do, too.

Suddenly nervous, and certain that Landover would soon send for her, she paced, wondering what she would say, wishing she had enough courage to tell Darrow she had made a mistake, certain she could never do so.

It occurred to her that the marquis might assume she would want to give Darrow her decision personally. What on earth would she do then? It might be easier; then again, it might be a thousand times more difficult. She did not think she would be able to say no, knowing as she did how much it would hurt him. She had thoughtlessly led him on. She could see that now. The whole awful business was her fault. If he were the hateful sort, she could send him about his business without a qualm. But he was not, and since she had brought the whole thing on herself, it was only fair that she be the one to suffer, rather than poor Darrow. And, after all, it was not as though he would make a dreadful husband.

The door opened midthought, and Bet popped her head in. "'is lordship be wishful t' see ye in the study, miss," she said quickly. There was a glint of sympathy in her eye, and Gillian guessed that Landover had made no secret of his displeasure over the entire business. She drew a deep breath and went downstairs, feeling somehow as though she were leaving a haven of safety to walk into the lion's jaws.

To her utter astonishment, the marquis was alone, sitting grimly behind his desk. Her eyes widened when he bade her enter and sit down.

"Where is Lord Darrow?" she asked, despising the tremor in her voice.

"He has gone."

"Gone!"

"Indeed. I am afraid I have decided you are too young for marriage, Miss Harris. Your behavior last night left me in no doubt of the fact. And so I have told his lordship. He is leaving London today to spend a week or so at his country house. We agreed that it might be wise to let things cool a bit between the two of you."

Nearly limp with relief at the thought that she need not even face Darrow right away, Gillian could think of little to say other than to parrot Landover's own words. "You . . . you told him I was too young?"

"I did. But you need not fly into a pelter about it. I explained that you are not averse to the notion of matrimony and that if the two of you are of the same mind a year from now, there would be none to stand in your way."

"A year!" She wanted to thank him but could think of no way to do so. It occurred to her that she ought to apologize, to explain that she had made a mistake.

"Yes, a year. It may seem like a long time now, but it will pass quickly." He had misunderstood her. He thought she objected.

"Please, my lord—" How to apologize? How to let him know how grateful she was to him?

"We'll not debate this matter, Miss Harris," he said stiffly. "Next you will remind me that I am not your guardian and have no right to do this. But, believe me, I feel strongly about it and would have no hesitation about forcing your compliance. And do not be so foolish as to think your brother would support you against me. He will not."

"You have discussed this with Avery?"

"I have."

Her cheeks flamed. Good God, she wondered, how much had they discussed? Surely, even Landover, arrogant and unfeeling as he could be, would not discuss intimate details with her brother!

"What did he say?"

"He agrees with me that you behaved very badly last evening and deserve to be punished."

"Punished!" He had no notion, could not have an inkling of how much she had been punished already. But whatever compunction she had had to beg his pardon vanished as in a puff of smoke. "What will you do?" Her own voice was stiff now, her expression apprehensive.

His harsh gaze softened noticeably. "I daresay you'd just as soon hear the penalties your doting brother suggested for making such a goose of yourself. But I am not an ogre, child. I will simply ask that you keep to this house today and tomorrow, without visitors, and spend the time giving some deep thought to what transpired last night. On Saturday, you may return to your normal activities. It is scarcely harsh justice, since there can be very little on your social calendar at the moment."

"But I haven't seen anyone in a fortnight!" Gillian protested automatically. "And we were going to Drury Lane with Lady Harmoncourt tonight!"

"Abigail will excuse you," he retorted, his voice hardening again. "Have you anything further to say?"

"No, sir." She looked away, ashamed of her outburst. She had sounded exactly like a child denied a treat, and he was perfectly right. The penalty was a fair one, lighter than she deserved. She had protested out of habit, no doubt simply because he always seemed to stir her to rebellion. She sighed and rose gracefully to her feet. "May I be excused now, my lord?"

He nodded, watching her narrowly as though he questioned the ease with which she submitted to his decree. But she said nothing further, merely dropping a small curtsy before letting herself out the door.

Back in her bedchamber, however, Gillian did not feel so acquiescent. Despite the fact that her better judgment told her she was being let off easily, she could not help being provoked by the way Landover so peremptorily assumed control of her life. It was true enough that her actions the previous night had been disgraceful, and she had to admit that had any of her friends been discovered in so compromising a position, their punishment might have been a good deal more severe. It was not unheard of for fathers to beat their well-beloved daughters for such an offense. She tried to imagine what Lady Harmoncourt's reaction might have been, had it been Sybilla who was discovered in Darrow's arms instead of Gillian. The thought brought forth a small shudder. Poor Sybby would no doubt have been locked in her room for a month on a diet of bread and water.

But even such thoughts as these did not reconcile her to her own lot. Landover was scarcely her father, and if she had behaved badly, well then, so had he, and he certainly had no intention of remaining cooped up until Saturday. She realized now that he had not even apologized for his actions, and Lord knew they were far more reprehensible than Darrow's had been. Blushing at the memory, she nibbled on her lower lip. If she deserved punishment, so too did his lordship.

The chambermaid popped her head in a few moments later

to announce that a light nuncheon was being served in the dining room.

"I'm not coming down, Bet. I'll have something here—a bowl of soup, bread, cheese, and some fruit." She was famished, but she certainly didn't feel up to a meal with Landover and no doubt her brother as well. In fact, if she had her own way about it, she would just as soon avoid the marquis altogether for the time being. Her eyes gleamed. That was it. If he wanted her to stay home, she would obey him, but his lordship would soon discover that she would never march tamely to his piping!

The maidservant brought her meal on a tray, and Gillian set to with gusto. It was delicious, and when Bet returned for the dregs, she asked that the fruit and a small basket of sweet biscuits be left to nibble on later. The girl smiled at her.

"Ye shouldn't stay cooped up on such a day, miss. The ol' sun's been peepin' out this hour past, and the day be gettin' warmer. Like as not ye'll be wantin' a stroll in the park a bit later."

Gillian glanced outside. The girl was right. The sky was clearing. She sighed. It would be a good afternoon to ride with her friends in Rotten Row. Giving herself a mental shake, she got up and went in search of paper and ink. Whatever else she did or did not do, she must reply to Princess Charlotte's note. While she was explaining that she was mildly indisposed but would visit her highness early Saturday afternoon, Ellen entered to discover her mistress's plans for the rest of the day. Gillian explained that she had been ordered to keep to the house until Saturday.

"Oh, my poor lamb!" exclaimed Ellen in suitable outrage. "That beastish man! Whatever possessed him?"

Gillian made a wry grimace. " 'Tis a punishment, Ellen, and not undeserved, I'm afraid. But it means you will have little to do for a day or two, so if you'd like to have the time off . . ."

Ellen, grateful for the offer, said she really had no place to go but that she wouldn't mind a free afternoon or two for shopping or just a leisurely stroll. Gillian grinned at her and agreed that it sounded like heaven.

"If you wait but a moment or two until I finish this note to her highness, perhaps you might send one of the footmen with it to Warwick House."

Ellen agreed cheerfully, and a moment later, Gillian was alone again. She curled up in the window bay with *The Castle of Otranto*. The book held her attention easily, sending delicious shivers up her spine from time to time, and the afternoon passed quickly until Mrs. Periwinkle's return. That lady sailed blithely into the room and greeted her charge with a cheerful smile.

"I won three pounds at silver loo!" she announced.

"Good for you, ma'am." Gillian marked her place and set the book down upon the seat beside her, quite ready for some conversation. But Mrs. Periwinkle had returned only in order to prepare for the evening ahead. When Gillian informed her of Landover's orders, the old lady was quite taken aback.

"Not go! Then I shall remain with you, of course, my dear. 'Tis only an impromptu outing, after all. Her ladyship will quite understand."

"Nonsense, ma'am," Gillian protested. "It is a family party, and you know Lord Harmoncourt has promised to take everyone to dinner at the Clarendon Hotel after the play. You will not wish to miss such a treat. I shall be perfectly all right here by myself. A light supper and an early night will be good for me, I expect. You are not to worry."

Mrs. Periwinkle was easily persuaded, and Gillian went back to Mr. Walpole's thriller until Ellen returned to ask what she would wear to dinner.

"I'm not going down," Gillian said. "Please ask Mrs. Trueworthy to send up a tray. Then you may do as you please for the rest of the evening. I shall not want you."

She glanced at her book again until Ellen had gone, but deciding she had done enough reading for one day, she got up and went to the washstand, pouring cool water into the basin to wash her face and hands. Then she stepped over to the dressing table and smoothed her hair into place. But after that, she was at a loss. She had, all protests to the contrary aside, already had a good deal more solitude than she was used to, and the thought of another full day of it was rather daunting, to say the least. But everyone else was going out anyway, so even if she went downstairs, it would be to a solitary supper. And if she should chance to encounter Landover, he would expect her to be civil, submissive. Far more sensible to remain safely in her room.

The door opened, and plump, gray-haired Mrs. Trueworthy stepped inside, a worried frown on her usually placid face. "Miss Gillian, the master says . . ." Her voice faded slightly, and she stilled her hands in the folds of her bombazine skirt. "I'm sorry, Miss Gillian," she went on more firmly, "but his lordship has ordered that meals be served only at the table. He said to tell you dinner will be served at eight in the dining room, as usual, and that he will look forward to your company."

"I thought he was dining out with Lord and Lady Harmoncourt."

"No, miss. He sent his regrets. I suspected that might have been why you ordered a tray sent up, and so I told his lordship. Shall I send Ellen to help you dress?"

"No, thank you, Mrs. Trueworthy." Dine *tête-à-tête* with Landover! Never! At any rate, certainly not while she was out of charity with him. Let him have a taste of solitude. It was better than she could have hoped. "You may tell his lordship, if you please, that I am indisposed. A headache, I think," she added musingly. "Yes, I feel sure a headache is coming on."

Mrs. Trueworthy was distressed. "I don't think he will allow me to send up a tray, my dear, even for a headache. And there's some lovely roasted partridges," she added temptingly.

"I'm sure they will be delicious, but don't worry. I shan't starve overnight," Gillian answered with a twinkle. Mrs. Trueworthy returned a smile, albeit a weak one, and went off to face her master.

Gillian found the next half hour oddly unnerving. She could not sit still, nor could she seem to think straight. Finally, she realized she was listening for Landover's approach. Somehow she had not expected him to accept her indisposition lightly but to storm the bastions, so to speak, to demand her attendance at table. But the time passed by, however slowly, until she knew he would not come. She ate the fruit and biscuits left over from her lunch and finally, after a good deal of searching, discovered some working candles in a drawer, and took up a piece of embroidery she had begun some weeks earlier, but it was not long before she was thoroughly bored, and by ten o'clock, she was in bed and sound asleep.

A twinkling Bet brought extra hot rolls and quince marmalade with her morning chocolate, and Gillian fell upon the feast hungrily, wondering what on earth she would do for lunch, not to mention dinner! Perhaps Ellen would be willing to visit a bakeshop for her. But when Ellen came to help her dress, and the suggestion was made, she shook her head unhappily but firmly.

"I dare not, Miss Gillian. His lordship's made it plain as a pikestaff that such a thing would be worth my place."

"Nonsense, Ellen. You don't work for Landover!"

"He pays my wages, Miss Gillian," replied the maid simply. "It may be Harris money, but 'tis his lordship who decides where it goes and how much be spent. I send half my earnings to my family in Sussex, and much as I love you, I cannot afford to take such a risk."

"No, of course not," Gillian said contritely. "I wasn't thinking properly."

"I'm right sorry, Miss Gillian."

There were tears in Ellen's eyes, and it took some time to coax her into a sunnier temper. Gillian was upset, too. Landover was ill-using her and his power over her. Well, it would do him little good. She would not give in.

She ordered a bath and washed her hair, which effectively disposed of the morning. But by noon, she was certain she would swoon if she did not soon have a decent meal. Mrs. Periwinkle came in scolding and extracted an apple from her flowered knitting bag.

"I am a very foolish, fond old woman," she twittered fretfully, smiling a moment later, however, at Gillian's pleasure. "You are being very naughty, my dear. Landover did not confine you to your room, after all, and he is most displeased by your stubbornness."

"It's good for him," Gillian replied, munching her apple. "Perhaps he will learn that the sun does not rise and shine by his rule."

Mrs. Periwinkle shook her head. "I think you will only vex him further, which will make us all uncomfortable. But we shall not harp upon that string," she added, rallying herself. "I have brought two new magazines for us to examine. I know you must be bored, and it will cheer you no end to argue the merits and demerits of the latest fashions. We had not made any particular plans for this afternoon or evening, you know, so we are not missing a thing, and I know you will prefer my company to your own."

Gillian could only agree with her, and the long afternoon ahead began to look a good deal brighter. No sooner had they gotten their heads together with *La Belle Assemblée* spread out before them, however, than the door opened unceremoniously and Sir Avery stood upon the threshold. His expression was grim.

"Cousin Amelia, will you excuse us, please? I want to speak privately with Gillian."

"Of course," she agreed, rising at once. "I shall be in my own sitting room when you want me, dear."

As Mrs. Periwinkle passed by him, Gillian watched her brother appraisingly. He seemed irritated but not really in a temper. She relaxed. "What is it, Avery?"

He shut the door carefully and stepped nearer. "What game are you playing now, Gillian?"

"Game! 'Tis no game, sir. 'Tis merely that I have no mood for company."

"You refuse to eat."

"That is not the way of it at all. Landover refuses to feed me."

"Don't quibble." He paused, pushing agitated fingers through the windblown look he had striven so hard earlier to achieve. "Dash it, Gillian, you have set up his back just when I need to have him in good spirits!"

"You need!" Her eyes widened. "What has happened, Avery? Are you in the briars again?"

He shook his head, pulling out a straight chair and straddling it backward, folding his arms across the back. "Nothing like that. My slate is a good deal cleaner than yours, my girl. Why, I've scarcely touched this quarter's allowance, and we're nearly ten days into the month!"

"Then, what is it?"

He seemed hesitant to explain but then, gathering himself, took his fence in a rush of words. "I want to marry Sybilla."

She grinned at him. "An admirable ambition."

"You think so?" He seemed boyishly grateful for her approval.

"Of course I do. But I cannot see what it's got to do with me."

"Well, it's because of Landover, of course. We can scarcely afford to set up housekeeping on the pittance he allows me, and if you continue to keep him at odds, what chance have I got to convince him to loosen the purse strings?"

"Have you discussed it with him?"

He nodded. "As soon as he got back from Sussex. He said I must show I can behave myself responsibly for six months before he will consent to a betrothal. But, dash it, Gillian, I don't even care about behaving any other way, and I know I could persuade him to allow me to make an offer if only you weren't so intent upon putting him in a temper."

Gillian knew he couldn't make a valid offer of marriage without knowing what sort of income Landover would allow him. And in a good temper, Landover might eventually consent to a reduction of the six-month time period. But even if Avery could convince him to change his mind, Gillian didn't think her behavior would influence the marquis one way or another. And certainly the next day or so shouldn't prove to be particularly crucial. She said as much, but it merely served to set Sir Avery off again.

"Dash it, it ain't just the two days! It's the way you have of constantly plaguing him. It's as though he has only to say the sky is blue for you to attempt to refute it. It wouldn't hurt you to behave in a civilized manner for once, my girl!"

She didn't want to make him any angrier, but Gillian could not feel that her brother had made much of an attempt to see things from her point of view. In his opinion, it was "dashed unfeminine" to refuse to let herself be "guided" by the two men—namely, himself and Landover—who cared only for her best interests, and "damned foolish" to be always insisting upon making her own decisions. Gillian sighed. She could make him no promises, she said at last, though she would agree to think matters over. With that, Sir Avery had to be content, but his attitude when he left her was not that of a man who thinks he has won any great victory.

Gillian did try to think. At least, she thumbed through the pages of *La Belle Assemblée* without paying much heed to the fashion illustrations. She knew she was being stubborn, and aside from showing Landover that he could not command her every move to his liking, she didn't know exactly what she meant to prove. The notion that she was merely sulking passed through her mind and was summarily dismissed, but its memory lingered, and Mrs. Periwinkle, returning a half hour later, was no help. Her attitude showed quite plainly that she was merely bearing Gillian company, not supporting her stand.

At six o'clock, when the elderly lady had departed to change for dinner, Ellen entered, bearing a folded sheet of notepaper which she handed to her mistress with hesitant hand and downcast eye. Gillian unfolded it curiously, experiencing a sudden nervous tremor somewhere in the region of her stomach when she recognized the firm black copperplate hand:

I have warned you before that I shall deal with childishness as it deserves. You will dine with us this evening or be prepared to answer to me.

Landover

There was no way to mistake his meaning. Gillian sighed, folding the note again slowly. "Fetch my green silk, Ellen. The one with the white sash and embroidery 'round the hem."

"Yes, Miss Gillian," Ellen replied with heartfelt relief. It was clear that she had dreaded another sort of response to the message.

Promptly at eight, Gillian descended the stairs to the dining room. Her breathing was regal, her manner calm. She behaved herself prettily, responding warmly whenever Mrs. Periwinkle or Sir Avery spoke to her, but replying to the marquis in polite monosyllables. She took great care not to be rude to him, to give him no valid cause for rebuke, and as soon as the port decanter was placed at his elbow, she excused herself and returned to her room. She learned later that the marquis, after scarcely half a glass of port, had flung himself from the table, muttering oaths and an intention to spend the rest of the evening at Brook's Club.

XII

The following morning, Gillian awoke to a sense of freedom. Today she could do as she pleased. The morning disappeared quickly in a series of visitors, and after a hasty luncheon, she ordered a carriage to take her to Warwick House.

When she arrived, there seemed to be some hesitation on the part of Charlotte's servants as to admitting her, but this was soon set right, and Miss Knight herself came to conduct Gillian into the royal presence. The princess was sitting quite alone at a writing table, quill in hand, obviously in a state of agitation.

"Miss Harris!" she cried. "How wonderful to see you today! You may leave us," she added firmly to her companion.

"Very well, madam," replied Miss Knight, clearly reluctant, "but pray remember that the letter must be delivered today."

"Yes, yes, Notti! Am I not doing my best?" Charlotte gestured almost angrily at the scattered sheets of notepaper on the table before her. She turned with a rueful smile to Gillian when they were alone. "They have given me an impossible task, as you see."

"May I inquire, your highness, what it is you are attempting to write?"

The princess chuckled. " 'Tis a letter to my father." Gillian blinked. "Yes, already you perceive the difficulty. He has been prodigiously angry ever since I returned that stupid invitation list to him, and now it seems that I must submit to him. He has said so."

Gillian's eyes began to twinkle in response to the princess's infectious grin. "Must you, madam? Your mood does not seem compatible with such a task."

"It is not. Oh, I have written much that is submissive—all about a daughter's duty to her father and such stuff as that—but I cannot and will not submit to his ridiculous demand that I marry the Prince of Orange in September."

"Oh dear." The princess's mood matched her own feelings so exactly that Gillian could only commiserate.

"Indeed. I asked to see the marriage contract, you know, and my dear father refused—said it was no business of mine! Or William's either," she added conscientiously. "It is between Papa and the King of Holland, he says, and I am merely to submit. Submit! I detest that word! Particularly since I have it on excellent authority that I am meant to *live* in Holland, not merely to visit the place." Her skirts moved, and she bent to pat the little white greyhound as it emerged from under her chair. The dog looked curiously at Gillian, but then moved off to find a quieter spot to sleep. Charlotte went on bitterly, "They even say my firstborn son will be returned to England at the age of three to be raised as crown prince, whilst my second will be raised as future monarch of Holland. Can you imagine? All this decided without a word to me. Heiress to the throne of England, and not only must *I* submit, but I am to have nothing to say to the future of my own children!"

"It is vastly unfair, your highness," Gillian agreed sincerely.

"More than that, it is intolerable," said her highness flatly. "I won't do it."

Gillian felt a tremor of fear. Surely the princess meant to stir up a wasps' nest! A maidservant brought refreshments, and Gillian, hungry again despite her large luncheon, helped herself to a date bun, nibbling daintily as she watched the princess frown over her task. At last, Charlotte sat back with a sigh and laid her quill aside. Scattering silver sand across the paper, then blowing it clear, she picked up the result of her labors for a final appraisal.

"There," she said with satisfaction. "That will do." Handing the paper to Gillian, she grinned. "See what you think."

Rapidly, Gillian scanned the letter. Its tone was as submissive as could be. The princess declared herself the Regent's obedient subject and affectionate daughter whose only wish was to serve and obey. There was a great deal more to the same effect, but not by the longest stretch of imagination could her words be construed as an agreement to wed the Prince of Orange.

"Your highness," Gillian said hesitantly once she had done reading, "does not the Regent expect something a trifle more specific?"

Charlotte chuckled. "I daresay he does, but he'll not get it from me. I have quite made up my mind. I will never wed William of Orange. I might have succumbed to Papa's wishes earlier, particularly if he had not been so adamant about my going to live in Holland. But now . . . now that I have met dear Leopold, no matter what concessions Papa might make, I could not agree to marry Orange."

"I think the Regent will be displeased."

Charlotte's bubbling laughter filled the room. "I think you must be a mistress of understatement, Miss Harris." Her laughter faded soon enough, though. "He will be apoplectic. Nevertheless, I know of no way by which he can force me to wed where I wish not to do so. They tried to tell me otherwise, you know."

"Otherwise?"

"Indeed." Charlotte nodded. "Some minion of Papa's said I must obey, said it was the law. But when I asked him to put the notion in writing that I might show it to Lord Brougham and others amongst my advisers, he refused, so it came to naught."

"I am glad of that, your highness, but in point of fact, if your father orders you to marry, will you not have to obey?"

"I suppose I would, if he were truly to force the issue. But," she added, shrewdly, "I daresay he will not, for he greatly fears the scandal. Our subjects tend to support me against him anyway, you know, and on an issue like this one, there is no doubt but that they'd rally to my banner."

Gillian could only agree. There was no comparison between the princess's popularity and Prinny's lack of it. "But I still think you are very brave to stir his temper like this, madam, because he is bound to fly into a pelter when he receives this letter."

Charlotte sighed. "I know," she said, "but I must defy him. I cannot consider any other man for my husband—not since meeting Leopold." She clasped her hands, and there was a hint of girlish rapture in her voice. "Ah, Miss Harris, if only you might meet him, you would see for yourself!"

Miss Harris agreed that Prince Leopold of Saxe-Coburg must be very handsome and a pearl among gentlemen, but by the time she left Warwick House, she could only be worried about the princess's future. She did not have Charlotte's confidence in her ability to flout the Regent's wishes, and she very much feared that her highness was riding for a fall. So great was her worry, in fact, that she herself braved Landover's potential displeasure in order to raise the subject at the dinner table that evening.

She did not plunge straight into the heart of the matter, of course, for she was uncertain what his attitude toward her might be. She had not seen him at all since the previous night's dinner and had half expected him to dine out tonight. But he had not, and her spirits lifted when she and Mrs. Periwinkle descended to find that he was waiting to escort them into the dining room.

Gillian was at pains to show him that she was no longer angry with him, and Landover was not so tactless as to make reference to her behavior of the past two days, so by the time they had finished off the vermicelli soup, tender veal cutlets, and mushrooms in béchamel sauce, Gillian was in perfect charity with him again. The footmen began laying the second course, and she wrinkled her nose at a side dish of potted lampreys but brightened at the sight of the strawberry tarts.

Landover himself provided her with an opening by commenting that things seemed almost dull in town now that all the hubbub over the visiting monarchs had died away. "I only hope you ladies will not be bored by the comparative inactivity before Prinny's Vauxhall fete," he said. "He put it off to the first of August in order to separate his own celebration of peace from the state visits. Besides, after all he put up with from his guests, I think he will welcome some peace and quiet."

"I doubt he'll get it," Gillian said with a small frown, as she tried to decide between a dish of haricots and a dish of broccoli. She chose the broccoli, then looked up to discover both her companions looking at her expectantly. "The Princess Charlotte is about to stir coals," she said with simple directness.

"I was given to understand that she's already stirred some,"

Mrs. Periwinkle said with a little smile. Gillian looked at her curiously. "Whilst we were away," she explained. "Broadsides. Even one caricature they labeled 'the Devonshire minuet' that showed her dancing with Prince Leopold. Others that suggested she was toying with his highness of Orange."

"Oh dear," Gillian said, distressed. "No wonder her father is displeased."

"He is furious," contributed Landover. "Those little gems greeted his return to London. My personal favorite was one of the most blatant, called 'the Dutch toy.' It shows the princess whipping a top with the letters P.O. painted on it, while Prinny is entering the room behind her, armed with a birch rod. I'm sure his highness was tempted to emulate his own caricature when he saw that one."

"Well, he may do so yet," Gillian replied frankly. "She was ordered to write him a letter of submission, and I'm certain he meant that she must submit to the marriage, but she says she cannot and will not do so. And I for one don't think she should have to marry that dull stick when she could have someone as romantic as Prince Leopold."

"Gillian!"

"Never mind, ma'am, I'll deal with this." Landover waved away a dish of chocolates and nodded to the footman offering to replenish his wineglass. "You are to stay strictly out of this business, Miss Harris, and you are not to let me hear you refer to his highness of Orange in such terms again." He was not angry, and his voice was gentle, but there was an unmistakable undertone that told Gillian he meant to be obeyed. She subsided immediately, having no wish to fight with him and fearing he might forbid future visits to the princess if she was not careful.

"I'm sorry, Landover. I should not have said that. But her highness is easily as stubborn as her father, I think, and you must admit that to force England's crown princess to live in Holland is going beyond what is permissible."

" 'Such duty as the subject owes the prince,' " quoted Mrs. Periwinkle, shaking her head gently, "so does the daughter owe her father."

Landover's eyes twinkled. "Surely that refers to the duty a

wife owes her husband," he teased. "Matters have not yet progressed so far, my dear ma'am."

Nothing daunted, Mrs. Periwinkle insisted that it was all of a piece. "For when they do marry, she must go where William wills, and if a daughter does not owe her father the duty a subject owes her prince, then things have changed a great deal more in this world than I was aware of, Landover. And the Princess Charlotte is both subject *and* daughter, much as she would like to think of herself only as future monarch. She owes him double duty!" She turned to Gillian as though she expected protest, which indeed was already forming itself on that young lady's lips. "It is true, my dear. Prinny is no more a favorite with me than with most folks, but he has had a hard life, and despite the fact that people tend to rally round the Princess of Wales and her daughter, they have both given him as much grief as he has given them. And furthermore, in this instance, he is in the right. It is as much his duty to arrange a suitable marriage for her as it is hers to submit. He has done his part."

"Well, if that's all there is to being a father—"

"That's enough, Gillian," Landover interrupted firmly. "No one thinks much of Prinny as a father, and everyone feels sorry that the princess is not given more freedom to behave as other girls her age behave. But it is no affair of yours, and if you wish to pursue your friendship with her highness, you must agree to stay out of it." She shot him a mutinous look, but instead of taking her to task, he merely shook his head with a little smile. "Don't look at me as though you think the end of that friendship would be my doing. Just use your head. How do you think Prinny will react if he thinks you are influencing his daughter against him?"

"But I wouldn't!"

"Your own interpretation of your actions is of very little consequence, I'm afraid. His is the only one that would matter."

Mrs. Periwinkle nodded in agreement, and the subject was dropped. Gillian was certain that they were mistaken. The Regent had never been anything but kind to her, and she could not believe that he would punish her for a friendship with his daughter. She would certainly exert every effort to avoid "influencing" Charlotte, as Landover had called it. She did not do that sort of thing anyway. Had she not tried to impress upon her highness that she was about to enrage the Regent? Surely, that could only be seen as an attempt to support him. It could in no way be interpreted as support for the princess.

Landover was only trying to interfere with her activities again. He had never approved of her visits to Warwick House, and now he was simply trying subtler methods to curtail them. But she would be loyal to Charlotte, no matter who tried to come between them. She liked her and felt sorry for her. A girl Charlotte's age ought to be enjoying life, ought to be dancing till the small hours and falling in and out of love. Just because she was a royal princess was no reason to treat her as though she were some sort of hostage to be auctioned off to the highest bidder!

Yet that was just what Prinny did, and there seemed to be nothing anyone could do about it. Consequently, for the next few days, Gillian lived in a state of trepidation, wondering what would happen as a result of Charlotte's so-called letter of submission. Rumor was rife, but everyone seemed to agree that the Prince Regent was in a grand fury. He had heard that Prince Leopold virtually haunted Warwick House, that he shadowed the princess's carriage whenever she drove in the park. Then word flitted about that it was not Prince Leopold at all but another prince, Augustus of Prussia, who followed the princess about, that the Prince Regent actually liked Prince Leopold. Gillian hid a smile when she heard that one.

On Monday evening, she heard that the princess was ill, and on Tuesday morning she sent her a note, wishing her a speedy recovery. Her own day was spent paying calls with Mrs. Periwinkle, as usual, and there were plans to attend a rout and then a small, select supper party followed by dancing at Lord and Lady Cowper's in the evening.

Landover decided to dine at White's with some of his friends and invited Sir Avery to join them. Avery accepted the invitation with alacrity, bound to show his mentor how well he was behaving, while Mrs. Periwinkle and Gillian enjoyed a cold collation early in the evening and then retired to their separate bedchambers to prepare at leisure for the entertainments to follow. Ellen was putting the finishing touches to Gillian's hair when Bet, hesitantly and with a puzzled countenance, stepped inside the room.

"Beggin' yer pardon, Miss Gillian, but there be a young person below as is wishful to speak wi' ye."

"A young person, Bet? For heaven's sake, who can it be at this hour? Someone's servant?"

"No, miss. She be dressed well enough, but Elbert, the younger footman, ye' know, he says she come in a hackney, miss. She wouldn't give a name either, miss, just says she must speak wi' ye. Says tell ye it's urgent." The maidservant spread her hands with a small shrug that denied responsibility for such odd goings-on. Gillian smiled at her.

"Where have you put this young person, Bet?"

"In the side parlor across from 'is lordship's study, miss. Do I tell 'er t' come back tomorrow?"

"No, no, if it's urgent, I must at least speak with her," Gillian said.

"I'll come with you, Miss Gillian." Ellen spoke firmly, but Gillian shook her head slowly.

"I have the oddest feeling, Ellen, that I should deal with this business alone. I'm quite sure I shall be perfectly safe." Ellen was reluctant to let her go, but Gillian brushed aside her worries and hastened downstairs to the tiny parlor. The sight that met her eyes upon opening the door justified all her odd feelings.

"Your highness!"

Charlotte turned a tear-ravaged face to greet her. "Bless you, Gillian! I was afraid I'd be turned from the door, but I dared not give my name. There will be a great enough dust over this as it is, I'm afraid."

"Sit down, madam." Gillian literally pushed the younger girl toward a chair. "You look dreadful. Something awful must have happened." Another thought occurred to her. "The maid said you came in a hackney coach!"

A tiny smile forced its way through Charlotte's pain. "All the way from Cockspur Lane. 'Twas a great adventure." She sighed. "I ran away, Gillian. I could think of nothing else to do. But once I got away, I could think of nowhere to go that would be safe from him."

"The Regent?"

Charlotte nodded. " 'Tis that stupid letter. It put him in a towering rage."

"But you expected that!"

"I know." She sighed again. "I found, however, to my personal shame, that I could not face him in such a fury. He sent for me yesterday."

"We heard you were ill."

With a shrug, her highness explained that it seemed the thing to say at the time. "My brave Notti went to see him by herself. She said he was very cold, very bitter, and very silent. Poor Notti tried to explain that all the rumors about Leopold and me are simply not true, and he said he knew that much, thank you, that Leopold is an honorable man. Oh, Gillian," she added, leaning forward in her chair to emphasize her words, "I must tell you that I was pleased to hear even that much from him."

"But he has not given his approval to a marriage between you, I daresay."

Charlotte sagged backward again. "No, of course not. That would require a miracle. He commanded that I go to see him today unless Dr. Baillie went to him personally to say that I was not capable of walking over."

"Oh dear."

"Indeed," Charlotte grimaced. "Dr. Baillie quite naturally said I was perfectly capable. But really, Gillian, I was too ill, too affected—it was impossible. Notti persuaded me to write to him instead, entreating that he come to me. We hoped that once he saw I was truly ill, he might have some sympathy and would not begin by blasting away. But I might as well have gone to him."

"He blasted?"

"For three quarters of an hour! The things he said! I tell you, I was in agony over them. But that is not the worst. He has dismissed all my ladies, all my servants!"

"Not Miss Knight!"

"Even Notti. And oh the pain of telling her, Gillian. She has been so devoted to me, and he said she must leave tonight! At once! He apologized for the *inconvenience* but said he had need of her room!" Tears welled in the princess's eyes again, and Gillian was at a loss for words. But Charlotte dabbed her face with a lacy handkerchief and sniffed. "He has appointed a new household for me, but I am to be confined at Carlton House for five days and then remove to Cranbourne Lodge. That's smack in the middle of Windsor Forest, Gillian, and I am to be allowed to see no one but the Queen! And she is to come but once a week. Papa said if I did not go immediately tonight to Carlton House, he and the new women would remain with me. And, Gillian, he says if I do not submit properly this time, he will thrash me. Me!"

Gillian caught her breath, and a momentary thought of what Landover might have to say to all this sent shivers down her spine. She collected herself with difficulty. "Are you not perhaps making matters all the worse by running away, your highness?" she asked gently.

"Perhaps," Charlotte agreed, "though I fail to see what else he might do to me."

"Why did you leave, highness?"

Charlotte slumped a little more in her chair. "It was almost as though I were possessed," she said slowly. "As though there were nothing else I could do. It was after I spoke to Notti. She was going in to face Papa herself, so I just left. I hailed the hackney and ordered the coachman to drive here. It was the first place I thought of."

"Well, you cannot stay here," Gillian said flatly. "Landover would murder me."

Charlotte smiled a natural smile for the first time since her arrival. "I do not think the noble marquis would be quite so violent as that."

Gillian returned the smile. "No, perhaps not, but he would be vastly displeased. That I am sure of. He told me in no uncertain terms just two nights ago that I am to stay well clear of your affairs, highness."

With a deep sigh, the princess arose from her chair and gathered her cloak about her shoulders. "In that case, I must leave at once." She took but one step toward the door, however, before turning helplessly. "I have dismissed the coach, and I don't know where to go."

Thinking quickly, Gillian said, "You must go to your mother. She will know what to do, and she will support you against your father, too. No doubt there will be others to help you as well, but you will find them better from Connaught House than from here."

Charlotte nodded. "But you must come with me. I have had

enough solitary travel for one night. Please, Gillian, say you will."

Without hesitation, Gillian agreed. Landover would have a great deal to say, and she truly didn't want to annoy him, but the princess was her friend, and what was more, her highness was presently just another young girl in deep trouble. Gillian could no more have abandoned her than she could have abandoned an injured puppy on the highroad. Calling the younger footman, she gave him a vague message to be delivered to Mrs. Periwinkle after their departure, excusing herself from the evening's entertainments, then sent him for one of Landover's carriages to convey them to Connaught House.

Once they were safely on their way, the princess's spirits rose mercurially. Gillian could not help thinking from her attitude that she did not seem to have much fear of the future. On the contrary, now it seemed that Gillian was the only one who did fear it. Landover was likely to be quite as furious as the Prince Regent, for not only had she disobeyed him again, but he would think she had done so out of defiance. She would never be able to explain her actions satisfactorily.

Though Gillian noticed that she said nothing whatsoever about the Regent or her forthcoming difficulties, the princess talked of all manner of things, chatting about plans for the forthcoming Vauxhall fete, wishing hopefully that she might be allowed to attend such a function, and asking for Gillian's impressions of the Burlington House masquerade. Gillian followed her lead as best she could, but she could not help feeling relieved when they finally reached Connaught House.

The princess bounded out of the coach the moment the steps were let down and flew up the stairs to the front door, pulling the bell with the fervor of a child or a madwoman. The door was opened quickly enough, and a very imposing butler bowed her in.

"Pennyfeather," said the princess grandly, "inform her highness that I must see her at once."

"I am afraid her highness is not at home, madam," said the butler in dignified tones. Not by the flicker of an eyelash did that stately fellow indicate curiosity at the fact of the crown princess's unexpected arrival.

Gillian felt her heart plummet. What on earth would they do now? "Where is she?" demanded Charlotte in similar dismay.

"Her highness should be on her way home from the Blackheath villa, madam, but I could not presume to say when she will arrive."

"Then we must send to intercept her at once," declared Charlotte. "She must return with all speed. Knowing Mama, she will stop off to visit Earl Grey or another friend just because the journey bores her. Send someone at once, Pennyfeather."

"Of course, your highness. Might I suggest dinner whilst you wait?"

Charlotte agreed promptly, and although Gillian was certain she wouldn't be able to eat a thing, it seemed much better to dine than to sit about trying to convince each other that everything was going to be a bed of roses. In no time at all, a table was spread, and she found herself sitting *tête-à-tête* with Princess Charlotte over mock turtle, partridges, sherried mushrooms, dumplings, fried anchovy toast, French cut beans, spinach pudding, and ginger valentines. Before they had half finished the splendid repast, her highness of Wales was announced.

"What on earth!" Caroline exclaimed, blinking rather owlishly at the two of them. "Good evening, Miss Harris." Gillian got quickly to her feet, but she might have spared herself the exertion. The Princess of Wales had directed her attention to her anxious daughter.

"Mama! What am I to do?"

"*Liebchen,* I've no notion, since I do not know what passes. Tell me."

Haltingly, and leaving a good many things out that then had to be explained, Charlotte got most of the tale told. As her voice died away, her mother shook her head sadly.

"Why do we fight him? We should learn better. You cannot win this battle, *Liebchen.* The best we can hope is that you will not lose the war. We need Brougham. He will advise us."

A message was despatched at once to Lord Brougham, and when the dining-room doors opened not twenty minutes later, all three ladies looked up with pleased expectancy, only to hear Pennyfeather announce sepulchrally, "The honorable Marquis of Landover to see you, madam."

Gillian's air of grateful expectation fell away ludicrously, and she watched the marquis's entrance with not a little apprehension. Even so, she had to admit that he was looking particularly handsome in dark pantaloons and a well-fitting jacket. A small ruby glinted in the folds of his neckcloth. As he approached the two princesses and bowed, his expression was unreadable.

"Greetings, my lord." It was Caroline who recovered first, and she did not seem overly displeased to see him.

"Good evening, your highness. I have come to collect Miss Harris. I doubt you will want her in the midst of all the uproar descending upon this place."

"Assuredly not, my lord," Caroline agreed before either Charlotte or Gillian could express a different opinion. "Uh . . . *is* there an uproar descending?"

"Absolutely, madam. His highness has sent for his ministers, and a council is being held in the Foreign Office as well as at Carlton House. In fact, that you may judge properly the gravity of the situation, I need only tell you that when she heard the news of the Princess Charlotte's flight from Warwick House, her majesty the Queen immediately left a card party she was giving!"

"Indeed!" Princess Caroline clutched her breast at news of such unprecedented action, and Charlotte glanced anxiously at Gillian. The latter was watching Landover, still trying to gauge his mood. Amazingly, she suspected a certain amount of levity. She could not for an instant tell why she suspected it, but she became certain when he went on.

"I am afraid the Regent knows as well as I do where her highness is, madam. Your messenger to Brougham was intercepted on the road. Not that Brougham will not come. He will." Landover paused, and there could be no denying the twinkle in his eye as he continued, "So will the Bishop of Salisbury, the Duke of York, the Lord Chancellor, the Chancellor of the Duchy of Cornwall, his grace the Duke of Sussex, and quite possibly Lord Liverpool himself."

"The Prime Minister! *Mein Gott im Himmel!*" exclaimed her highness of Wales.

"Gillian, don't leave me!" wailed Charlotte.

Landover smiled kindly at the distraught princess. "Miss Harris has no place in all of this, as I am sure you must agree, and the sooner she is well out of it, the better. However, perhaps the Princess Charlotte would be willing to hear a word or two of advice before the others arrive."

XIII

"Won't you sit down, Landover?" Charlotte invited regally. "This mock turtle is delicious. Help the Marquis of Landover to a plate, Pennyfeather."

To Gillian's surprise, Landover accepted the invitation, pulling out a chair at Charlotte's right hand. "I shall be delighted, your highness, but I warn you, my conversation will be aimed at persuading you to return to Carlton House."

Charlotte laughed at him. "But, sir, I've only just run off!"

"This is not a time for levity, *Liebchen*," stated Princess Caroline brusquely. "You must return at once."

But Charlotte had no wish to listen, preferring to believe she might be allowed to remain with her mother. Gillian, watching her, thought she was making a particular effort to maintain the lighthearted air she had affected in the carriage from Landover House.

"Your highness," put in the marquis, speaking rather sternly, "it would be far better to go now than to wait until your father forces you."

"He cannot do so," replied Charlotte blithely. "I shan't allow it."

"The law is on his side, I'm afraid."

"What law is that?" demanded Gillian.

He turned that stern gaze upon her, and she shivered involuntarily. "A law laid down in the reign of George I, which gives absolute power to the King or the Regent to dispose of the persons of all the royal family whilst they are underage."

"Oh," Gillian said. She glanced at Charlotte, who shrugged resentfully.

"My people will support me. I have only to tell them how he treats me. He has, after all, threatened to thrash me, has he not?"

"Quite true, madam," Landover said quietly. "We have only to gather a crowd and tell them of your grievances. They would most certainly rise in your behalf."

"Exactly so!" agreed Charlotte, her spirits lifting noticeably. "Why should they not?"

"The commotion might be a trifle excessive," Landover warned. "If the crowd were large enough, rowdy enough, Carlton House itself might be attacked—even pulled down about your father's ears. Soldiers would be called out, blood would be shed, and many lives would be lost." He paused briefly, giving time for each of his listeners to visualize the drama he described. Then his brows drew together, his voice grew rougher. "If your highness were to live a hundred years, it would never be forgotten that your running away caused the mischief."

Gillian privately thought he was overdoing it, but even as the thought passed through her mind, she realized that the color had drained from Charlotte's startled face. If the princess cared nothing for her duty to her father, she cared much for her duty to her people. Stupefied and a bit lost, she turned a bewildered gaze upon Landover, speaking in a much smaller voice.

"You truly think such a thing might come to pass?"

"Indeed, highness," he replied solemnly, "you may depend upon it. Such is the English people's horror of bloodshed that you would never get over it. I know it will be difficult, but the most admirable course for you to follow is the one requiring the most courage on your part. You must return to face your father."

"He said he would beat me," Charlotte muttered as though to herself. Landover said nothing, but his gaze—gentler now, more compassionate—locked with hers.

"Begging your pardon, madam," Pennyfeather said woodenly from the doorway, "but my lord Brougham, his grace of York, and the Lord Chancellor have arrived. I have taken the liberty of putting them in the blue drawing room, since they seem to think there will be further arrivals."

"Nonsense, Pennyfeather," said Princess Caroline, taking a

deep breath and shooting a sidelong glance at Landover. "Show them in, and lay three more places for dinner."

The butler looked at his mistress, who merely shrugged, but as he turned away, Landover spoke quickly to the Princess of Wales.

"One moment, if you please, madam."

"You have made your point, my lord," Charlotte interrupted bleakly. "I shall accept your advice, but you must let me handle matters in my own fashion."

"Indeed, highness," he replied, turning back to her, "I had no other thought in mind. I merely wish, as I mentioned before, to see Miss Harris out of this."

"Of course," agreed the Princess Caroline. "Pennyfeather, show the marquis and Miss Harris out by the west door before you bring in our other visitors."

The stately butler bowed as though such goings-on were perfectly normal, although the younger princess looked for a moment as though she might debate the matter. Evidently she thought better of it, for she merely gave a tiny smile of farewell when Gillian rose to take the marquis's proffered arm. But just as they reached the door, Charlotte spoke.

"Landover!" He turned back to find her watching him almost helplessly. "You will come back, my lord." It was a statement, not a question.

"It will be my pleasure, your highness. Just as soon as I've seen Miss Harris safely to her carriage." She nodded, a glint of relief showing clearly in those expressive blue eyes.

They went quickly, and Gillian soon found herself tucked up in the carriage. He had said nothing at all to her. As he moved to shut the carriage door, she spoke his name, her voice nearly betraying all the pent-up anxiety she had been feeling since his arrival. His face was shadowed, unreadable, but his voice was grim.

"We'll speak of all this later," he said. "Right now, you are to go home and go to bed, whilst I see what remains to be done here."

"But I—"

"No arguments!" He shut the door firmly. "Take her home, Jason!"

The horses were whipped up immediately, and Gillian fell

back against the squabs, resigned to her fate, whatever it might be.

Mrs. Periwinkle was waiting for her when she returned and promptly began to fuss and scold, but Gillian knew perfectly well that the old lady had been worried about her. She gave a weary smile.

"You should have gone ahead without me, ma'am."

"As if I would. ' 'Tis not in the bond,' as the bard would say." Mrs. Periwinkle swished her puce satin shawl and smoothed the beige lace of her skirts as she sat with regal dignity upon the French seat in Gillian's window bay. "Tell me what happened, my dear. And don't, for mercy's sake, leave out any of the good bits."

Gillian complied, and Mrs. Periwinkle's eyes twinkled with delicious glee when she described the number of potentates descending upon the princess.

"All honorable men," she chuckled, "but talk about the cat amongst the pigeons! Oh, my dear, this scandal will reign supreme for days, for it is sadly true that 'greatest scandal waits on greatest state.' Poor Prinny must be well-nigh beside himself. His daughter has given the unkindest cut of all, whilst all the powers that be are making tedious old fools of themselves, each wanting to be the one who tames the princess. The sad thing is that I don't believe one of them cares a groat for her. They merely want Prinny to think they've managed a miracle on his behalf."

Gillian nodded, preoccupied with her own thoughts, and Mrs. Periwinkle gazed at her pensively for several silent moments before she got to her feet with an air of purpose and swished toward the tapestry bell pull near the bed. She gave it a hearty yank, and shortly afterward, Bet put her head in at the door.

"Yes, miss?"

Gillian looked up, bewildered, and Mrs. Periwinkle said, "Fetch Ellen to Miss Gillian at once, Bet, and have them send up a tray with some cheese and biscuits and a pot of hot chocolate. And I want that chocolate well laced with peppermint brandy. Mind you don't let them forget."

"Right away, miss!" Bet's eyes were round.

The maidservant's expression made Gillian chuckle, and

once the door had shut behind her, she turned with a fond smile at her companion. "She thinks we mean to become tipsy on hot chocolate, ma'am. I thank you for your kindness, but I really don't need a restorative."

"Restorative, my foot," scorned Mrs. Periwinkle. "We don't want you as drunk as Shakespeare's sailor on the mast, but if I find that those dolts belowstairs haven't put enough of Landover's brandy in that chocolate to send you straight off once I get you to bed, I shall have a few words to say to them. I don't want you tossing and turning all night, wondering what he's going to say to you tomorrow. And unless I miss my guess, that's precisely what you would do if I weren't on hand to take steps."

"Perhaps," Gillian agreed with a rueful smile.

"What sort of mood was he in when you left him?"

"Rather grim."

"Dear me." Mrs. Periwinkle shook her head. "Well, he can't eat you, after all. And his bad humors are generally quickly over and done. Seems to be sunny-tempered enough when no one's trying to vex him."

Gillian wrinkled her nose at the implication. "All I did," she said carefully, "was to help a friend in need. And I would do it again at the drop of a hat."

"No need to snap my nose off, I'm sure," rebuked Mrs. Periwinkle sharply, although a glint of amusement lit her pale blue eyes seconds later. "Save your temper for his lordship. I daresay he'll know how to deal with it."

Gillian stared at her hands, and spoke contritely. "I beg your pardon, ma'am. I shouldn't have spoken so to you. It is just that I think Landover would like to mount my head over the postern gate for this. At least, he would if Landover House *had* a postern gate."

"Well, it hasn't, and that's sheer poppycock anyway," retorted her companion. "Things will not look nearly so dim, come morning. That is," she added acidly, "if we ever get to bed. Where is your Ellen, for mercy's sake?"

As though she had heard her cue, the door opened, and Ellen entered breathlessly. "Oh, Miss Gillian, we didn't expect you home so early! Forgive the delay, but I was walking in the back garden, and Bet didn't find me right away. She says to tell you the chocolate and biscuits are on the way."

It was evident from Ellen's flushed cheeks that she had not been alone in the garden, but Gillian forbore to tease her in Mrs. Periwinkle's presence. Mrs. Periwinkle did not approve of familiarity with one's servants. Consequently, she only smiled sweetly and asked Ellen to help her prepare for bed. The chocolate arrived moments later, laced potently enough to satisfy the old lady and potently enough to make Gillian think she would be lucky to escape a shattering morning headache.

Nevertheless, the tasty brew did its work. By the time Ellen tucked her into her bed, Gillian felt as though she were floating. Thoughts of Landover and his probable lectures wafted through her mind but had no substance, nothing to make them stick. There was a vague thought that it was only fair, since Princess Charlotte would have to reap the consequences of her actions, that she, Gillian, must do likewise. The thoughts jumbled until she fancied herself a princess marching up to the Prince Regent to tell him quite rudely that he ought to go soak his head. But the Regent most unfortunately had Landover's face and was brandishing a thick birch rod while he threatened to send her immediately home to Sussex. Then the birch rod disintegrated, to be replaced by a glass of bubbling champagne, and she thought, How magical. He can do anything. Landover lifted his glass in a toasting gesture and winked at her, smiling, before he faded away into a gray fog.

There were other dreams or wisps of dreams, but morning came soon enough in a blaze of sunlight that lit up the room. Gillian opened her eyes carefully, half expecting to feel the effects of the peppermint brandy. But there was nothing. She stretched, much as a lazy cat might stretch, beginning with her toes and working up to arms, hands, and fingertips. Then she wriggled back into her pillows and adjusted the down comforter to wait for her morning chocolate. Bet entered a few moments later, bidding her a cheerful good morning.

"Good morning, indeed. It looks glorious outside."

"Looks like bein' a scorcher, miss," replied the maid. "Summer's settin' in. like as not. All the nobs'll be leavin' town soon, I'm thinkin'."

"Right after the Vauxhall fete," Gillian replied. "The Prince Regent intends to leave for Brighton the day after, and I imagine a good many of us will soon follow."

"Aye, his lordship has a house on the Marine Parade, don't 'e, so he'll be goin', like as not." Bet set the tray across Gillian's knees, then helped plump a rebellious pillow into place. "Will that be all, Miss Gillian."

"Yes, I think so, Bet. Has the early post come yet?"

"Yes, miss, but his lordship said he wanted to look it over. Just took the whole lot into the study afore it was sorted."

"His lordship is up already?"

"Indeed, miss. Been for a ride in the park 'n' all. Don't know how 'e does it neither. Jeremy said 'e didn't be gettin' home till after four. Looks well though, I'll give 'im that. A bit smudgy under the eyes, perhaps, but chipper enough for all that."

"Thank you, Bet," Gillian said dismissively. The girl bobbed a curtsy and departed, not the least offended by the tone. Gillian stared at her empty cup for a moment, then lifted the silver pot to pour out. So Landover was chipper, was he? The thought was a confusing one. She had expected him to be in the devil's own temper, crying for her blood, and determined to hustle her off to Sussex. Her curiosity well aroused, she swallowed her chocolate quickly, then rang for Ellen to help her dress. A short time later, elegantly attired in cherry-sprigged muslin with a cherry satin sash and matching sandals, her long, soft curls tied back with a red ribbon high at the back of her head, she tripped briskly downstairs, subduing trepidation as she approached his sanctum.

The footman Jeremy saw her coming and sprang to open the doors for her. Landover looked up from his desk. He smiled.

"Come in, Miss Harris. Sit down."

"I thought you might wish to speak with me, sir," she said, outwardly calm but spinning inside at the thought of what might lie ahead.

"You did, did you?"

"Yes, sir." She sat in one of the Kent chairs, arranging her skirts with special care. "I . . . I expect you might have a thing or two to say about last night, my lord. I should prefer to have the matter behind us as quickly as possible."

"I see." He watched her carefully for a full minute. She shifted uncomfortably, looking down at her hands, then forced herself to meet his gaze, wondering if he meant for her to say more than she had already said.

"Gillian," he said softly, "are you afraid of me?"

Her eyes flew wide. "Afraid of you?"

"Yes. Are you?"

"No, my lord," she replied firmly. "Of course not." He was silent, and she licked her lips nervously. Was she afraid of him? The answer came quickly, and she looked back at him directly, more sure of herself now. "I am not afraid of you, Landover, but I confess to a certain amount of fear regarding the action you mean to take. I do not wish to be sent home."

"What makes you think I might send you home?"

His voice was quite gentle. Was he toying with her? Why would he do such a thing? Her eyes narrowed as she gazed searchingly into his. "Last night," she said slowly, "I thought you were furious with me. I expected your wrath to descend this morning."

"Why? What did you do that was wrong?"

Gillian sighed, staring at him, wondering if he had gone demented on her or if he was merely playing some stupid game. Her expression seemed to amuse him, which only made matters worse. "Do you expect me to condemn myself out of my own mouth, Landover? 'Tis simple enough, I should think. You forbade me to mix in her highness's affairs, but I did exactly that, and I am afraid I should not hesitate to do it again under similar circumstances."

"And for that you expected me to punish you?" She nodded, watching him warily. He shook his head, smiling, then got to his feet and walked toward her. It was clearly a game, a game of cat and mouse. Her tension mounted as he neared her. He reached down and, taking both her arms, gently pulled her to her feet. His touch was electrifying. She trembled. "Gillian, sweet Gillian," he said quietly, "it is true that you disobeyed me, but I cannot think—all things considered—how you might have done otherwise. What you did was done out of friendship, and you wrong me deeply if you think I would condemn the sort of friendship you have given to her highness. Such a gift is a precious thing, not given lightly. If I was angry last night—and I cannot deny it—it was anger directed at the situation, at the Regent if anger must be directed toward a person. Not at you."

"But you were seething when you put me in the coach," she protested, looking up at him, her face flushed at his nearness, too conscious of his hands on her bare arms to be able to think clearly. But he had been angry, and it was difficult to believe that that anger had not been aimed at her.

"I was furious," Landover admitted, "too furious to trust what I might say to you, which is why I couldn't discuss the matter then. But I was infuriated by my own helplessness," he added, and there was a sound of anger mounting again even as he spoke. She cocked her head in puzzlement.

"I thought you managed things rather neatly."

"To be sure. *After* the damage had been done."

"Damage! What damage?"

"Your friendship, my dear. That precious, open friendship. It is as good as ended now."

"No! You cannot!"

Landover drew closer despite her attempts to pull away from him. "Gently, child." His voice was a caress, and she relaxed, trembling in his grasp. His arms slid around her shoulders. "'Tis none of my doing," he muttered, "but 'tis a fact nonetheless. Prinny knows that Charlotte fled here first and thence to her mother. He will no doubt draw the logical conclusion, simply because he will prefer to pretend that Charlotte would never have thought to turn to her mother without outside influence— namely yours. I wish it had never happened, Gillian, but it did."

"You think I should have turned her from the door," she accused.

"Don't be daft. Of course I don't. You could have done nothing other than what you did do. You might have done better to have sent for me instead of accompanying her high-ness personally to Connaught House," he added honestly, "but I quite understand why you didn't feel that you could do that. And that is my fault. I should have made it clear much earlier that you can trust me."

Suddenly, she could think of nothing to say. She was conscious only of his compassion, of a desire to nestle her head against that broad chest, to insist that of course she trusted him. Without warning, tears welled up into her eyes and spilled down her cheeks. Landover shook his head ruefully and held her away only long enough to dislodge a large linen handkerchief from his waistcoat pocket and hand it to her. Then he pulled her close again.

"Poor Gillian. It has all been rather tempestuous, has it not?" She nodded miserably, and he bent her head against his chest again, holding her, letting her cry. "It isn't over yet, either," he added when her sobs diminished. "Prinny will very likely give you the cut direct. I don't imagine it will hurt your social standing much. Not when folks hear the whole tale. But things could be a mite uncomfortable. No more invitations to Carlton House for you, I'm afraid."

Gillian blew her nose, then looked up at him, tears still sparkling on her lashes. "What about you, Landover? Will he cut you, too?"

He chuckled. "Not likely, I'm afraid. He may glower a bit and fume. He may even tear a strip or two off me for my insolence, for involving myself. But he does know I sent her back, and sooner or later there will be a treasure he covets desperately. I may be in the shade for a short while, but I shall come about." He paused, watching her, then smiled. "Would you like to hear what happened after you left? It makes excellent entertainment, I promise you."

She nodded with a watery sniff. "If you please, sir."

The smile widened to a grin. "I please. But I think you should sit down. I recommend the settee, however, in case your spirits need further support. Come." And he led her gently to a settee in the corner away from the desk. Gillian made no protest when he sat beside her, his arm still around her shoulders. It seemed only natural to snuggle against him while she listened.

"You've never seen such a commotion," he began. "Not only did Brougham, the Duke of York, and the Lord Chancellor arrive, but also Mercer Elphinstone—one of Charlotte's previous ladies, you know—as well as the Bishop of Salisbury and the Duke of Sussex!"

"Did the princess not tell them she had decided to return?"

"Not a bit of it," Landover chuckled. "I think her highness enjoyed herself hugely. It isn't often she gets a chance to be the center of attraction, after all. She kicked and bounced as though she meant to dig in her heels and defy them all, and when Brougham informed her that she would be obliged to entertain the lot of them until she capitulated, she only grinned at him and, going on as she had begun, ordered her servants to serve them all dinner."

"She didn't!" Gillian sat up straighter and stared at him in disbelief.

"She did indeed, and when dinner was served, she practically commanded them to eat it."

"And did they?" Her eyes began to twinkle.

He nodded. "To humor her they sat whilst she played hostess. She drank wine with her baldheaded uncles, chattered, cracked jokes, and laughed with all of them. I daresay she's had few happier moments." He paused, then added musingly, "She was like a bird set loose from a cage. Brougham said that, and it was as apt a description as anyone could give. Her spirits were absolutely soaring."

"I daresay she had her wings clipped soon enough, though."

Landover grimaced. "Very true. It was Sussex—cautious, kindly Sussex—who asked Brougham whether or not they could legally resist if the Regent made an attempt to carry Charlotte off by force. They couldn't, of course. So Sussex, in that fussy way of his, advised her to return with as much speed and as little noise as possible."

"Is that when she told them she had already decided to do so?"

"Not then. There was a good deal more fuss and bother, with her mother supporting the others in no uncertain terms. But there was method in Charlotte's stubbornness. When she agreed at last to go, it was only on the condition that Brougham would draw up a formal declaration of her refusal to marry the Prince of Orange. Then she made him promise to see it published immediately upon the announcement of any such marriage, so that her people might know she had been forced against her will. The declaration was written on the spot and signed with all of us as witnesses."

"How . . . how brave of her," Gillian whispered.

"Brave indeed. Prinny will have her head for it. I must say I felt sorry for her when she climbed into that coach with Brougham and Miss Elphinstone. She looked for all the world as though she were climbing into a tumbrel, on her way to face the guillotine."

"Do you think his highness really thrashed her?"

Landover shrugged. "I'm sure he was angry enough, and he's certainly capable of it, but I daresay a thrashing is the least of her worries."

"What else?"

"There's no saying. Prinny's capable of nearly anything when it comes to either his wife or daughter."

"I think he's hateful."

"I daresay. I've certainly heard you voice that opinion upon more than one occasion." He stood up and pulled her to her feet. "But don't let me hear you say so again anywhere but here, if you please. You are in enough trouble with his highness without that. Have you made plans for this afternoon?"

She shook her head, surprised by the abrupt change of subject.

"Well, see if your Cousin Amelia would fancy a trip to Hampton Court. I've a mind to try my luck with the maze, and it isn't nearly so much fun if one is alone."

XIV

"The thing is being buzzed all over town," Sir Avery said at the dinner table several nights later, "and all are against the Regent, of course."

"Never had a princess so many champions," smiled Mrs. Periwinkle, "and everyone behaves as though her punishment were totally unmerited."

"Well, I certainly think he was unnaturally harsh," said Gillian.

"Don't believe half of what you hear," advised her brother loftily. "I, for one, prefer the stuff one reads. The broadsides have been positively merciless to his highness. And the comic prints! Well, I ask you."

"They are dreadful," said Gillian flatly.

"Do you truly think so? I find them amusing. Particularly the one I saw today by that George Cruikshank fellow. 'Tis entitled 'The Regent Kicking up a Row,' or 'Warwick House in an Uproar,' and shows Prinny flourishing a thick birch rod whilst Charlotte runs shrieking off to Mama. The faces are especially good, I thought. Poor Miss Knight is kicking her heels on the floor, whilst the other ladies are falling all over one another in their haste to get out of harm's way, and the Bishop of Salisbury is exchanging absurdities with John Bull in the background. Dashed amusing!"

"I doubt her highness finds such things at all amusing, Avery," Gillian retorted angrily. But he only grinned at her and demanded to know if the other two at the dinner table did not find the news sheets entertaining. Neither one deigned to answer him directly, but Mrs. Periwinkle reminded Gillian

184

that there are more flies to be caught with honey than with vinegar.

" 'Tis a point our dear princess seems never to have learned," she added. "Only look how she dragged her poor Sussex into the matter, a move that can only have been calculated to turn the Regent's fury in a new direction."

Landover was the only one who had given no opinion regarding the public furor over the Princess Charlotte's flight and the consequent penalties. As Gillian's gaze met his now, his expression seemed to be a mixture of sympathy and mild amusement. She glared back at him, then angrily attacked the roast squab on her plate.

Perhaps, she thought, it was a bit unfair of Charlotte to have dragged the gentle Duke of Sussex into the mess, but what else could she have done? After a few no doubt miserable days' solitary confinement at Carlton House, the Regent had sent her to Cranbourne Lodge in the charge of the four grim ladies who had replaced her own beloved attendants.

A small silence had followed Mrs. Periwinkle's observation, but Gillian broke it now, declaring indignantly, "They say she is watched day and night, that her desk is rifled, her letters intercepted, that she is not allowed to write letters herself or have friends to visit. Why, 'tis even said she had to steal the very paper and pencil she used to write his grace of Sussex."

"A letter full of piteous complaints of her ill treatment," observed Landover, speaking for the first time, his tone ironic. "Does that sound like the princess you know?"

Gillian gave the matter some thought. "Perhaps not," she admitted, "but it seems to have answered the purpose well enough, and that must count for something."

"So you presume to know her purpose," he replied, watching her carefully. "I confess that I do not. I know only that the duke, poor fellow, hastened straight off to the House of Lords burning with righteous indignation and clutching his list of questions."

"There is nothing wrong with asking a few pertinent questions, Landover," Mrs. Periwinkle pointed out briskly. "'Tis how one learns to tell a hawk from a handsaw, after all. And her people have a right to know whether their crown princess is being held prisoner or not."

"And whether her physician ordered sea air for her health?" chuckled Sir Avery. Gillian shot him a withering look, but Mrs. Periwinkle acknowledged the relevance of the remark with a small nod of accord.

"That was indeed carrying things a bit far," she agreed, "for how can her physician have made any such recommendation if she has been held *incommunicado*, as it were?"

"Just so," replied Sir Avery, still grinning. "But the Prime Minister squashed old Sussex flat, you know, saying there were certain 'disagreeable implications' in his questions. What a phrase! But it sent the duke about his business quick enough. And now the precious news sheets are full of Princess Charlotte's daily rides in Windsor Park and the visits paid by Mercer Elphinstone and the rest of her dearest friends, so I for one think the whole affair has been little more than a hum from the outset."

"It was no such thing!" cried Gillian hotly. "I am a friend, and I have not been invited to visit her highness at Cranbourne Lodge, so she cannot have very much to say about who does visit. And furthermore, that drivel about the daily rides—if it is true, which I find difficult to believe myself—merely shows that the Regent is allowing her highness some small freedom as a result of what must have been prodigiously awkward gossip."

"Enough, child," Landover said gently, but he turned a sterner eye upon Sir Avery when Gillian had subsided into silent indignation. "It would be far wiser, young man, if you were to refrain from voicing dogmatic opinions when you know few of the facts involved. It was not the Prime Minister but the Bishop of Salisbury who persuaded his grace of Sussex to withdraw the questions he had asked in the House."

All eyes turned toward him, for this was news. "How is this, sir?" inquired Mrs. Periwinkle, speaking for all of them.

"His eminence has let it be known that he is prepared to offer statements of Prinny's many kindnesses to his daughter, including eyewitness descriptions of tearful scenes between the two. Quite touching, I thought."

"How . . . how could he!" Gillian demanded. "A man of the cloth!"

"Nevertheless, that is the situation as it now stands," stated the marquis matter-of-factly as he nodded to a flunky to refill his wineglass. "Sussex can scarcely make a successful fuss whilst Salisbury supports Prinny as a doting parent. But since there is nothing any one of us can do to alter things," he added firmly when Gillian opened her mouth to continue the debate, "I suggest we change the subject. I confess to becoming slightly weary of her highness's misadventures."

Gillian swallowed the retort that flew to her lips. Nothing could be gained by irritating him. And as a matter of fact, she had been basking in the light of his goodwill for some days now and had no wish to change that state of affairs.

The outing to Hampton Court had been a complete success. At Sir Avery's suggestion, Lady Sybilla had been included, whereupon Mrs. Periwinkle had declined the treat, saying that she was sure Sir Avery would look after Gillian, and that she had no wish to play gooseberry. Gillian tried to convince her that she would enjoy the outing, but Landover had chuckled and said he for one was relieved, since even the barouche was uncomfortable for more than four people.

Both he and Sir Avery proved to be veritable founts of information with regard to the history of the famous residence. Gillian rather thought her brother must have swotted up a bit in order to impress Sybilla, but she was just as certain that Landover had not done anything so silly.

On the road, Sir Avery informed them that the magnificent palace had been a gift to King Henry VIII, but he couldn't for the moment put his finger on the name of the previous owner. It remained for Landover to provide the information that Cardinal Wolsey, then Lord Chancellor of England, had given it in an unsuccessful attempt to regain royal favor.

Gillian didn't care much about the history of the place, but she was fascinated by the building itself and particularly by the huge astronomical clock over Anne Boleyn's Gateway. It was a full eight feet in diameter and was so cleverly devised as to tell not only the hour, but the date and month, the number of days since the beginning of the year, the phases of the moon, and the time of high water at London Bridge! The gardens were lovely, and the maze, just as Landover had promised, was truly fun. All four disdained help from the guard on his viewing tower and were vastly pleased with themselves when they found the center. Finding their way out again, they discovered, offered an equal challenge.

The day following that pleasant excursion, Sybilla came to call, announcing rather sadly that her mama had fallen victim to a chill that seemed determined to set up forces of occupation in her lungs. Sir Avery rallied her, insisting there was no need to fall into the dismals about it, since Mrs. Periwinkle would be only too happy to escort her as well as Gillian to whatever parties she wished to attend.

"But Avery, I cannot possibly think of attending parties whilst Mama is taken to her bed!"

"Nonsense, Syb, you are being entirely too nice. Your mama would be the first to agree that you ought not to allow her indisposition to spoil your season," Sir Avery replied bluntly. The others, knowing that Lady Harmoncourt intended to see her lovely daughter married before a second season was needed, especially in view of the fact that Sybilla's younger sister was to be fired off the next year, had no hesitation about supporting Sir Avery's views on the matter. Thus, it became quite the usual thing for Sybilla to make one of the Landover House party when entertainments began to flourish again in prelude to the Regent's grand fete, which was scheduled for the first of August.

What had originally been planned as a festive party at Vauxhall Gardens had blossomed into a Grand Jubilee. There would be a balloon ascent as well as varied entertainments at all the parks. Scarcely anything else was talked about by the citizens of London in the final days of July.

It no longer occurred to Gillian to disdain Landover's escort. In fact, since Darrow had been down in the country, she realized she had come to depend upon the marquis. Word seemed to have gotten around that he had declared her too young to marry, which seemed to have been interpreted by most of the gazetted fortune hunters to mean that Landover had no intention of turning over the purse strings until he absolutely had to do so. Thus, it put the finishing touch to whatever lingering shadow remained of the Harris Heiress stakes, but Gillian had no difficulty filling her dance cards regardless of that little detail. Still, she found that lately most of her escorts seemed either a trifle immature or distinctly boring. It never occurred to any of them to contradict her or to tell her she was chattering too much or to order her to sit down at least long enough to catch her breath. They were far and away too busy flirting and telling her how beautiful she was ever to be so tactless as to inform her that she'd got smut on her nose or wine on her gown.

Somehow it was a good deal easier to trust a man who snapped that her bodice was too daring than one who told her her eyes were liquid pools reflecting the distant stars, while at the same time he seemed to be drowning his gaze in her cleavage. It was certainly more comfortable to have an escort who lifted her unceremoniously over a puddle than to listen to another wishing rapturously that he were Sir Walter Raleigh with a cloak to spread at her dainty feet. Her temper still soared at his slightest nudge, but she found, also, that without Landover at her side or at least within smiling distance, the evenings tended to pall.

It crossed her mind now that tomorrow evening threatened to be rather boring, for the Regent was holding a reception at Carlton House to honor the new Duke of Wellington, recently returned from the Continent. Landover had been invited to attend, but the invitation had not included any other member of his household.

Tonight, however, they were to attend an informal evening at Lord and Lady Jersey's. Not a grand affair, but there would be dancing and a card room, so it promised not to be dull. The carriage was waiting a half hour after they adjourned from the table to drive them the short distance to the Jerseys' townhouse.

Gillian was surrounded immediately by a group of young hopefuls who began to fill in the spaces on her dance card. As one gentleman moved to pass it to another, however, a long arm swooped in from behind the crowd and practically snatched it away. Gillian looked up straight into a pair of familiar gray eyes.

"Darrow!"

"At your service, Miss Harris. And just in the nick of time, it seems. Only three spaces left, but I see that none of these halflings has had courage enough to take the quadrille, so I shall. And perhaps you would grant me the pleasure of your last waltz?" There were groans from several of the gentlemen who had not yet had the privilege of signing her card, but Gillian smiled.

"'Twould be my pleasure, sir."

He bowed, returning her card with a graceful flourish and leaving her in something of a quandary. One dance left and several hopeful admirers. She sighed, trying to decide which one to accept.

"I trust you've managed to save at least one dance for me, child," Landover said behind her. She turned to him in relief.

"Oh, I have, sir. The gavotte. Just here." Pointing out the empty space, she handed it to him, amazed to hear him chuckle as he scrawled his name. "You find something amusing, sir?"

"Indeed, minx," he responded in an undertone. "Do you think me so blind as not to recognize a damsel in distress?"

"Ah, of course," she retorted sweetly. "My knight in shining armor. 'Twas the dark coat that put me off, my lord."

"Nevertheless, Lady Impertinence, I quite look forward to our dance."

He disappeared into the crowd, leaving her to stare wide-eyed after him. His voice had been low, nearly gruff, but there could be no mistaking the ring of sincerity in his statement.

Her spirits seemed to take wing. She saw her brother in a corner talking avidly with Lady Sybilla and beamed at them just before her first partner came to claim her. As the evening wore on, it seemed to Gillian that this was one of the finest parties she had attended in London. Everyone seemed so relaxed and gay.

There was a flurry at the main door just before the dancing couples adjourned with the rest of the guests to partake of a light buffet supper. The reason was quickly ascertained. His highness the Prince Regent had deigned to put in an appearance to honor Lady Jersey. He moved from group to group, gathering an entourage as he went, and Gillian saw soon enough that Landover had been correct, for although the Regent came to an abrupt halt just in front of her, she might just as well have been so much air. As she sank into a low curtsy, he turned pointedly to the tall, thin gentleman at his side and spoke as though he were continuing a previous conversation.

"Petersham, I tell you I am the victim of bedevilment.

Throughout this sorry season, I've been dogged by one ill-fated circumstance after another, but this last has been by far the worst. With the damned Whigs to brand me monster, who knows what unspeakable brutalities I stand accused of? Cruelty to a helpless child, they say. Helpless! Ha! My own daughter, sir, and they make me sound as ogreish as Caligula. Now, I ask you!"

Lord Petersham—it would be Petersham, she thought—made soothing noises and glanced accusingly at Gillian, which did nothing to reduce her blushes. Nor did his words seem to quell the Regent's whining, although he did, thankfully, move on at last. Gillian had do doubt that Prinny had staged the scene for her benefit. He quite obviously knew exactly what role she had played in his daughter's flight, and she was certain now that if she was ever to further her friendship with the princess, the chance would come only when her highness finally came into her own. With a sigh of relief, she rose slowly to her feet and saw Landover watching her. Her chin went up immediately, at which he smiled so encouragingly that although her earlier sense of gaiety had completely evaporated, she couldn't help but smile back.

Her supper partner materialized out of the crush a moment later, and the evening went on. At last, it was time for the quadrille, and Darrow found her quickly, although she had scarcely laid eyes upon him since he had signed her card.

"I confess I am not much in the mood for *coupés* and *entrechats* at the moment, Miss Harris," he said with a smile as he adjusted a fold of his intricate neckcloth. "Will you be vexed if I suggest we sit this one out?"

"Only if you try to drag me off into a private chamber, my lord," she teased, taking his arm. Despite her attempt at lighthearted banter, however, Gillian realized that she was decidedly nervous. Darrow seemed to know it, too, for his tone was gentle.

"I'll not deny I'd like a private chat, my dear, but a pair of empty chairs will do as well as a withdrawing room. May I fetch you some refreshment first?"

She was tempted, simply because it would delay their conversation, but she shook her head. Better to get the first awkwardness over as quickly as possible. They found a group of empty chairs and sat down.

Darrow wasted no time coming to the point. "I have recently been engaged in much quiet reflection," he said somberly.

"I, too, have been thinking, sir."

"Was it true what Landover said? Do you truly wish to marry me, Gillian?"

She hesitated, but his question was too blunt to be parried with anything other than an outright falsehood, and she liked him too well for that. "Not . . . not exactly, sir. You are a dear friend, and I would do nearly anything to protect that friendship. But—"

"*Nearly* anything," he repeated pointedly.

"Only that, my lord." She looked down at her fingertips, unable to meet his eyes. "I . . . I am most sincerely conscious of the honor you do me, and I am most frightfully sorry if my actions or attitudes led you to believe—"

"Rubbish. Put a sock in it, my girl."

She stared at him. He was smiling, a sad smile, but still a smile.

"You don't mind?"

"Of course I mind. I mind like hell. I cannot imagine anyone I'd rather have for my lady wife. But you are not to blame yourself for the fact that I jumped to a hasty conclusion. It was my own wishful thinking led me on, not you. I knew by your response when I kissed you. You behaved as though you were performing an interesting experiment. There was nothing more, save what my imagination provided. You've no reason to feel responsible."

Her throat seemed suddenly tight. "Shall we still be friends?" she muttered.

"Always." He spoke gruffly. "But I hope you will understand if I take you back to Mrs. Periwinkle just now."

"Of . . . of course." They skirted the dancers rather quickly, and Darrow made his farewells with more speed than charm. Gillian found to her dismay that she was watching his departure with tears streaming down her cheeks. She felt a gentle touch on her arm.

"Come with me. 'Tis my dance, so no one will miss you."

Landover led her quickly to a curtained balcony overlooking

the back garden. As she stepped through the curtains, the soft night air touched her cheeks, chilling them slightly. Then Landover took her by the shoulders and turned her around.

"Let me see." His handkerchief was soft linen, his touch gentle. He chuckled when she sniffed. "Better?"

"Yes, thank you. You seem always to be mopping me up lately."

"Nonsense. That little scene must have been very difficult."

"What would you know about it?"

"You were hardly falling into each other's arms, my dear, and I know for a fact that this is the first time you've seen him since he offered for you. There is only one alternative."

"I told him I had made a mistake."

"Exactly."

Gillian sighed deeply, finding it very comforting when he put his arm around her. She leaned her head against his shoulder. "Landover, am I fickle?"

"Very likely. It has been my experience that most females are."

"Your *vast* experience."

"Precisely."

She grinned. A comfortable silence fell between them while they watched a crescent moon that seemed to dive in and out of scudding black clouds. Gillian shivered slightly in the chilling breeze, and Landover sensed it, drawing her closer as though to share the warmth of his own body.

His hand moved up until it was just beneath her breast, and the movement created a sudden, mad wish that she could throw herself into his arms, to surrender to a burning assault on her body similar to the one she had experienced the night he caught her with Darrow. She looked up at him, and he smiled. There was a warmth in his expression that she hadn't seen before. Her lips parted. Suddenly breathless, she was not at all surprised when he bent his head, capturing her with a kiss so gentle, so tender that it seemed almost to be a figment of her imagination.

Her reaction was not nearly so mild, however. Every nerve responded. It was as though his very tenderness teased her senses, provoking a passion deeper than anything she might have imagined. She pressed closer, lifting her arms to return his embrace, driving him to greater urgency. He held her more tightly, and her conscience stirred even as she returned the embrace. His hands began to move, caressing her, first gently, exploringly, then more firmly, sending her feelings to even greater heights.

Gillian told herself that she had no business to allow such behavior, that she must be wanton to enjoy it, but it was no use. She reveled in it, delighting in each new sensation, gasping with pleasure as his fingertips brushed the tips of her breasts. Really, she thought to herself, she had been absolutely right about his expertise. It was a prodigious shame he wasn't the sort of man she wanted for a husband. But despite his good behavior these past days, he was entirely too overbearing and dictatorial. Not at all the proper husband for a girl who knew her own mind as well as she did! She sighed, and Landover set her firmly back on her heels. This time, however, he looked down at her with a rueful little smile.

"Forgive me. I should never have allowed that to happen."

"Why not?" she demanded.

"Because you are entirely too vulnerable tonight. I wouldn't want you hurt by these little games we all play."

"Games! Why, you insufferable— Ooh!" Too angry to think of anything sufficiently rude to say to him, Gillian turned on her heel and flounced back inside, blinking furiously in the sudden blaze of light. She avoided the marquis for the rest of the evening and was perversely gratified when Darrow, with a rueful smile, showed up to claim her hand for his waltz.

The following day she continued to ignore the marquis and made a point the day after that of not asking how Wellington's reception had gone. She was naturally curious, but she didn't have to suffer long, for she met Mr. Brummell at the Berry sisters' that very afternoon, and he was only too pleased to describe the affair.

"Prinny's usual deep planning, of course. And the usual outrageous expeditures," he added wickedly. "Everything was white. He built a great brick thing in the garden and swathed the whole in white muslin. It held two thousand guests, they tell me. All I know is it was a sad crush. There were mirrors all over the place, so it looked like a multitude, and everything was so hideously *virginal*. Busts of Wellington all over the place, of course, but even so, one had to keep reminding oneself that one was attending a fling for a rugged military hero and not the Princess Charlotte's come-out. Of course, the new duke made the rounds, and there was no missing that stupendous nose or his abysmally foul language. All in all, I suppose I should call the evening a qualified success."

Landover, who had uncharacteristically chosen to accompany Gillian and Mrs. Periwinkle to the little house in Curzon Street, had been watching her while she chatted with the Beau, so Gillian was not particularly surprised when he made his way to her a few moments later. She wanted to ask him if he had actually spoken with the national hero, but she was still angry and would not allow herself to be more than civil to him. And she was just as glad she had not when he demanded to know what she and Brummell had been discussing so avidly.

"Mr. Brummell was kind enough to tell me about Wellington's reception, my lord," she replied, carefully polite.

"Well, if he expressed them, I hope you were not so unwise as to agree with any of his opinions regarding the Regent," he replied sharply. "To do so would only arouse George's contempt, you know."

Gillian controlled her temper with difficulty. "I am confident, my lord," she replied in chilling tones, "that Mr. Brummell would never be so rude as to express such opinions to me." Then, before he could contradict her as she knew he would—and with excellent reason, since she had just spoken a great piece of nonsense—she gave him a fine view of her back by turning to speak to Mrs. Periwinkle, who stood just behind them. Therefore, she did not see Landover's slight, mocking bow, but moments later, she realized he had gone. In the next few days, Gillian watched as his reaction to her continual snubbing passed through mild amusement to irritation, and was oddly satisfied with the change.

XV

The morning of the Grand Jubilee dawned through a thin
drizzle of rain, but the people of London, having long antici-
pated the treat, were not about to allow such a minor detail to
damp their holiday spirit. Even the servants at Landover House
went about their duties humming and laughing, and when the
sun's rays began to slip through the clouds at noon, Gillian
could have sworn she heard cheers from the kitchen. Nearly
everyone was to have a half day off, and the house rapidly
emptied after luncheon. Only a skeleton staff remained, including Jason, who would drive the Landover party to the parks.

They began with Green Park, where a mysterious structure
known as the Castle of Discord had suddenly appeared with a
round tower and ramparts a hundred feet square. The fortress
had been made to revolve so that it could be viewed from every
angle, and at midnight it was to be transformed amidst flames
and smoke and thundering artillery in a symbolic destruction of
the horrors of war into a beautiful symbol of peace, the Temple
of Concord. Booths and flying barracks and open stands of a
more humble description had sprung up everywhere, with all
sorts of refreshments, and the atmosphere was similar to that of
Bartholomew Fair, with great crowds everywhere.

From Green Park, they went on to St. James's Park, where
they met Lord and Lady Harmoncourt and Lady Sybilla. As
they wended their way through the crush toward the canal in
order to view the magnificent Chinese bridge designed especially for the occasion by John Nash, the Regent's favorite
architect, Lady Harmoncourt, now fully recovered from her
illness, took her brother's arm and leaned toward him confidingly.

Her voice carried easily enough, however, to Gillian's sharp ears.

"I have a special treat for you tonight, Landover."

"Indeed?"

"I daresay you will remember Lady Henrietta Armitage?" Her tone was nearly coy, her eyebrows lifted teasingly.

"Don't be silly, Abigail," Landover replied, glancing at her quizzically. "But I thought Hetta meant to spend the Season in Paris now that peace is at hand."

"Perhaps she said as much," Lady Harmoncourt chuckled, "but she must have got bored, because she is back in town. She called upon me only yesterday, and seeking to surprise you, I took the liberty of inviting her to join us for dinner. We are engaged to collect her on our way to Vauxhall. But I shall let you have the honor, for I know she would prefer to go by water with the rest of you, whilst I shall, as always, take the land route." She turned, smiling, to the others. "I knew Landover would be pleased. He and dear Henrietta have been *such* good friends for such a long, long time." And to Gillian's astonishment, her ladyship actually winked at Sybilla.

Gillian herself felt a strong sense of dismay. It had been so long since her ladyship had produced a possible bride for Landover that she had quite forgotten their plot. Even Sir Avery, content in his courtship of Sybilla, had ceased to complain of the marquis's interference in his life. She stared at the immense seven-story pagoda in the center of Nash's bridge, too preoccupied to be impressed by the magnificent blue-and-yellow structure with its flanking temples and stately columns.

"Nash has an unerring sense of the monumental, has he not?" observed a familiar voice. She turned to find Darrow at her side and did her best to gather her wits.

"Good afternoon, sir," she replied. "I suppose he must be very good, since everyone says so, but I find his work a trifle overblown."

"Perhaps you are right," he agreed. "This is hasty work here, and slick, too. But you must admit the man has a certain breadth of vision. His notions for the transformation of Marylebone Park quite take one's breath away."

"Do they?" She smiled weakly. "I am afraid that I know very little about it."

He grinned at her tone. "And you care even less. The subject interests me, however, so I'm afraid I do tend to get carried away. Good afternoon, Lady Harmoncourt, Mrs. Periwinkle."

Her ladyship nodded regally. "How nice to see you, my lord. Is this not a splendid sight?"

"Indeed, ma'am, but not nearly so splendid as it will be tonight when they light the pagoda up. They are using those new fangled gaslights, you know."

"Yes, so I had heard. Do you know, Harmoncourt thinks to see those dreadful things inside our townhouse before the decade is out?"

"Very likely, ma'am. 'Tis the coming thing."

"But so messy," she objected, "and quite lacking the elegance of candlelight."

"Or the dimness," Landover chuckled, coming up behind her. He shook hands with Darrow. "Won't you join us as we walk, sir?"

"No, thank you, my lord," Darrow replied, "though I'm glad to have crossed your path." He cast an oblique glance at Gillian. "Something has come up, and I find I must return to the country this afternoon. I was merely taking a rapid survey of the sights when I saw your party."

"Then you are not following the world to Brighton?"

"No. I'm going to take care of business at home until the hunting season begins. But then I shall no doubt see you with the others in Leicestershire."

"No doubt," Landover replied. They shook hands again, and Darrow made his bow to the ladies, then disappeared into the crowd. Sir Avery and Sybilla wandered up to the others a moment later.

"I say, wasn't that Darrow?" Sir Avery inquired. "I wonder he did not join us." He winked at his sister.

"He has business to tend to at his country house," she replied evenly.

"Bad luck. He will miss all the fun, especially the reenactment of the Battle of the Nile on the Serpentine."

They were all looking forward to that spectacle, but first

came the balloon ascension. Gillian nearly held her breath while she watched the intrepid Mr. Sadler climb into his tiny flag-bedecked gondola. The ropes were cut, and the great meshed red-yellow-and-blue-striped balloon, rising slowly at first, gained speed as it mounted to a chorus of cheers from the gentlemen, timorous shrieks from the ladies, and high-pitched squeals of delight from the children. With a gallant gesture of reassurance, Mr. Sadler leaned over the side of the swinging gondola and waved his cap to the upturned faces below. Giving a little shiver at his courage, Gillian watched until the balloon had floated away into space, then moved on with the others to find the carriages for the drive to Hyde Park, where the next entertainments would be found.

The afternoon passed quickly into dusk while the Battle of the Nile was presented with much realistic banging of guns to the complete annihilation of the enemy. Gillian could see very little of it for the press of people, but she could hear well enough and, long before it was done, wished she could cover her ears against the din. It was rapidly growing dark, and she was tired and hungry. Therefore, neither she nor anyone else demurred when Landover suggested that if they wished to obtain a good view of the lighting of the pagoda, they had best return to St. James's Park before the masses took it into their heads to do so.

They could still hear the distant thunder of battle even as they found excellent seats at the canal side; however, at long last, the roar of cannon ceased, and suddenly it was as though a necklace of jewels had been strung amongst the trees, where Chinese lanterns, silver crescents, and golden moons came sparkling to life. At the same time, at the center of Nash's Chinese Bridge, from every one of the pagoda's seven pyramidal stories, light poured a reflected sheet of flame upon the water, providing the signal for the grand fireworks display. As the first curving snake of color whizzed heavenward to burst in fountains of falling stars, a gasp went up from the crowd. It was a magnificent display, and they had an excellent view of competitive displays from the other parks as well, but Gillian soon discovered it was necessary to beware of falling and drifting sparks, and she learned later that before the show was done, four ships of the Serpentine fleet had been set ablaze! It was said that the resulting flare-up was hailed as part of the fun by all except a wedge of frightened swans that fluttered screeching to safety.

It was over at last, and the crowds began to mill about while thoughts turned to dinner. Many people had brought picnics and merely spread themselves and their blankets and baskets wherever they could find room. Others could be heard streetside, shouting for hacks and carriages. Landover soon gathered his party, although it took a moment to find Sir Avery and Lady Sybilla, who had managed to wander off together in hopes of getting a better view of the sea battle. Then there was another moment or two while a sternly frowning Lady Harmoncourt imparted a few private but, judging from Sybilla's downcast countenance, well-chosen words to her daughter.

When Sybilla turned away from her mother, Gillian noticed that the younger girl's lips, though held in a tight line, were trembling, and it was as much to draw the others' attention to herself as for any other reason that she spoke up to Lady Harmoncourt. "Perhaps it would be best, ma'am, if Cousin Amelia and I were to travel with you. You know how Landover abominates a crowded carriage, and there will be six of us with Lady Henrietta."

"Nonsense, my dear," replied her ladyship. "You will much prefer to cross the Thames to Vauxhall by water. I don't mind the longer route across Westminster Bridge, because I find the boats a bit fragile, but you young things always think them romantic. If the carriage is too crowded during the drive to the boat landing," she added on a note of asperity, "your brother can ride up with the coachman."

Sir Avery opened his mouth to protest, and Sybilla looked more wilted than ever, but Mrs. Periwinkle chuckled. "There will be no need for such a sacrifice as that. The girls are slender enough that the three of them may sit together, and if I ride with you, dearest Abigail, there is no reason to think the gentlemen will not be perfectly comfortable as well. No one will think you unprotected, my dear," she added kindly to Gillian, "whilst you ride with both your brother and your trustee."

Everyone else seemed to approve the idea, and Landover turned away to send a boy for the carriages.

"No," Gillian said firmly, surprising herself as much as everyone else.

"Why ever not?" asked Lady Harmoncourt. "Seems a perfectly logical solution to me." Even Landover looked back at her, his eyes narrowed speculatively.

Gillian was embarrassed. How could she explain to them all that she had suddenly realized she would feel like a fifth wheel with Sir Avery paying heed only to Sybilla and Landover only to Lady Henrietta? Even to suggest such a thing would make her sound self-centered and sulky at best and like a veritable shrew at worst. And how on earth could she expect the others to understand such feelings when she didn't even like the thought of them herself? She felt perilously close to tears. No doubt it was because it had already been such a long afternoon and because she was tired and hungry, but she felt completely unable to cope with the problem of thinking up an acceptable reason for her attitude, so she simply replied that she wished to have Mrs. Periwinkle's company.

"She is my companion, after all," she added, thinking miserably that she sounded childish and stubborn, but unable to stop herself. "Since it matters not one whit to me whether I go by water or in your carriage, ma'am," she went on lamely, "I—I cannot see what all the fuss is about."

"Well, you must do as you please, of course, Gillian," answered her ladyship with profound reluctance, "but I am not sure Henrietta's parents will approve of her going just with Landover. They are very protective, as indeed they should be. I do not worry about Sybilla's being with Sir Avery, because she will also be with her uncle. But Henrietta's parents cannot say the same, of course. An extra female always makes such things more conformable."

"Don't bother your head about it, Abigail," interjected Landover harshly. "We can all survive one carriage squeeze. If worse comes to worst, I can always take a turn at tooling the horses myself, you know. Do you and Harmoncourt go ahead, and we shall be there to meet you when you arrive. All of us," he added with a speakingly stern look at Gillian. She turned away unhappily and felt rather small a few moments later when he handed first herself and then Sybilla into his carriage. Mrs. Periwinkle came next and sat between the two girls, while the

gentlemen sat on the opposite seat, their backs to the horses.
There was silence until they reached the Armitage family town
house on the south side of Grosvenor Square. Landover jumped
down and strode up the steps to the front door.

Light from the carriage lamps lit the faces inside. Sybilla
looked herself again and smiled once or twice at Sir Avery.
Mrs. Periwinkle was placid, her slim blue-veined hands folded
in her lap, but Sir Avery's head rested against the corner of his
seat as he watched, not Sybilla, but his sister. Gillian glanced
at him, found his look a bit discomfiting, and turned away
again, shifting slightly in her seat. At that moment, the front
door of the house opened, and a blaze of light poured down the
steps to the street. Gillian heard a trill of husky feminine
laughter and turned to watch Landover and his companion
hurry down to the carriage. A footman carrying a torch paced
beside them, and in the flickering torchlight, Gillian got a good
look at Lady Henrietta Armitage.

Her ladyship was slender and tall, so tall in fact that with
her high-piled nutbrown curls and heeled sandals she lacked
only three inches or so of Landover's height. Her figure in the
flowing and clinging draperies of an exquisitely low-cut amber
satin gown could be seen to be full-busted with a tiny waist and
well-curved hips and thighs. She moved with the supple grace
of a woman who is well used to commanding the full attention
of everyone around her, and as they neared the carriage,
Gillian became aware of twinkling topaz eyes, a straight, gently
flaring nose, and a generous, laughing mouth. Lady Henrietta
was a beauty, and it was clear from his smiling expression that
Landover liked her very well indeed.

The footman held the door while Landover handed her ladyship inside. Sir Avery squeezed into his corner, but even so it
looked as though there might not be room for his lordship. He
grimaced.

"It seems I shall ride the box, after all."

Lady Henrietta chuckled, her voice delightfully low-pitched.
"Nonsense, my lord. I shall promise not to bite, so that you
may wedge yourself in however you may."

"But your lovely dress will be crushed!" protested Mrs.
Periwinkle. "You must change places with me, your ladyship."

"No, no, ma'am, you are not to trouble yourself," laughed

Lady Henrietta. "If the gown is ruined, then Daddy must simply buy me another, and I promise, 'twould only be to serve him with his just deserts for making me miss all the grand fun this afternoon. I am Henrietta Armitage, you know," she added, "but I don't believe we have met. Do get in, Landover, and do these introductions properly, else we shall leave you where you stand."

How very pushing she was, Gillian thought, succumbing to an unexpected flash of anger as Landover obeyed with a grin and introductions were made. The others all seemed to like her well enough, though. She watched as Sybilla acknowledged having met Henrietta once before.

"But you must call me Hetta, you know," laughed her ladyship. "I promise, all my best friends do. Only Daddy calls me Henrietta, and then only when I am in the suds with him."

"Is that what happened today?" teased Landover.

"Today?" She looked puzzled for a brief moment, but then her brow cleared, and she chuckled again. "You mean because he made me miss the fun! No, no, I promise 'twas nothing of the sort. He was merely worried about my safety in the crowds. Can you imagine?"

"Easily," responded his lordship. "I confess to having had a qualm or two myself on behalf of Lady Sybilla and Miss Harris."

"But you didn't forbid their going! Daddy let me come out tonight only because I was to be with you and because he expects nearly all the rabble will stay in Green Park to watch that castle-temple thing explode from Discord to Concord. Otherwise, I expect he would have forbidden this venture as well."

"You missed everything else?"

"I promise you, Sir Avery, I did indeed, so you must—all of you—tell me all about it. Every last detail!"

Everyone except Gillian seemed only too delighted to comply with this request. She could find Lady Henrietta only irritating, however, and decided it would be far safer to tune out their merry chatter before she inadvertently said something rude. Really, though, it was quite ridiculous the way they were all toad-eating her precious ladyship! Recognizing this thought as an uncharitable one, she made a firm effort to subdue it and turned her mind instead to anticipation of the pleasures that lay ahead.

She had been to the famous gardens only the one time before, with Darrow; but after having been rowed up the Thames from the Whitehall Stairs to Vauxhall landing in a wherry so light that she had felt like a fairy in a nutshell—quite delightful—they had dined together in one of the arcaded booths, and she remembered the Vauxhall menu easily. There would be quarts of arrack punch, as well as wafer-thin slices of ham, *petits poussins*, outrageously expensive lettuce salads, and delicate, mouthwatering cheesecakes. It made her hungry just to think of it. There would also be music and dancing, as well as magical strolls past the triumphal arches of the Grand South Walk or along the Cross Walk to the cascade.

The others tried to include her in their conversation, but her contributions were monosyllabic at best. She knew she was being rude and had no doubt that she would hear about it later, but with her emotions unquestionably if unexplainably in a turmoil, there appeared to be nothing she could do to stop herself. The drive to the Millbank Road seemed to take forever. Sir Avery asked Landover why they were not to embark from Whitehall Stairs.

"After all, sir, half the pleasure of a visit to Vauxhall is the water passage."

"I've a good notion the Whitehall Stairs will be a mass of rabble tonight," replied the marquis. "Since it costs nearly as much to cross from the old Ranelagh landing, we will miss most of the great unwashed. Besides," he added with a twinkle, "I wanted the liberty of reserving a barge for the entire night, and by the time I checked at Whitehall, those who are willing to do that sort of thing were already booked."

Sir Avery gave an appreciative chuckle, and a few moments later, the Ranelagh landing came into sight. Music drifted across the river, and the famous "fairy lights" of Vauxhall twinkled a welcome. There seemed to be a number of persons and a good deal of noise down below on the torchlit landing, and as they alit from the carriage, one shadowy figure detached itself from the others and walked toward them.

"Yer lordship?"

"Yes," Landover replied. "That you, Jack? What's up?"

"Naught of significance, m'lord, but y' best hold the ladies 'ere a mo' or two. Seems we've got a spot o' bother wi' a couple o' flash coves, who wants a wherry t' cruise wi'. Got a mind t' go ahuntin', if y' take m' drift."

"I do. Scarcely unusual."

"No, m'lord, but ain't one of us wants t' gie 'em a boat. Too muddled by half, they be, and the river too crowded. We'll get 'em sorted out quick enough, though. Won't keep y' waitin' but an eyewink."

"Hunting, Landover?" Lady Henrietta grinned at him.

"For beautiful women, Hetta," he retorted. "They cruise up and down the river searching for the willing sort."

"So why are you hiding us?" she challenged archly.

"Sometimes, particularly in their cups, they are not so choosy." But he grinned back at her, then looked toward his carriage. "I think I'll ask Jason to keep the carriage here instead of setting a time for him to meet us. He won't mind, since I know he's got his dinner in a basket under the box. He can jabber with the boatmen or have a nap, as he wishes." He stepped away to attend to the matter, and Lady Henrietta moved closer to Gillian.

"I say, Miss Harris," she said quietly. "Are you feeling quite the thing? You've been awfully quiet, and I'd hate to think you'd been suffering a headache through all our silly chatter."

"I am quite all right, thank you," replied Gillian stiffly, a quite unreasonable anger rising within her at the older girl's solicitude.

"I see." Lady Henrietta frowned thoughtfully as though she might say something further, but Landover called to her just then, asking if she wanted the reticule she had left on the floor of the carriage. She turned toward him gratefully. "Oh my, yes, how stupid of me! But you mustn't carry it, Landover. Too, too girlish! I'll just come and fetch it."

Watching her retreating figure, Gillian thought how silly Hetta was. But a moment later, she found herself insisting to Mrs. Periwinkle, Sir Avery, and Sybilla that she was neither tired nor sick, but just didn't seem to be in a mood for idle chitchat.

"Well, you'd best lighten up, my girl," her brother advised. "You're casting a damper."

Gillian glared at him and turned away toward the landing, where the trouble seemed to have been settled, and several people were being handed into wherries and barges. Landover had reserved a four-oared barge, a heavier craft than the wherry she had ridden in with Darrow, but she noticed when she boarded that it still listed most precariously. It took the combined efforts of Jack in the boat and Landover on the landing to hand each one of the ladies in safely. Nonetheless, being rowed across the Thames was very nice.

Sybilla, Henrietta, and Mrs. Periwinkle made suitable exclamations of pleasure, and even Gillian had to admit she was enjoying the ride. The fairy lights reflected on the water, dancing and sparkling on ripples stirred by the rhythmically splashing oars. The music grew louder, and soon laughter and other noises of revelry could be heard. Then, as they neared the Vauxhall landing, the fireworks began. Huge fountains of color, as beautiful as those in the other parks earlier, exploded overhead to be reflected in all their splendor upon the surface of the water.

"Magnificent," breathed Lady Henrietta, and Landover smiled at her. Unfortunately, Gillian's own enjoyment seemed to disintegrate at the sight of this shared enthusiasm. She found herself nearly gritting her teeth instead.

The barge bumped against the landing, and both Landover and Sir Avery leaped out to assist the ladies. Mrs. Periwinkle, being nearest, went first. Then Henrietta, who had sat next to her, took Jack's hand and stood up. Gillian, one seat back with Sybilla, moved over, and as a light wave disturbed the boat, she realized she had rested her arm, not upon the gunwale as one might have supposed, but upon the landing itself. Lady Henrietta, reaching toward Landover's outstretched hand, began to step from the boat, and just at that moment, a huge rocket exploded in a thunder of noise directly overhead, startling everyone. As they looked up at sparks of red, yellow, green, and white flashing in a giant spiral above them, Gillian, whether by startlement or subconscious design, shoved hard against the landing. Poor Lady Henrietta, thrown off balance by the sudden movement, caught her heel, missed both her step and Landover's outstretched hand, and despite Jack's efforts to save her, pitched forward with a shriek of dismay and an appalling splash straight into the icy Thames.

With a start of horror at what she had done, Gillian snatched her guilty hand from the landing to her mouth. Deeply conscious of the cries of astonishment from the others and a veritable surge to help rescue Lady Henrietta, she dared not look at anyone. No one said a word to her.

Jack had managed to retain his hold on Henrietta's hand, so she had not submerged entirely, and they got her out onto the landing easily enough. Nevertheless, her dress was ruined, and it was apparent to any but a blind man that she was on the verge of tears. Such mishaps were not uncommon, however, and the boatmen were prepared for them. Jack promptly produced a voluminous blanket from a locker in the stern and handed it to Landover.

"Wrap 'er la'ship up good, m'lord, and y'd best get 'er back quick, afore she takes a chill."

"We will indeed, Jack." He helped Henrietta back into the barge and saw her well wrapped before turning to his niece. "Here, Sybilla, up you go," he commanded, handing her safely up to Sir Avery. Gillian stood silently, expecting to follow her, but found herself firmly and unceremoniously pushed back onto her seat instead. "Don't even think it!" Landover muttered savagely, causing her breath to catch in her throat. He knew what she had done!

"I'll see to Sybilla and Cousin Amelia, Landover," Sir Avery said from above, and by his tone, Gillian knew that he, too, had either seen everything for himself or merely assumed her to be responsible for the mishap.

Landover was silent for a moment. Then he spoke to the boatman. "Can you find me a second coach, Jack? A hack will do."

"No problem, m'lord. Plenty comin' in and out t'night. Might 'ave to wait a mo' or two. Or y' might 'elp yerself t' m'lord Alvanley's rig. His man's got it up on the road there, and 'is lordship'll not be back till midnight or later. Seein' it's you, 'is lordship'd be the first t' offer, I'm thinkin'.'"

"Right you are. That's what we'll do." He glanced up at Sir Avery. "Sorry lad. I know you'll not thank me, but I'm sending you home with your sister. You'll take Alvanley's carriage and either come back with it, or not, as you please."

"What! Why cannot you take her?"

"Because Hetta must get home as quickly as possible, and she does not deserve to suffer your sister's company the entire way."

Gillian gasped at the harshness in his tone and involuntarily looked up at him. The expression on his face could only be described as ominous. She looked quickly down again, but not before she caught a glimpse of Henrietta's face above the thick woolen blanket. At first, her eyes seemed accusing, but then the look changed to something nearer puzzlement. Gillian turned away, her thoughts numbed.

"Why can Cousin Amelia not go with her?" Avery demanded furiously. "She is her companion, after all."

"Because *my* sister would have my head on a platter were I so lacking in sense as to leave you here alone with Sybilla," the marquis replied flatly. "And we cannot all return, because someone must remain to explain what has happened."

"He is quite right, Sir Avery, so do stop quibbling," Mrs. Periwinkle said briskly. "We must not keep Lady Henrietta in this cold night air. Come, Lady Sybilla. We are to meet your mother near the prince's pavilion."

"Wait!" Sir Avery said sharply. He drew Sybilla to one side and spoke with her briefly, then turned back with a sigh and a narrowed glance at his sister. "Very well, sir, let's go."

The trip back across the river was accomplished in silence. Sir Avery fairly jerked Gillian from the barge and ignored her when she protested that he was hurting her. Jack sent a boy to find the two carriages, and Lady Henrietta was soon tucked up in furs and lap robes in Landover's carriage. The marquis turned briefly, one foot on the carriage steps.

"Take her home, Avery. She is to await my return in the study. And, Avery," he added softly, "don't dare to murder her before I get there."

XVI

Alvanley's coachman had accepted the marquis's command that he drive Miss Harris and her brother to Berkeley Square without a blink, and Gillian soon found herself in a carriage nearly as luxurious as Landover's. Her position was scarcely a comfortable one, however. Sir Avery had well-nigh shoved her inside before climbing in himself to sit opposite her, and he waited only until the vehicle lurched forward before telling her what he thought of the whole affair. He spoke with barely controlled fury and did not mince his words.

"I'm disgusted with you, Gillian, and the only reason I have not already given you the thrashing of your life is that I wouldn't think of denying Landover the privilege. And don't think he won't do it, either. As angry as he is, I wouldn't put it past him to take a whip to you."

"He won't, though," she muttered, fighting tears. "Not that I don't agree I deserve it, Avery, but he said he has not got the right. He . . . he has threatened before, but he has never d-done it. He will l-leave it to y-you." The tears spilled over, but Sir Avery ignored them.

"He shall have the right, my girl, for I'll personally give it to him. I kept mum when you dosed Lady Sharon's punch, and I said nothing about that nonsense with Miss FitzWilliam and Lord Linden, but by God, this business is carrying things entirely too far! I didn't even like the other two chits, and no lasting harm was done, but I dashed well think Lady Henrietta would make Landover a fine wife. How could you do such a dreadful thing to someone who has been only kind to you? She might have caught her death!"

Since Gillian didn't know why she had done it, there was nothing she could say to defend herself. With silent tears streaming down her cheeks, she gazed wretchedly down at her lap while Sir Avery blazed away at her. From time to time he demanded to know what she had to say to this or that, but Gillian couldn't answer him. She could only shake her head helplessly as the tears flowed freely, punctuated by barely repressed sobs. She heard every word he said, however, and could deny nothing. On more than one occasion before they reached Berkeley Square, his temper rose to such a pitch that she expected him to box her ears at any moment, but somehow he restrained himself, and the carriage drew up in front of the house at last.

Jumping down instantly, Sir Avery hauled Gillian out after him with bruising force, then turned to dismiss Lord Alvanley's coachman.

"You . . . you are not returning?" Gillian whispered.

"No point in it," he grumbled. "Syb says her mother will doubtless turn right about and drive home, since the party's been spoiled."

"Oh, Avery—"

"Not here," he growled. His grip on her arm had not slackened, and now he pulled her after him up to the door, where, after a hearty knock, an astonished Jeremy admitted them. Sir Avery strode toward the study, whereupon the footman hastened past him to open the doors.

"Will you be wanting refreshment, sir?" he inquired, recovering his customary aplomb.

"No," replied Sir Avery gruffly. But he changed his mind almost immediately, ordering Malaga. Once the door had shut, he rounded on Gillian. "Now, my girl—"

"Oh, Avery, no more," she pleaded. "You have said everything there is to say, and nothing that is not perfectly true. I know I've spoiled the day for everyone, and I'm sorry, but—"

"Save it," he ordered harshly. "I recognize these symptoms well enough. You are in deep trouble, my girl, and you are about to tell me how sorry you are and to beg my forgiveness. But whether you're sorry for what you did or sorry you got caught, I've no way of knowing, since I cannot begin to understand any of your behavior these last weeks. So keep your sob stories for Landover. Not that they'll help you there either," he added, moving toward the desk, "for they won't. If he follows my advice—and I've a strong notion that, for once, he will—he'll make you wish you'd never been born." He began to pull out drawers. "Where the devil does that man keep his letter paper? Ah, here it is."

When Jeremy entered a few moments later, Sir Avery was seated at the desk busily scribbling, and Gillian, thinking the footman had already seen enough of her ravaged countenance to keep him in gossip for a week, was holding aside one of the curtains and staring fixedly out upon the empty square.

The tray was set down, the wine poured out, and the footman departed once more before Sir Avery laid aside his quill and sat back to read over his efforts. "That should do it," he said at last. "Do you wish to read it?"

"No, thank you," she answered, having had time finally to recollect herself. She dropped the curtain back into place and turned to face him. "I'm certain whatever you have written will answer the purpose."

"Well, I hope it may," he retorted uncompromisingly as he folded the note in half and propped it against the inkstand. This done, he lifted his glass, but paused before drinking. "Just mind you see he reads it, puss. It's no use playing off any of your tricks, either, for I'll tell you to your head that if I discover Landover has not blistered you well, I shall attend to the matter myself tomorrow. Do you hear me?"

"I hear you," she sighed, "and you need not worry. I'll see he reads it. But I thought you meant to stay."

"Well, I don't. I'm famished, and I don't propose to dine here in solitary splendor, so I'm going to White's. I daresay someone or other will be there, despite all the celebrations." With that, he tossed off his wine and was gone, but not before warning her again to stay put until Landover's return.

Alone, Gillian sank down upon the settee, hands clutched in her lap. Despite her brother's warnings and her own promises, her first inclination was to run away, and it seemed to her as though she must physically hold herself in place. It would be ever so nice just to chuck it all, call for a hackney coach, and . . . and what?

The thought of a hack brought Princess Charlotte to mind.

No doubt one might follow her highness's lead. She could find a hack easily enough and have the driver take her to Cranbourne Lodge. The princess's people would probably be loath to admit her, but she was certain Charlotte would force them to take her in if she was actually at the door. Not that it would do her much good, of course, for it would not be long before Landover would discover her whereabouts, no matter whose protection she sought, and she had no doubt of his ability to reclaim her. And once he did—

She shivered. The outcome did not bear thinking of. He would be difficult enough to face as it was, but if she ran from his house and then had to face him anyway . . . The vision of his face as she had last seen it popped into her mind. She could not remember ever having seen him so angry, not even the day she had gone to visit the Grand Duchess of Oldenburg!

That had been a foolish thing to do, perhaps, but the thing she had done this night was far, far worse. What in the world *had* possessed her? She could not remember consciously deciding to dump Lady Henrietta in the river. It had simply happened. But she could not fool herself or anyone else into believing it had been an accident. Why had she not thought to cry out, to insist that a wave from one of the other barges or just pure startlement had caused the accident? She should have apologized on the spot, should have made a fuss over Henrietta. Instead, she had sat like a stock, the picture of guilt. Landover *would* murder her!

She got up and paced to the bookcase and back. It was chilly, and she wished Avery had thought to ask the footman to light the fire. She was hungry, too, but it would never do to order supper for herself. Avery had made it clear by his remark about dining in solitary splendor that he meant for her to go supperless, and she could not think it would aid her in the least if Landover were to discover her in the midst of a tasty repast. With a glance at the clock on the mantel, she realized she had been home for more than half an hour. Surely he would be here soon.

He liked Lady Henrietta. The thought came unbidden and lingered to tease her. Gillian scarcely realized the tears had begun again until she reached up to brush one from her cheek. Why was she crying? she wondered. Lord knew, there would be occasion enough for that once Landover was done with her. She didn't want to think about that, so she forced herself to think about Henrietta instead. Such a silly, stupid girl. But the thought stirred her conscience. It wasn't true. She walked back to the window and, drawing the curtain aside, looked out onto the square again. Still empty.

Avery was right. Henrietta had been only thoughtful and kind to her, and everyone else liked her perfectly well. She was not in the least like Lady Sharon or Clara FitzWilliam. She clearly knew Landover well and liked him for himself, not for his wealth or title. And she had not even seemed particularly possessive of him, merely friendly. So why had Gillian had such an overwhelming urge to hate her? It was incomprehensible.

She had done what she had done in those previous instances in order to protect Landover from possible unsuitable alliances forced upon him as a result of her own devious schemes. But she certainly could not claim that as a reason this time, for Lady Henrietta was eminently suitable. She would make him an excellent wife.

The tears were flowing freely again, and she turned angrily from the window. "Ninny!" she scolded herself aloud. "Why is the thought of a w-wife for Landover anything to blubber about? It is what you've wanted all along, is it not?"

But as she heard herself ask the question, the words suddenly took on another meaning. She caught her breath, thinking them over, letting the question glide through her mind a second, third, even a fourth time. And then, with a sense of clarity that shook her to the very core, she knew the answer. It *was* what she had wanted all along. She had only been fooling herself to think she disliked him. For that matter, it had been a good long time since she had even pretended to dislike him. That he was overbearing was indeed a fact. Dictatorial and arrogant as well. Unquestionably. But he was also kind, thoughtful, gentle, and wise. And she loved him. "Jealousy," she whispered. " 'Twas naught but jealousy."

She plumped down upon the settee, trying to digest the facts of the matter, and it was as though someone had lit one of those brilliant gas lamps, casting light into corners of her mind that she hadn't thought to investigate before. From the first, she had acted out of jealousy! Even when she thought she detested him, she couldn't bear the thought of him married to another woman. There really had never been a noble motive behind her actions, which was rather a lowering thought, taken all by itself. And what good did it do to acknowledge her love now?

Gillian sighed, remembering the exquisite sensations she felt at his slightest touch. She should have known at once. But he had only been playing games with her. He had admitted as much. No wonder his admission had made her so furiously angry! But had she not played games as well? Her childishness, her sulks, her uncertain temper—all could be explained by the simple fact of emotions set on end.

Surely he must feel something too. Had he not told her once that she was beautiful? She remembered moments of tenderness, those looks she had been unable to interpret, his ultimate feelings about her friendship with Charlotte. Was it possible? But no, even if he held a tenderness for her, she must have destroyed it by her dreadful actions tonight. She had been hateful, stupid, and utterly childish. She deserved whatever punishment he chose for her.

It was a full hour with thoughts such as these for company before she heard the carriage roll to a stop outside in the square. Hurriedly, she moved to the window and carefully parted the curtains. The marquis was just descending from the coach. She could see nothing of his expression, but as he hurried up to the house, his step seemed lighter than she might have expected. It was as though he were looking forward to dealing with her. Well, she thought, unhappily, she couldn't blame him for that.

She turned from the window and watched the study door apprehensively. There were voices briefly in the entry hall, then the latch began to turn. Her courage failing, Gillian's gaze dropped to the carpet. She heard him step into the room. The door shut gently. Then there was silence.

She hoped he would move to the desk where he would see Sir Avery's note for himself, but he did not. She would have to tell him, and if she did not do so bang off, she would never find the words. She cleared her throat and lifted her head, though she spoke to a point over his right shoulder, thereby avoiding his eyes.

"M-my brother left a message for you, Landover. It is on your desk."

"My God, Gillian!" he exclaimed, stepping toward her. "You—"

"The note, sir," she insisted in a strangled voice, gesturing toward it. "P-please. I promised."

Pausing, he glanced toward the desk, then back at her. He opened his mouth to say something but, changing his mind, strode to the desk and picked up the note. Flipping it open, he scanned it quickly while she watched him. His mouth tightened, and she thought he must be angrier than ever, but then he looked up. dropping the note back to the desktop, and she realized he was doing his utmost to suppress amusement. His eyes fairly danced.

"Do you know," he said carefully, "it never occurred to me that I ought to ask his permission?"

She frowned, bewildered. "It is scarcely a point to laugh about."

"Do you dare to scold me?" he countered, lifting an eyebrow.

"N-no, sir." She eyed him warily. Something was amiss. His eyes still twinkled, and the note in his voice had been a teasing one. "Wh-what game do you play now, my lord? You came in shouting, and now—"

"I never shouted."

"You did. You said, 'My God, Gillian!' Like that. And you started toward me as though, as though—"

"I was appalled by the way you looked when I came in," he explained. "You have obviously been attempting to drown the wind with tears, as your cousin might say, and I thought you looked miserable. What on earth did your idiotish brother say to you?"

"Nothing I did not deserve to hear, my lord. And nothing you will not say yourself. What I did tonight was despicable. I only hope Lady Henrietta will suffer no lasting harm." She swallowed, trying to retain the small bit of poise she had left. "I deserve whatever you choose to . . . to—"

"Put your mind at rest," he cut in on a gruffer note. "Hetta is fine, and despite Sir Avery's thoughtfulness, I shan't beat you."

"You won't?"

"I'll not deny it was my original intention, you abominable girl, but Hetta would not let me leave her until I gave my word that I would not."

"Hetta!"

"Yes, Hetta. You didn't expect aid from that quarter, I daresay."

"No, indeed." She turned the notion over in her mind, examining it, and not at all sure she liked it. It was a facer, to say the least. She looked up at him. "By rights, she should be demanding retribution. I never expected kindness."

Then came the very last sound she had thought to hear. Landover chuckled. "Not kindness," he said. "She *promises* me it is no such thing. Says she's only being practical, and chose to remind me of a time while we were children when I pushed her into the lake at Landover. I was well flogged for my impudence, of course, but according to Hetta it can't have done much good, since I repeated the offense the following day."

"Surely she doesn't expect me to do it again!"

He moved toward her. "Of course not, although by her reasoning, the possibility does exist." He stood over her now, and she stared at the middle button of his waistcoat. "Why did you do it, Gillian?"

"I . . . I don't know." She simply couldn't tell him the reason, so she tumbled over herself in a spate of words, trying to divert his attention. "It was kind of Lady Henrietta to support me, sir, whatever she says to the contrary. She is beautiful and . . . and kind and . . . and I'm sure she will make you a fine wife."

"I think you do know, my dear," he said quietly, his hands coming to rest upon her shoulders. "I should like it very much if you could find the courage to confide in me. I promise I shall not— Wife! What wife?" His fingers dug into her shoulders.

"Why, Lady Henrietta, of course," she replied a good deal more calmly than she had thought possible. "You are looking for a wife, after all, and she would be—"

"She would be impossible," he laughed. When Gillian's eyes widened, he gave her a little shake. "Foolish child. So that's what you thought. Hetta and I have known each other since she was in the cradle, and despite admittedly fond hopes on the part of both sets of parents, as well as my loving but interfering sister, we decided years ago that we should not suit. We like each other well enough, but there is no spark between us, and we are both incurable romantics."

"Spark?" She thought of the electrifying impulses that shot through her at his gentlest touch.

"Yes. Now, why did you douse her?" he demanded unyieldingly.

"I tell you, I don't know!" She tried to pull away from him, but he would not let her go.

"Gillian, Gillian, how can I make you trust me? Hetta tells me she knows why you did it."

"She . . . she does?" She looked up, searching his face.

He nodded, his eyes filled with tenderness. "She says it was the same reason you laced a cup of punch with spirits and the same reason you manipulated the fickle Clara into Linden's willing arms."

"They only wanted your money and your title," she said without thinking. "But how did Lady Henrietta . . . I mean, I cannot think what you are—" She broke off, flushing deeply.

Landover chuckled. "She knew because I told her, and don't deny you did those things, because it won't wash."

"But how did you know?"

"I didn't at first, you little wretch, or there would have been hell to pay. I suspected the first incident only after the second, but the penny didn't really drop until tonight when I began railing about your misbehavior. You see, I couldn't think why you would sabotage your own scheme. It was Orison," he added kindly, when she stared at him in astonishment. "My lamentable heir's name flitting between your lips and Sybilla's one day and being flung at me by Abigail the next . . . well, even a simpleton might have figured that part out. But then, the business with Darrow rather put me off the scent."

"Darrow!"

"I thought you loved him," he answered simply. "But Hetta says that cannot have been the case."

"Does she?" Suddenly, she seemed short of breath. There was an odd sort of tension, a mental tautness strung between them almost as though there were wires, like those in a pianoforte, vibrating in the tiny space between their bodies.

"Must I say it first, Gillian?" he asked.

"What would you say, my lord?" she whispered to his waistcoat. "You and Hetta seem to know more about my feelings than I did myself, certainly more than I know about yours. You said you were only playing games."

"That is not precisely what I said, but I'll admit I behaved foolishly that night. I was afraid of confusing you. You had just come from a difficult scene with Darrow, and I had already been at pains to convince you that you could not trust your passions. I wanted you to learn to know your heart instead."

"I do now, sir."

"Then you know mine as well." He lifted her chin and lowered his head to hers. The kiss was gentle, and she responded slowly, letting the feeling of warmth it generated spread with delicious fingers of flame throughout her body. His arms came around her, and she lifted hers to him, standing on tiptoe when his kisses became more urgent. A moment later, he drew her to the settee.

As he pulled her once more into his arms, his gaze met hers commandingly. "Say it, sweetheart."

"I love you," she whispered. Then her voice grew stronger as she saw the response to her words in his eyes. "Oh, my lord, I love you so very much! But I didn't know you cared a button."

"From the first," he replied, nuzzling her curls. "But I only knew I cared. I didn't know how much until the night I found you with Darrow."

"You were livid," she remembered. "I suppose if I ever need to test your love in the future, I must arrange another scene like that one."

"Not unless the gentleman is entirely expendable," Landover growled.

She trembled, but not so much from his threat as from the delightful music his hands played on her body. Silently, she let her fingers slip under his coat to stroke his broad chest, fiddling with the buttons of his waistcoat as she came to them. His hand caressed her throat, fingers tracing lines along the delicate blue veins, moving lower to tease at the lace edging her low-cut bodice, pausing when they encountered the silken bow in the center. Deftly, he untied it, then loosened the lacing until the bodice gaped, exposing the delicious curves of her satin-smooth breasts.

Gillian gasped as he slid his hand under one soft mound, cupping it, sliding the cloth away to expose the rosy nipple. He lowered his head, and she gasped again when his lips touched her flesh. But suddenly he tensed.

"What is it?" Then she too heard the voices from the entry hall. They seemed to be coming nearer, and she grabbed, panic-stricken, for the lacing at her bodice.

"No time for that!" Landover grinned. "Unless I miss my guess, that's Amelia and she's coming straight in." He chuckled at the look of horror on her face, then relented. "Come here then, and hide your face in my coat. Leave this to me." And just as the study door opened, he gathered her to him and looked over her lowered head to greet a rather anxious-looking Mrs. Periwinkle.

"Oh, Landover," she cried. "Is she all right?"

"Indeed she is, ma'am. Just a trifle undone over all this business. 'Twould be best if you leave her to me for the moment." Gillian, aghast at his play on words, had all she could do to stifle her merriment in Landover's waistcoat. But to Mrs. Periwinkle, it must have looked as though she were sobbing her heart out.

"Well, if you think so," she replied, eyeing her charge's shaking form doubtfully. "I . . . I hope you did not find it necessary to beat her, Landover. I know what the Bible says about sparing the rod, but 'tis also true that nothing becomes a man with half so good a grace as mercy does."

"Not to worry, my dear ma'am. I have discovered a far more trying punishment. She is going to marry me."

"Marry you! That is . . . I mean, how wonderful. I . . . I wish you both happiness, I'm sure. But . . ." She seemed reluctant to go on, but then she faced him squarely. "Does Gillian *wish* to marry you, Landover?"

He grinned. "She does. Do you think I could force her? To quote your faithful bard, 'Though she be but little, she is fierce.' I doubt I could marry her against her will."

"Don't fling Shakespeare in my teeth, sir! The Devil can cite Scripture for his purpose, after all. Not but what you haven't made your point." She sounded relieved, but now she peered at them both carefully, and when next she spoke, she did so as though it were a reluctant duty. "I wish you both every happiness, of course, but there are those who would hesitate to call marriage to you a punishment, Landover, those who would think she had accomplished something rather clever at Lady Henrietta's expense."

"Oh, no!" Gillian's voice was muffled, but when she turned her head quickly to look at Mrs. Periwinkle, the tears glistening on her lashes were no longer tears of merriment. "They mustn't think that, ma'am," she said quietly. "I do wish to marry him, for I love him dearly. But I should hate for anyone to imagine I did anything clever tonight. I behaved very badly."

"Yes, well, we needn't say more about that now, my dear. Not but what you will be hearing more, no doubt—especially from Lady Harmoncourt, I'm afraid. She is most displeased."

"Oh dear," murmured Gillian wretchedly.

"I'll deal with Abigail, my love. Enough has been said about this business already." Gillian looked up at him gratefully, and Mrs. Periwinkle expressed approval.

"Her ladyship must listen to you, my lord. And now, if dear Gillian is recovered, I shall take her up with me." Gillian stiffened. What on earth would dearest Cousin Amelia say if she were to stand up in all her dishabille? But Landover rescued her again, albeit with an unmistakable touch of amusement in his voice.

"Not just yet, ma'am, if you don't mind. There are one or two things I still wish to say to her."

"As you wish, my lord, but I beg you will not be too long about it. It grows late." With another sharp look at them, she turned on her heel, only to pause again with her hand on the latch. "I shall await you in your bedchamber, Gillian dear."

The door shut behind her, and Landover lifted Gillian to a sitting position. "I think we have had our marching orders, my love. Now that we are to be wed, it is no longer proper for us to be alone together, a point your chaperone has made quite clear. So you'd best fasten your dress again, else I shall lose my head, and we'll be in the briars. Next time it could be your brother who walks in."

Gillian began to obey him, but thought of her brother made her fingers tremble. Landover noticed and spoke gently. "What is it, love?"

She looked up at him. "You may call marriage a punishment,

sir, though I know you meant it in jest, but Cousin Amelia is quite right, and if it weren't for the fact that I must face Avery tomorrow, I *should* feel as though I'd done something clever. Still, I wish he weren't—"

"I shall deal with Avery as well as Abigail," he said firmly. "I think the simplest method would be to allow him to announce his own betrothal when we announce ours. Do you agree?" When her eyes lit, he made himself look stern again. "Don't think you are getting off scot-free, however. Tomorrow morning, as early as you can manage it, you are going to present yourself in Grosvenor Square to make an abject apology to Lady Henrietta."

"Oh, I will, I will," she promised.

"On your knees, I think," he added with a teasing grin. "That would make a nice touch."

"If you think I should, I will even do that," she agreed, smiling at him. "And I shall thank her, too, for understanding things I didn't even understand myself until tonight."

Landover nodded. "There is one other thing, love," he added, looking quite stern again. "If you should ever do such a corkbrained thing again, to anyone, I can safely promise you won't sit for a week. Do you understand me, Gillian?"

"Oh yes, sir." She looked up at him shyly, then as his expression warmed, her eyes began to twinkle, and she flung herself into his willing arms. "You may coerce me and scold me and no doubt use me abominably, but oh, my lord, it will be lovely to be a wealthy marchioness!"

Landover chuckled appreciatively, but a few moments later, the sound had changed to a low moan deep in his throat, and he could be heard directing a rueful curse at the waiting Mrs. Periwinkle.

About the Author

A fourth-generation Californian, Amanda Scott was born and raised in Salinas and graduated with a degree in history from Mills College in Oakland. She did graduate work at the University of North Carolina at Chapel Hill, specializing in British history, before obtaining her MA from San Jose State University. She lives with her husband and young son in Sacramento. Her hobbies include camping, backpacking, and gourmet cooking. Her previous Regencies, *The Fugitive Heiress* and *The Kidnapped Bride*, are also available in Signet editions.

More Regency Romances from SIGNET

(0451)

☐ **AN INTIMATE DECEPTION** by Catherine Coulter.
(122364—$2.25)*

☐ **LORD HARRY'S FOLLY** by Catherine Coulter.
(115341—$2.25)

☐ **LORD DEVERILL'S HEIR** by Catherine Coulter.
(113985—$2.25)

☐ **THE REBEL BRIDE** by Catherine Coulter. (117190—$2.25)

☐ **THE AUTUMN COUNTESS** by Catherine Coulter.
(114450—$2.25)

☐ **THE GENEROUS EARL** by Catherine Coulter.
(114817—$2.25)

☐ **AN HONORABLE OFFER** by Catherine Coulter.
(112091—$2.25)*

☐ **AN IMPROPER COMPANION** by April Kihlstrom.
(120663—$2.25)*

☐ **A SCANDALOUS BEQUEST** by April Kihlstrom.
(117743—$2.25)*

☐ **A CHOICE OF COUSINS** by April Kihlstrom. (113470—$2.25)*

☐ **A SURFEIT OF SUITORS** by Barbara Hazard.
(121317—$2.25)*

☐ **THE DISOBEDIENT DAUGHTER** by Barbara Hazard.
(115570—$2.25)*

*Prices slightly higher in Canada

Buy them at your local
bookstore or use coupon
on next page for ordering.

SIGNET Regency Romances by Clare Darcy.

(0451)

☐	CAROLINE AND JULIA	(120086—$2.50)*
☐	LETTY	(098102—$2.25)*
☐	ALLEGRA	(096118—$1.95)
☐	CRESSIDA	(082877—$1.75)*
☐	ELYZA	(110234—$2.25)*
☐	EUGENIA	(112741—$2.50)*
☐	LADY PAMELA	(099001—$2.25)*
☐	LYDIA	(082729—$1.75)
☐	REGINA	(111133—$2.50)*
☐	ROLANDE	(085523—$1.95)
☐	VICTOIRE	(097289—$2.25)*

*Prices slightly higher in Canada

Buy them at your local bookstore or use this convenient coupon for ordering.

THE NEW AMERICAN LIBRARY, INC.,
P.O. Box 999, Bergenfield, New Jersey 07621

Please send me the books I have checked above. I am enclosing $_____
(please add $1.00 to this order to cover postage and handling). Send check
or money order—no cash or C.O.D.'s. Prices and numbers are subject to change
without notice.

Name_____

Address_____

City _____ State _____ Zip Code _____
Allow 4-6 weeks for delivery.
This offer is subject to withdrawal without notice.